Miss Louisa's Final Waltz

Merry Spinsters, Charming Rogues

Sofi Laporte

Chapter One

THE SLAP RESOUNDED THROUGH THE BALLROOM.

Miss Louisa Highworth, diamond of the first water and much sought-after heiress, stood in front of her hapless suitor, the implication of her action slowly dawning upon her. The strains of the music subsided, the dancers paused, and silence fell as every pair of eyes in the room focused on her.

The fellow before her froze like a marble statue, barely believing what had just happened. Fascinated, Louisa watched as the red imprint of her hand appeared on his white cheek, and his already watery blue fish eyes bulged out even further, his mouth half gaped open.

Lawks, she'd really done it now. This would have severe consequences. For one moment, a feeling of queasiness washed over her.

But Louisa never did anything by half. Now that everyone was watching her, she had to rub it in even further; make a statement, get the point across, get it over with for once and for all.

Seeing the shocked look of disbelief on the man's face, a tiny twinge of remorse shot through her, which she quelled immediately.

"So terribly sorry," she whispered, only for him to hear. "But on second thought, you really do deserve this." Then she raised the hand holding a glass of ratafia and splashed the contents into his face. She watched with satisfaction as the sticky liquid sloshed down his cravat and onto his well-cut waistcoat.

He blubbered.

The entire room gasped.

There, Louisa thought resignedly. That should do it.

If that hadn't ruined her reputation once and for all, nothing would.

THERE WAS scandal at Almack's of epic proportions, the likes of which had never been seen before in the history of the assembly hall, the gossip sheets gleefully proclaimed the next day. It was caused by none other than the beautiful and proud Ice Damsel, otherwise known as Miss Louisa Highworth, the famous heiress legendary for turning down every single suitor who ever approached her. According to the latest *on-dit*, the number of rejected suitors must be approaching at least fifty-five, as one scandal sheet conjectured. Nonsense, it must be closer to seventy-three, said another, before proceeding to list them all.

"It was the hundredth suitor, exactly," Louisa muttered, then crumpled up the paper and threw it into the fireplace. Despite the warmth of her boudoir, she shivered as she drew up her legs on the chaise longue and looked out of the window from her father's house in Park Lane. It had a splendid view of Hyde Park.

One hundred suitors in seven seasons. She calculated. That was an average of about fourteen marriage proposals per season for the last seven years. She stared darkly into the fire, watching the flames lick up the paper and turn it to ash.

One hundred men who, with varying degrees of desperation, wanted to marry her.

Gentlemen with and without titles, Corinthians and dandies, nonpareils and rakes; the tall, the short, the ugly and the handsome all flocked to her. She'd run the whole gamut.

Military officers, too many to count. Undoubtedly, the occasion was the victory celebration, marking the defeat of the feared emperor Napoleon at Waterloo. They all had convened in London for the victory parade, followed by the ensuing celebrations. Everywhere one looked, the vibrant scarlet uniforms flooded the ballrooms.

There'd even been a duke—short, fat, and intolerably high in the instep. She'd dubbed him Duke Blubber Cheeks because he had the fat cheeks of a whale. Her father had nearly had an apoplexy when she'd turned him down.

"You could have been a duchess!" he'd roared.

"I could have," Louisa agreed. "But I chose not to."

Then there was Sir Twiddlepoops, as she called him, because for the life of her she couldn't remember his face or his name. He'd been an annoyingly persistent officer, dashing in his regimental regalia, much admired by the society ladies, for he claimed to be some sort of hero with medals and all. Her father had been much incensed when she'd turned him down rather rudely.

"It is easy for a man to boast of bravery on a battlefield from the safety of a drawing room. Truly, it sounds to me like the majority of those tales of valour one hears might be overly exaggerated, more fiction than fact." She'd brushed him off. "Other women may want to marry a tin soldier, but I'm certainly not one of them."

"He's a bloody hero!" her father had shouted. "He's the Hero of Vitoria! He saved not only his general's life, but an entire company! Even Wellington bows to him, saying they wouldn't have won the battle without him, and he's just been knighted! What more do you want?"

"Then why don't you marry Twiddlepoops yourself if he's so great!" Louisa had cried, her voice carrying through the ajar door to her father's study. Her stepmother had been having afternoon tea with some society ladies in the adjoining drawing room, all of whom had soaked in every word with scandalised delight.

Alas, word leaked out, and the next day there was a dashing Cruikshanks' caricature displayed in the print shop windows, depicting a wedding scene with her short, bald and plump father in a bridal gown, marrying the medal-laden Hero of Vitoria, while she herself, stick-thin with icicles hanging from her pointy nose, crept out of the church with a finger on her lips.

All London roared with laughter.

It was a shocking scandal, and Twiddlepoops' humiliation couldn't have been more complete.

"*La Belle Dame sans Merci* even dared to give our beloved Hero of Vitoria a freezing set down. The ton cannot help but wonder: who will be next?" proclaimed the gossip sheets. *La Belle Dame sans Merci*—The lady without mercy. That was what they called her, after the 15th century French poem by Alain Chartier. In everyday English, it was reduced to the more epithetic "Ice Damsel."

To Louisa's surprise, the scandal blew over quickly, and within a fortnight the suitors were wooing her again.

Sir Twiddlepoops was soon followed by Sir Frippery Fop, an impeccably dressed dandy and Corinthian, a gentleman with perfect looks and address, charming to a fault, the catch of the Season, the darling of the ton.

She'd decided he was too perfect and too boring and therefore had no compunction about turning him down with a group of her father's cronies as witnesses.

Then there was Lord Muttonhead, Sir Stuttervoice, Baron Slowtop, Lord Sweatyhands, and Mr Death's Head Upon a Mop Stick. There were many more, but she'd lost count.

The last one whom she'd soaked in ratafia had been a viscount whom she'd called Viscount Carrothair. Rather handsome and not a bad catch if one thought about it, even if he had red hair. His vile personality had been the problem.

The ton, of course, was highly entertained by *La Belle Dame*'s antics. It had become a running jest that one wasn't a man unless one was rejected by the Incomparable. The Prince Regent himself was said to have slapped his thigh with mirth and exclaimed that he must be the only man in all of England who had not had the honour of being rejected by the Ice Damsel. It was something to be rectified and he very much looked forward to it, he was to have said.

Louisa sighed. The many, many suitors she'd turned down all blurred into a uniformed mass of unidentifiable faces. The truth was that she had never been particularly good at remembering faces. She was so terrible at it that chances were good she wouldn't recognise the Prince Regent himself if he were to stand in front of her.

"Which is, of course, arrant nonsense," her stepmother had proclaimed in her defence. "One cannot help but *not* recognise the man. Chances are, if you ever see a wine barrel with legs approach you in the ballroom, that it might be his Royal Highness. Forewarned is forearmed."

Louisa had smiled weakly but stored that bit of information away just in case for future reference. Heaven forbid she really did accidentally cut Prinny like she had cut so many of her male suitors.

As for all the other men ... they were all the same. And their manner of courtship was nearly identical. First the introduction: always the same scripted compliment, usually pertaining to her looks. Then a dance, followed promptly by a bouquet of flowers the next day, then a carriage ride in the park. They sought her father's permission to court her, which was always granted. Then, the embarrassing marriage proposal in the drawing room, as inevitable as thunder following lightning.

One hundred suitors. One hundred marriage proposals.

Her hand shook slightly as she raised it up to shade her eyes.

Good heavens. How could she have let it come to this?

It was time to put an end to this never-ending farce, and one hundred was as good a number as any. In fact, it was an excellent number, nice and round.

For if she didn't do something, they simply wouldn't stop. They would continue to hail from every corner of the country with their badly written love sonnets, flowers, and proposals of marriage. She seemed to be the only woman in all of England who could go on having Season after Season after Season, and still the offers would come.

And why?

Because she was an heiress. They wanted her for her notorious Highworth fortune. And possibly also for her looks, but only secondarily.

What else? Certainly not for her personality or her intellect.

She stared tight-lipped at the flame of her candle. Any other woman of her age would have been declared on the shelf long ago. But not Louisa Highworth. She would continue receiving offers when she was a rickety old hag.

Let us call a spade a spade, wrote one vitriolic gossip sheet. *If she weren't so beautiful and worth twenty-thousand pounds per annum, she'd be known for what she was, a mere ape-leader, an old maid long on the shelf. For what spinster of her advanced age (she was about to reach a shocking six-and-twenty soon) still had a Season? What woman could boast of seven Seasons in a row? It was* unheard of. It was a shocking embarrassment, unless one was a Highworth heiress, of course. Only a Highworth heiress could afford it. Only a Highworth heiress had the means.

Only a Highworth could get away with it, wrote another in more positive terms. Mark it, but our Incomparable will surely return next Season, even more beautiful, even more celebrated, with even more proposals. Nothing could ever harm her, not even her passionate temper. A slap in public? But how charming. Surely, she would return, as beautiful and untarnished and desirable as Botticelli's Venus, rising from the frothy sea.

The betting books were open in the gentlemen's clubs. The stakes were high.

A sick feeling ran through Louisa.

Were they right? Had she not done enough? What more must she do to get them to leave her alone? Should she have allowed Carrothair to kiss her in public? Should she have lured him into a secret antechamber to be discovered by some dowager?

No. That would have been the surest way to get herself caught in parson's mousetrap. Her father would have dragged in a clergyman and forced them to marry on the spot.

Louisa shuddered. Given the alternatives, what she'd done had been for the best. A dramatic, public statement. A slap.

Her stepmother had, predictably, had a fit of the vapours.

Her father, also predictably, had had an explosion of wrath that was, admittedly, unprecedented in its fury.

"You'd best hide in your room for a while," Penny, her abigail, had told her the next day. "He's smashed some valuable crystal vases in the library. It is best to stay out of his way today." The maid frowned in concern. "For the next few days, even, miss. Perhaps even weeks."

Louisa laughed hollowly. Her choleric, loving father, who wanted nothing more than for her to have a titled husband, was throwing a temper tantrum like a toddler.

"He'll get over it," she muttered. Then she curled up on her sofa, opened her book of sonnets and read, pretending not to hear the explosion of crystal in the library.

Chapter Two

The next morning, her stepmother sat at the breakfast table with red-rimmed eyes and dabbed her nose with a laced handkerchief drenched in lavender.

"Good morning, Sarah," Louisa said, dutifully planting a kiss on her wet cheek before sitting down.

Sarah did not respond, hiding her face behind her handkerchief and sobbing theatrically.

Unimpressed, Louisa sat down and proceeded to eat her breakfast.

Sarah lowered her handkerchief. "But what shocks me more than anything, Louisa..." she said, always in the habit of starting in the middle of a conversation.

"What?" Louisa continued to butter her toast.

"...is that you took your glove off in the middle of the ballroom. At Almack's. With all the patronesses looking on." Sarah shuddered.

Louisa's butter knife hung suspended in the air. "Ah, so I did." She'd done it on purpose of course, knowing full well that there could never be a satisfying slap resulting from a gloved hand. If one was to slap someone in public, one had to make sure it was done properly. She decided she'd done a good job of it.

Her stepmother moaned, "The indecency! The humiliation! It is tantamount to undressing in public. You might as well have stripped off your dress for everyone to see."

"I do think there's a difference between taking off a glove and taking off a dress," Louisa mused. "Removing a glove exposes the arm up to the elbow, whereas removing a dress exposes one's shift and corset. I dare say the latter is marginally more scandalous in a ballroom."

Sarah groaned. "How can you even mention shift and corset at the breakfast table?"

"Of course, if one were to take off one's stockings in the middle of the ballroom that would make a statement indeed. Perhaps I ought to have tried that—"

"Louisa!"

She laughed at her stepmother's scandalised tone.

"In all likelihood, it would only have accomplished the opposite and attracted even more suitors." Louisa cut her toast into rectangular strips and dipped them into her egg, suppressing a smirk. She had lovely, shapely legs, and she knew it, too.

"Louisa!" It sounded more like a moan now. "Horrible, unnatural girl. Haven't you a grain of humility in your body? Why am I even talking to you? The shame! What on earth did that poor boy ever do to you to deserve this kind of treatment?"

It was a fair question.

"He's neither poor, nor a boy," Louisa replied briefly. "He questioned my virtue."

Sarah gasped. "How ungentlemanly of him. No doubt he must have provoked you. But to dash the ratafia into his face? Was that justified?"

"If I'd been a gentleman, I'd have called him out. We'd be having a duel right now in Hyde Park as we speak. The slap and the ratafia weren't nearly enough. I should've poured an entire bowl of punch over his head and rubbed in some cream cake on top. But alas, Almack's refreshment room provided neither," Louisa lamented.

Sarah's eyes widened. "What on earth did he say?"

"I'll spare you his exact words. It would be demeaning to have to repeat them."

After she had repeatedly rebuffed his advances, Carrothair had sidled up to her and slurred into her ear, "I must say, it's become quite a sport amongst the gentlemen to wager on your next rejection. One might think you enjoy the power somewhat too much. Or is it that no man can live up to your deluded expectations? Hm? What do you say? I wonder what it takes to melt the Ice Damsel?" He'd trailed a finger down her neck.

Louisa slapped his hand away.

"Why not just place a wager on yourself?" she'd replied in a voice that could've frosted over hell itself. "Oh, I forgot. You've already joined the ranks of the rejected, haven't you? Like leftovers of a lavishly set table that no one wants. What does one do with them, I wonder? Surely one throws them to the pigs in the gutter, where one will find oneself in good company."

Ah, that had been a sharply clever rejoinder. She'd been rather proud of herself.

He'd grown pale with fury. "It's fascinating how a lady of your ... 'experience'... still manages to maintain such an air of innocence. One would hardly guess the number of suitors who've graced your drawing room," he whispered into her ear. "Or should we say bedroom?"

She'd rolled down her glove and slapped him, followed by the ratafia.

And she didn't regret it in the least. One might even say that Carrothair had done her a favour by giving her the excuse to make a dramatic public statement to extricate herself from the suitors' dilemma.

Phibbs, their butler, entered at this moment with a mournful expression on his face, carrying a letter on a salver.

Sarah wiped her nose, took it, read it, and promptly burst into tears again.

Louisa patted her shoulder. "There, there. I'm certain it can't be as bad as all that." She took the letter from Sarah's shaking hand and perused it.

It *was* as bad as all that.

A crumb of toast stuck in her throat as she read it. She coughed, took a sip of her tea, reread the letter, folded it, and replaced it on the salver.

"They've revoked your Almack's voucher!" her stepmother moaned when she was capable of talking again. "It was a unanimous decision made by all the patronesses. Oh, the shame! I vow, I shall not survive this day."

Well, that was what she wanted, was it not? To be

banned from the hallowed grounds of Almack's, the temple of the ton. As certain as the amen that followed a prayer, this would be irrevocably followed by further withdrawals of invitations to other major balls and events. The doors to the ton would close in her face, one by one. Gossip would grow rampant. People would shun and snub her in the street. No one would ever speak to her again.

Her reputation was tarnished. Her ruin complete.

Well done, Louisa. Well done.

Her teacup shook slightly as she set it down.

"Phibbs, where is my hartshorn salt?" Sarah asked with a weak voice.

Phibbs rushed to fetch it.

The door crashed open, and her father burst into the room, whip in hand. "Where is she?" he roared.

Like a flash, Louisa shot from her chair to the other side of the table.

"Come here, Louisa, and I will give you the thrashing of a lifetime." He raised his whip.

"Hector!" her stepmother cried out in alarm. "Surely you cannot mean to whip the child with that brutal instrument. She is not a horse!"

Her father flexed the whip in his hands. "Why not? If nothing else, it will get through to her. At least my horses are more obedient than she is. At least they win races! And my daughter, what does she do? She rejects all her suitors, all perfectly fine men, and slaps a lord in the middle of a dance."

"We were not dancing, Papa," Louisa corrected. "We were standing in the refreshment room."

"Bah! I am done pampering this spoiled, self-indulgent, proud and hard-hearted creature. Nothing good has come of it, as one can very well see."

Louisa ducked behind the footman standing by the sideboard and held him in front of her like a shield. The poor man gulped and trembled with fear.

"Come here!" her father roared, smacking his whip on the table, causing the porcelain cups to jump.

"Calm yourself, Papa." She lifted a beseeching hand. "I'm certain things will blow over soon."

"Not this time it won't," her father huffed. "You insulted Lady Jersey's nephew. It was as if you had slapped her personally."

Goodness. Oh, that was well done, indeed! But why did Lady Jersey have such an ill-bred nephew?

"You've made yourself a mortal enemy for life. Which is fine. Fine!" He tossed the whip on the table, to Louisa's great relief. "If you choose to make the most powerful society hostess your enemy, so be it. But that also means that her husband is withdrawing his invitation to a hunt that I've been looking forward to all year. And why? Per his wife's request. And following that, Mounteroy withdrew his invitation to his personal race, and you know"—he wagged his finger in the air—"you *know* how important that was to me."

Her father had a passion for hunting and horseback races. He'd been waiting the entire year for Mounteroy's invitation, and when it finally came, it was all he could speak of. With no title of his own, it meant a great deal to her father to receive invitations from the peers of the realm. Too many looked down on him, claiming that the

Miss Louisa's Final Waltz

fabulous glitter of his wealth smelled of the shop and was tarnished by the soot of his coal mines and textile factories. None of her father's business acumen and wealth made up for the fact that he was not a titled peer and therefore not seen as an equal. But they did rather desperately want to marry his daughter, hypocrites that they were.

"I'm truly sorry, Papa." She did sincerely feel sorry.

Her father, out of steam, had slumped into a chair, hunched over, both his hands on his head, looking like a crumpled bundle of misery. She hadn't considered that her disgrace would also affect her father and her stepmother. It had been short-sighted of her to not think of that.

Louisa bit on her lower lip. How foolish of her. Perhaps she should have given Carrothair his set-down in private after all. But now it was too late; what was done was done.

"Be that as it may, you've danced your final waltz in Almack's or any other ballroom." Her father lifted his weary head. "You might as well pack up and take yourself off to a nunnery."

"Not such a bad prospect." In a nunnery, they might actually leave her alone. She'd have her own room where she could read all day, and sew, and pray, and work in the garden, and whatever else it was that nuns did, and not be bothered by the rest of the world. It was a pity that Henry VIII had disbanded all convents and rid the country of nunneries. It had been a highly inconsiderate move on his part, she decided.

"Why, Louisa. Why? If you hate the prospect of

marriage that much, why not just pick the best of the bunch—preferably a titled one who likes horse racing and hunting—and just marry the chap and then ask him to leave you alone? You can send him off to some island. I'll buy you one specifically for that purpose."

Indeed, her father could afford to do so, for he owned more than one island in the West Indies.

A deep, dark streak of despair ran through her. A grief so old, buried in the farthest recesses of her soul, that she'd almost forgotten it existed.

How could she ever explain this? He would never understand. No one ever would. He would merely have another fit of anger if he discovered that she still hadn't forgotten the past.

"Let me turn the question around, Father. Why do you want me to marry so desperately?"

"Why do we want you to get married?" Her father and her stepmother exchanged speaking looks. "What kind of question is that? Our daughter did not just ask that, did she? It is simple. It's what any good parent would want for their child in this day and age. Marriage is a great blessing," he said eagerly, falling into a preachy tone. "In fact, it is the greatest blessing life can offer, especially when the union is crowned with children. And what greater joy is there to have than children?" He sighed.

Sarah's eyes glittered brightly as she nodded. Alas, her father's union with Sarah had not been blessed with children. Louisa was an only child and would also have dearly loved to have half-brothers and sisters, but it was not to be. She knew how much that pained them, even though Sarah put up a brave face. She awkwardly patted her stepmother's hands.

"I have always said I wanted you to experience the same kind of union I have had with your mother, and now with your stepmother." He grabbed Sarah's other hand. "I was lucky twice, which is why I gave you the freedom to choose your husband. I want you to experience the joy of marriage as well. And lastly, you are not just anyone, Louisa. You are an heiress of considerable fortune, burdensome as it is." He heaved a sigh. "Our family needs to secure this legacy. We deserve to become a dynasty. The Highworth dynasty. Which is why I keep saying a titled gentleman would be an asset. But you have taught me to lower my standards to such a degree that I will take anyone who will have you—provided you agree to him. And provided he takes on our name if he wants to inherit the business."

"The Highworth Dynasty." The words fell from her lips bitterly. "You have reminded me of this every single day for my entire life. Although, Father, let me ask you one question: this family legacy, this dynasty. Is it your dream or mine?"

"It is our collective dream, of course. As a family." Her father lifted a weary hand to wipe his forehead. "You know what? Forget the title. Forget the name. Just one chap. Any chap. It really doesn't matter who or what he does. Just get married. Have children. Be happy. That is all."

She stared at her father, wondering how it was possible to simultaneously love and hate a person so.

"Just one chap? Any chap? Very well, Father," she

drew herself up proudly. "I take you by your word. If that is your wish, I vow that I shall marry the first man who crosses my path. And I mean this very literally. I'll marry John the footman if he's the first."

The footman she'd just used as a shield earlier jumped back three feet away from her with a horrified expression on his face.

Her father pushed the chair back that it fell over with a crash and pointed a trembling finger at her. "Mark my words, if you do that, I will personally drag you to the altar, even if it is the lowest scum of the rookery you come across, if it is the last thing I ever do," he roared. "You will be married. And, just to be clear, you won't receive a single farthing from me." He slashed his hand in the air. "As of today, you are no longer an heiress." He stormed out of the room.

Sarah rushed after him, wringing her hands.

In the silence of the room Louisa remained sitting by the table, erect and pale, and sipped her tea as if nothing extraordinary had happened.

Chapter Three

The next day Louisa donned a high-waisted, white muslin dress with several rows of fine trimmings. Her thick, honey-golden hair cascaded in rich, glossy curls about her shoulders, framing her long, swan-like neck. Her features were striking; she had a proud nose and a sensitive mouth with pink, petal lips that rarely parted in a smile.

Long-limbed, lushly curved, and proud. She studied her figure in a mirror dispassionately. Yes, she supposed her appearance fulfilled the current beauty ideal. Many people would be surprised to learn that she did not like the way she looked. She would have preferred to look different, for she'd always admired the smaller, lither, Mediterranean type.

"Today is a special day, Penny," she said.

"Is it, miss?" Penny arranged the Kashmiri shawl around her and stepped back, satisfied.

"Yes." Louisa drew in a deep breath. "Today is my wedding day."

Penny stared at her with round eyes and clasped her hands together. "Oh! But who...?"

"I haven't the faintest idea," Louisa confessed. "It will be revealed in due time." She had to admit that she felt a sick churning in the pit of her stomach. "I have told my father that I shall marry the first man I encounter today." She swallowed. "I hope Phipps and John don't show themselves until then. Though I hold them both in high regard, I'd rather not marry either of them unless absolutely necessary."

"Phipps? John?" Penny's mouth dropped open. "You'd never do that!"

"Oh yes, I would," Louisa replied grimly. "I swore I'll marry the first man who crosses my path. Be he a beggar, servant, or soldier."

Imagine being married to Phipps! The man was well over sixty years old. She lifted her chin. Even if it came down to it, she would do it. She'd made a vow, hadn't she?

"But, miss!" Penny wailed. "What if you run into the chimney sweep? Or the coachman? Or, heaven forbid, the night soil man?" The night soil man collected the excrement from cesspools and privies and sold it as fertiliser in the countryside.

Louisa swallowed. "Then this shall be my fate, Penny. I have taken a vow, and I shall keep it." She was determined to become a martyr on her own altar of foolishness.

"In that case, miss, let me rush out and warn the household staff to stay out of your way today. Do not leave the room for the next fifteen minutes." Penny scampered out of the room before Louisa could stop her.

She waited for a quarter of an hour. Then, taking a deep breath, she opened the door and stepped out into the corridor.

As fate would have it, the first man she ran across was —her father. He wore a banyan, had a newspaper tucked under his arm, and looked thunderous.

"Today is the day!" He wagged the rolled-up newspaper at her.

"I haven't forgotten, sir."

Lifting her chin, Louisa marched down the stairs, noting that Penny had done her work, and all the male servants were indeed nowhere to be seen.

She flung open the front door. It was a bright morning, and Park Lane was deserted. Not a single carriage or coachman in sight. Not a single passerby, not a single caller.

Now that she'd finally decided to get married, had the entire male world of London suddenly decided to hide? Where were all the men?

Louisa marched down the street towards Piccadilly, followed by Penny, who ran after her, wringing her hands.

She supposed she could linger outside Apsley House, also known as Number One. It was currently owned by Wellington's brother, the Marquess of Wellesley, and had a steady stream of aristocratic male callers. If she waited long enough by the gates, there was a good chance one of them would cross her path. But that would be akin to cheating. It was likely that every gentleman who entered Apsley House had already proposed to her in the past and been rejected. She might as well have accepted Sir Frippery Fop's hand and spared herself the trouble.

The streets were oddly silent. Frowning, Louisa paused at the corner, and noticed that there wasn't a single vehicle on the road.

She narrowed her eyes.

Except for one.

Across the road stood a mule-drawn cart. Next to it was—eureka! Dressed in a rumpled, ill-fitting waistcoat with a cap crooked on his head, the man bent down to lift a crate onto the cart.

Her heart jumped, then raced.

There he was. A simple costermonger.

She swallowed. Her bridegroom.

It took every inch of her willpower to put one foot in front of the other and to cross the street. Her heart pounded in her ears, her stomach churned, and her hands trembled.

Yet she continued to walk straight towards him with singular determination.

He did not see her approach and only paused his activity when she stood right in front of him.

She crossed her arms and stared.

The man took a step back in surprise, almost dropping the crate. He looked over his shoulder, to the left, the right, then back at her again.

He set down the crate, pushed back his hat and scratched his head. He looked away again, then finally met her gaze.

He was tall with light eyes, a tanned and weathered face, uncombed hair, and a scruffy two-day beard. He didn't look any different to the many hundreds of costermongers who worked in the London markets. His stained waistcoat worn over a wrinkled shirt that was rolled up to the elbows revealed muscular arms. Louisa wrinkled her nose. He probably hadn't bathed in ages. If ever.

She wondered whether he could read and write.

She closed her eyes painfully for a moment, swallowed, then opened them again and nodded.

"Milady...?" he mumbled uneasily. "'ow can I 'elp? An apple, maybe, or a carrot?" He lifted one of each in his hand. He spoke in a thick accent spoken from the East End of London.

"What is your name?" she demanded.

"Robert Jones, milady."

"Are you married?"

"Nay."

"Do you have a sweetheart?"

"Nay."

"You'll do," she pronounced.

"Eh?"

"Follow me." Without much ado, she grabbed him by the arm and dragged him across the street back to her house, where the entire household had gathered at the entrance to watch the spectacle unfold before them.

The man recoiled at the sight of so many people inspecting him with various degrees of surprise. "Begging yer pardon, but what's the meaning of this?" he demanded.

"Come in." Louisa nodded at the door. "That is, if you please."

He threw her a suspicious look. The people at the entrance stepped aside.

"Why?"

"We'll explain things momentarily. If you could come inside, we can discuss it all in the drawing room."

"If yer meaning to order some fruit or vegetables, I daresay I can discuss it with the cook in the kitchen, not in the drawing room," he began, visibly ill at ease at setting foot into the expensive townhouse. Then he caught sight of Louisa's father standing in front of him with his arms crossed, scowling.

"Inside!" he thundered.

"Yes, s-sir," the poor man stuttered, tearing off his cap and clutching it to his chest as he made his way into the house, bowing crookedly to everyone, including Phipps, who gave him a scornful look and gave the footman a quick order to sweep after his trail of mud. He stood awkwardly in the drawing room, the centre of all attention.

He was uncommonly tall, Louisa noticed. He stood large and broad, easily a head taller than herself—quite a feat, considering her own stature as a tall woman. He even towered over her father.

Her father! Oh dear. He was breathing heavily, and his face had taken on a puce colour.

Her stepmother sank back on the sofa, moaning and holding her handkerchief to her face, as if the scene in front of her was too painful to watch.

The servants gathered at the door.

At a nod from her father, Phipps began to close it.

"Wait," her father ordered. "You"—he pointed at

Walker, his secretary, who was standing next to Phipps with a slack jaw—"and another person are needed as witnesses. And fetch a clergyman."

"Yes, sir," Phipps replied.

"As for you." Louisa's father turned to the costermonger. "What is your name?"

"Robert Jones, sir." He looked at her father uneasily. "Am I in trouble, sir? I was merely picking up some apple boxes. I swear I meant to move the cart immediately afterwards."

Her father cut him off. "Robert Jones. You have the honour of being chosen as my daughter's husband." He gestured to Louisa standing in the middle of the room, clutching the top of the chair for support so tightly that her knuckles were white.

"Eh?" The man's mouth dropped open.

At least he had a good set of teeth, Louisa noted. White and strong. She might have objected if half of them had been black and missing.

"You're marrying my daughter," her father repeated with exaggerated slowness.

The man stared. "Begging your pardon, sir. Do I understand that you want me to marry your daughter?"

"He appears to be a fool," her father growled. "But at least his hearing is in order. You have understood correctly. The clergyman is sent for."

The man backed away. "Is this a jest?"

"It is not."

"Her?" He pointed a thumb in her direction.

"Yes."

"What's wrong with her?"

His mistrustful attitude towards her, as if she were about to sprout horns and a tail, caused Louisa to snap. "Wrong? There's nothing whatsoever wrong with me."

"Beggin' yer pardon." He bowed in her direction. "But something must be if yer wanting me to marry ye."

His gaze swept appraisingly over her figure. Quite inexplicably, Louisa blushed.

"There's nothing wrong with my daughter. She is beautiful, as you can very well see. She is accomplished. She speaks five languages and plays the harp. The only problem is that she is unmarried. We are in the process of rectifying that."

"If she's such a paragon, why marry her to me?" the man protested. He slowly edged backward towards the door, where Phipps was standing guard, his arms across his chest.

"My name is Louisa Highworth."

The man's eyes widened. "No. The Ice Damsel?"

Louisa stifled a groan. Even the lowest costermonger had heard of her.

"Yer truly wanting me to marry the Ice Damsel?"

"Stop calling her that," her father said irritably.

"But, sir, yer honour, yer graceship, with all due respect, why should I marry the Ice Da—I mean, yer daughter? Can't you find another toff to marry her to?" He waved a calloused hand. "Some drawing room dandy more suitable to the task?"

Louisa cast him a sweet smile. "You're very suitable, Mr Jones. I choose you."

That apparently rendered him speechless, for he said

nothing for the next few minutes. When he regained his tongue, he said, "But why should I? What's innit for me?"

"Ah, we come to the heart of the matter. Sit down." Her father gestured to the armchair in front of him. When the man hesitated, Highworth snarled, "Sit!"

The man stumbled into the armchair and sat, but Louisa's father remained standing, appearing more at ease now that he could look down at him. "Make no mistake, my daughter has been disinherited. If you're expecting a fortune to come with her, get that out of your head, because it's not coming."

The man jumped up again. "Well, in that case—"

"Sit down."

The man ducked and quickly sat down again.

"As I said before, my daughter is an exquisite woman, refined, cultured, educated, and possesses all social graces."

A slight sneer crossed his face. "But what do I do with one like that? I don't need no society lady," the man argued. "All the graces and accomplishments are of no use to me if she melts like sugar in the rain. My kind of woman must be physically strong and robust." His eyes flicked over her dismissively. "She has to be able to lift a crate of turnips without batting an eyelid. Not a pretty china doll that breaks easily. She's entirely useless to me. I'm sorry." He shook his head and got to his feet.

Pretty china doll?

Melting like sugar in the rain?

She was not physically strong and robust?

She was of no use to him?

Louisa was outraged. "I can lift a crate of turnips," she declared. "Do you want me to prove it to you?"

The man pulled his mouth to a sarcastic smile. "That is entirely unnecessary, milady."

"Miss. The name is Miss Highworth."

The man shrugged and turned to go.

Highworth pressed him down again into the chair. "I understand completely. I'm a man of business after all. It's money you want."

The man pretended to consider. "Yes, sir, yer honour, yer graceship. I mean, no, sir. Well, money won't hurt neither ... but ye just said she ain't got no fortune. How much are ye offering, then?"

There it was again. Money. It always came back to that, didn't it?

She clenched her fingers into her palms, choking back the hot tears that shot into her eyes.

"As I said, she won't inherit, but to ease the first few months of your married life, as an incentive, I'm giving you a small financial bonus in the form of a dowry." He named a sum that, to Louisa, was small indeed, but it seemed to take the wind out of the costermonger's sails.

He gaped at her father as if the sum he mentioned was the biggest he'd ever heard of in his entire life. For a costermonger, it might well have been.

"Yes, sir. Very well, sir. I'll marry her, then. Gladly, sir. When? How?"

"As soon as the minister arrives. We have a special licence," her father responded.

Chapter Four

SHE WAS MARRIED.

With the arrival of Reverend Shaw, everything unfolded in a whirlwind. Louisa felt so overwhelmed by the rapid succession of events that she could scarcely comprehend it all. She barely heard the words spoken, she signed the papers in a daze, and before she knew it, Reverend Shaw was congratulating her and addressing her as "Mrs Jones."

There had been a moment of awkward silence during the ceremony where everyone had looked at her expectantly. A rushing sound filled her ears. She'd been so lost in her own thoughts that she hadn't heard a single word uttered by the minister.

Louisa blinked, shook her head as if to clear her mind, then said, "I will."

There was an arrested expression on her bridegroom's face, a curious mixture of alertness, bafflement, and unholy amusement. She briefly wondered if she'd missed something important. Perhaps she'd imagined it.

His demeanour quickly shifted as he hooded his eyes, and his face was as impassive as before. The minister continued as Robert placed a simple gold band on her finger, which her father had given him, and their marriage was solemnised.

That's how quickly one got married, Louisa thought as she hurriedly signed the register, without seeing a word on the paper.

She stared in disbelief at the stranger, that large hulk of a man standing next to her, who was now her husband.

A dirty costermonger she'd picked up on the street a few minutes earlier.

Good heavens.

What on earth was she supposed to do with him now?

Surely, in a few hours, she would heartily regret this course of action, but at the moment she felt merely ... numb.

Everyone was still giving her strange looks. A hushed silence had fallen over the room. Sarah had dropped her handkerchief and looked at her with wide eyes and half-parted lips. Phibbs wore a distinct expression of puzzlement, and footman John outright gaped. Only her father displayed satisfaction, puffing out his chest proudly as if he had accomplished some insurmountable feat.

"Well, finally. I thought I'd never see the day," he said with false heartiness as he rubbed his hands. "Now that you're a married woman, you will naturally follow your husband to his home. For that is the natural course of things. Say, where do you live, Roger? Robin? Richard?"

She didn't blame her father's inability to recall his name. She had already forgotten it herself.

"Robert. I rent a room in St Giles, yer graceship."

"Merciful heavens," Sarah groaned. "The rookery! The poor child will be living with the cadgers and thieves in the worst slum in London."

"It ain't that bad," Robert offered. "But I daresay my room might be getting a tad too tight, since I'm sharing it with two other mates. A chimney sweep and an ironmonger."

To this, Sarah found no answer but merely stared in mute despair at her new son-in-law.

It was a dream, Louisa decided. It was all just a dream. And since it was a dream, there was no harm at all in saying, "Let's go then to your home in the rookery."

Robert nodded at her in approval. "You'll like it. It even has a window overlooking Gin Lane."

Gin Lane was the most notorious part of St Giles, the hubbub of the gin sellers, which meant the street was teeming with drunkards, hardly something to brag about. But Robert seemed to think the contrary.

Mr Highworth cleared his throat. "I've already told the maid to pack a small trunk of essential items for you. You won't need much for your new life. This"—he lifted a purse so that its contents clinked—"is for you, the promised dowry." He tossed the purse to Robert, who caught it deftly with one hand.

"Yes, sir. Thank you, sir. You won't regret it, sir. Yer graceship." He beamed, flashing his teeth at him.

Louisa returned to her room and changed her thin muslin gown for a woollen one and her thin slippers for leather walking boots. She wouldn't need any of her silk ballroom dresses, but she made sure her maid had packed her shawls, coats, petticoats, and stockings. The pearl necklace and earrings were hers; she would take them with her and sell them. And she had some pin money left; not much, but it was better than nothing. That, too, she packed away in her reticule. She put on her bonnet and went downstairs where her father and husband were waiting in the hall.

Her father cleared his throat anew and patted her awkwardly on the shoulder, and Sarah had pulled her into a tearful embrace. Suddenly, Louisa found herself on the costermonger's cart, together with a small trunk—and her husband beside her.

"Hiyup," he told the donkey, and the cart began to move.

It dawned on Louisa this was truly happening. She had married a stranger from the street and now she would go live with him.

He drew the cart to a stop right in front of the Hyde Park Turnpike, lowered the ribbons, turned to her, and said something.

She didn't react until he repeated himself for the third time, when he snapped his fingers in front of her face. "Attention, Louisa. Look at me," he commanded.

When she finally snapped her eyes up, she met his flinty gaze, which bore intensely into hers.

"Well?" He had sharp hazel eyes, tinged with a hint of mockery and expectation as if—as if—he was waiting for something significant?

Louisa knitted her eyebrows together in confusion.

He seemed to be waiting for some sort of reaction from her. But what?

He crossed his arms and his mouth twitched.

She shook herself. "Yes? Did you say something?"

He stared at her intently a moment longer.

It crossed her mind that he didn't like her. She drew herself up and lifted her chin. It mattered not whether he liked her. Not even if he was her husband. She certainly didn't like him.

When she didn't react, he huffed and shrugged. "It occurred to me, with all the blunt, we're rather rich, now, yes?" He patted his pocket where he'd stuffed the purse her father had given him.

Money. Again. Louisa curled her lips into a cynical smile. "Rich is a relative word, but yes, I suppose in your world, we could be called thus."

"Well, now that we're rich, I was thinking we don't absolutely have to return to St Giles." He raised a hand to indicate the turnpike. "Not unless ye're keen on it. We could go somewhere else."

Louisa looked at him as if she were seeing him for the first time. "Are you saying we could leave London?"

"Why not? The whole world is open to us. No one will miss me if I don't return. And this," he gestured to the produce in his cart, "is mine anyhow. Don't have to sell it at the Fleet market, can sell it anywhere I want. How about an adventure, madame? Where to?"

As the impact of his words sank in, she almost lost her breath from the sudden sense of excitement that swept through her. "You mean, we could go anywhere? We could travel?"

"That's what I said! Where would you like to go? North? South? East? West?"

She didn't have to think long. "West."

"Yer wish is my command."

He made a mock bow and set the cart in motion.

HE ASKED her at every crossroad which way to go, and she directed him to the south-west. They drove in silence. Louisa stewed in her own thoughts, sitting upright, gripping the edge of the hard wooden seat to keep from falling off. Even though he snuck occasional sideways glances at her, he made no attempt to engage her in conversation.

Louisa was grateful for that. She feared that if he did, she'd either burst into tears, start howling, or, what's worse, curse her father, her life, her fate, and everything in between.

Judging from his wary, searching glances, she suspected that her husband was expecting precisely that sort of behaviour from her.

"Not tired yet? Would you like to go back? Just say the word and we'll return to London," he asked her at regular intervals.

Finally, she retorted in a waspish voice. "Stop it. I don't tire easily, and we're not going back. I don't tend to retract my decisions, ever."

"Indeed?" he drawled. "We shall see. Very well, then, Ice Damsel."

"Stop calling me that," she snapped, but he just grinned.

He was making fun of her. He expected her to turn into a watering pot. What had he said earlier? That she would be 'no use to him if she melted like sugar in the rain.' She gritted her teeth. Since that was exactly what she wanted to do more than anything else in the world right now, she decided it was better not to say anything at all and to hold on to her composure with an iron reserve for as long as it lasted.

After they'd passed safely through Hounslow Heath without being robbed or attacked by highwaymen, he pulled up the cart in front of a seedy-looking inn. The creaky sign above the entrance said, "The Red Rooster". Several horses and carriages stood in the muddy yard, and a stable boy was running back and forth with buckets of water for the horses. Louisa looked at the inn doubtfully. She'd never set foot in a place like this. It was much too inferior compared to the richer inns where the Highworths usually stopped to change their horses.

"It'll be dark soon. Might be a good idea to get a room for the night," he suggested.

Louisa's first inclination was to agree. She was uncomfortable on the hard seat, shaken to the bones by the bumpy ride, and she wouldn't mind a room, a soft bed, a bath, and a proper tea tray with almond cakes and cucumber sandwiches—but wait.

"We can't afford it."

That was the reality. True, her father had given him a small pouch with money, but it hadn't looked like it was much, and she'd rather not squander it on the first day of their trip. She was her father's daughter and had some business sense, after all. It was best to keep the money for later.

"I daresay we could at least afford a room for the wedding night," he drawled.

Wedding night!

Now that was something that had completely eluded her. But he was right, wasn't he? Where there was a wedding, there was a wedding night, as certain as the sun rising in the east, as certain as the letter B following the letter A, and as inevitable as death and taxes.

She looked at him with wide, horrified eyes.

He raised his eyebrow and smirked. To Louisa, it looked like he was leering.

"No," she said with alarm. "Out of the question." She shifted to the far end of the bench, as far away from him as possible without falling off the seat. "I mean, it's not a good idea. We can't afford a room. It's best if we spend the money wisely. If we start squandering it now, we won't have enough to rent a cottage later, when we settle down somewhere. It's better to invest the money in something that will last."

He weighed his head. "Settle down. Rent a cottage somewhere. That sounds nice. Is this our plan?"

"Yes. We must find a place to live, of course. It has to be affordable. So you see, we must save the money and not waste it on irrelevant things like"—she lifted a hand—"a room for the night."

He weighed his head solemnly, as if gravely pondering on her words. "Yes, that's rather irrelevant, to find a room for the night. Who needs a roof over one's head with a comfortable bed for a wedding night? Certainly not us."

Was he mocking her? But his face was straight.

"Tonight," she said, looking around at the fields that surrounded them, "we'll have to sleep outside."

There it was again, that hard, mocking look. But also, something more, as if he was assessing her. A hint of grudging respect, maybe? The man probably hadn't imagined that the Incomparable would have no qualms sleeping on the bare ground outside.

"Very well, then." A slight smile played on his lips, as if this situation amused him. "Let's make camp and bivouac under that oak tree over there. It's warm enough. And you'll discover that sleeping on the ground can be just as restful as sleeping on the softest feather beds."

Well, if he always agreed with her without any objections in that docile manner, they were bound to have a fabulously happy marriage, indeed, Louisa thought sourly. She was not oblivious to the challenge uttered in those words. This was her opportunity to prove to him that she was more resilient than people thought.

She climbed down from the cart and studied the field in front of them. There, under that tree, the ground seemed dry and suitable for sleeping.

"There's some moss on the ground over there. And for supper"—she turned to regard the cart and swallowed—"we have parsnips." She walked over to the side and lifted a box. It was heavier than it looked, but she managed. There, she'd done it. She gave him a challenging look. Had he seen that? She'd proved she was strong enough to lift the box.

But Robert was busy elsewhere as he began to rummage around, rearranging the contents in the crates. "I'll be back shortly." He hauled a crate filled with fruit and vegetables on top of each shoulder as if they weighed nothing, and before she could ask what he was planning on doing, he'd left in long strides towards the inn with a whistle on his lips.

Consider it an adventure, she told herself. A grand journey like the travels of Gulliver. Travelling to unknown, magical places. It was a clear summer night, and with some luck it wouldn't rain. She sat down on the mossy ground under the tree. At least it was soft. She leaned against the trunk.

What would the *beau monde* say now if they saw her now? What would they say if they saw the Incomparable camped out in the country like a regular country bumpkin?

She plucked a blade of grass from the ground.

Little did they know that once upon a time, she'd enjoyed doing that. Scrambling about in the forest, swimming in the lake, fishing in the brook, climbing trees, taking naps in the meadow. None who knew her as Miss Louisa Highworth would have thought it possible that she'd used to scamper about the countryside like a veritable peasant boy.

When had she last done this?

Memories surfaced; memories she'd long forgotten. Memories she'd wanted to forget.

She hadn't been alone, then, no. She'd had a companion then, a dear friend.

Will.

The only friend she'd ever had. They'd made promises to each other they couldn't keep.

She stared blindly into the distance.

It was so long ago.

A familiar, dull pain pressed down on her chest. She took a deep, shuddering breath and tapped her hand against her breastbone.

The costermonger, that is, Robert, her husband—she must begin to think of him in that way—came striding back from the inn, this time not carrying a wooden crate, but a basket. He had some blankets tucked under his arm.

Louisa scrambled up.

"I was able to sell all my apples," he reported cheerfully. "In return for some woollen blankets"—he threw them beside the tree—"and some food." He set the basket on the ground. It contained a tankard of liquid, a bowl with vegetable stew, bread rolls, and two spoons.

It smelled divine.

"What is it?" She sniffed the pungent liquid from the tankard.

He handed it to her. "Ale."

She took a tentative sip, grimaced, and took a second sip.

The stew was a thick soup consisting of indefinable vegetables and grains. It was poorly seasoned, and though Louisa made a face at her first taste, she ate until she was full. Meanwhile, he built a fire with quick, sure movements, as if he'd done it a thousand times before.

Then he sat down next to her, took the bowl, and shovelled the rest of the stew into his mouth, taking turns to bite into the bread. Then he finished the ale from the tankard and wiped his mouth with his sleeve. "Ahh, that was good."

Louisa watched him dispassionately. He had the manners of an uncivilised boor. But she supposed one couldn't expect anything less from a costermonger from St Giles.

"I am going to sleep," she announced.

"Do that," he agreed. "I'll keep watch and tend the fire." He lay down on the grass, his head on his arms, staring up at the night sky and chewing a piece of bark.

"Don't you want a blanket?" she asked after watching him for a while.

"No. You can have it. Don't mind me. I'm used to sleeping in all sorts of places, including the bare ground. This isn't the worst."

For a moment, Louisa wondered what kind of life he'd led to be used to sleeping like this. Then she shrugged, grabbed one of the woollen blankets, placed it on the ground at a safe distance from him and lay down on it. She covered herself with the second one, and then, for good measure, with her Kashmiri shawl. It was hard and uncomfortable, but she was warm.

She would survive.

The night sky was clear, and a billion stars twinkled above.

She would *not* cry.

Chapter Five

Louisa sat on the seat of the cart in a rumpled cotton dress, her uncombed hair tucked under her bonnet, her face hastily washed that morning from the bucket of ice-cold water that Robert had drawn up from the well in the inn's courtyard. How she longed for a bath, a change of linen, and fresh stockings!

A cup of hot chocolate. A piece of toast with soft egg. Her warm, comfortable bed. Her bookshelf! The list of things she missed kept growing.

She'd woken up that morning wrapped in more blankets and shawls than she could remember. She thought she'd pulled only one woollen blanket and a shawl over her shoulder when she went to sleep; but she'd woken up with three tucked tightly about her, in addition to her shawl folded into a small pillow placed under her head. Had he obtained more blankets and covered her? If he had, she did not recall when during the night he had done so. She reluctantly admitted that it was inexplicably thoughtful of him.

The initial sense of excitement and adventure of the journey had worn off. The last few nights had been the same—a makeshift bed in the field, the meadow or under a tree. Robert at a safe distance, tending to the fire. Her entire body was stiff, her shoulders tense, and her back ached. As hard and uncomfortable as her bedstead was on the ground, and cumbersome as the journey on the lumbering cart was, she was never cold or hungry. That was due to Robert. He was always able to obtain sustenance for them, wherever they were. He'd brought pasties and pies, mugs of tea and ale, and once, even several slices of apple cake that the innkeeper's wife had just baked. Otherwise, he treated her with wariness, as if expecting her to collapse any moment and beg him to take her home.

But as tempting as it was to cry and throw a tantrum, Louisa stubbornly refused to do so. She'd long since made up her mind to show him that she was no useless china doll, as he'd so contemptuously called her.

They had been travelling for several days. It had been painfully slow, the roads were bad, and she was exhausted to the bone, but fortunately the weather had cooperated, and it hadn't rained. The rolling hills alternated between meadows and farming fields. Under normal circumstances she might have enjoyed it, but she felt as if she'd been caught in a never-ending dream.

"How far d'you want to go?" he asked her once.

"Until we arrive," she'd replied.

"Where exactly?"

"Anywhere," she'd answered cryptically.

Southwest, she kept telling him. But when they'd

reached Salisbury, she'd paused for longer than usual, staring at the wooden signposts at the crossroads. This particular crossroad felt heavily symbolic for her life. Should she pursue the path west, towards Dorset, back into the past? Back into chapters of her life she'd long since closed? Or should she shrug it all off and venture north instead—towards Bath, perhaps, and then further north to Wales, or Scotland, even—to explore new paths and see new places? It would seem more fitting with her new life. Yet she felt a strange pull, a yearning to follow the road west. But what would await her there? What if she dug up old ghosts and scratched at the scabs that covered old scars? What if?

She wiped her perspiring hands on her skirt.

Robert leaned against the cart and chewed on a long leaf of grass. Seeing her indecision, he took the leaf from his mouth and threw it away.

"Let's go that way." He pointed to the road in the direction of Dorchester.

"Why?"

He shrugged. "Why not? It's as good a road as any. It looks solid and safe. Shall we, then?"

In response, Louisa climbed back on the cart, and Robert set it in motion.

During their journey, she'd been thinking deeply, reviewing her entire life, especially the last seven Seasons. Her hundred rejected suitors. Her father's choleric, volatile behaviour, which she couldn't understand. And then her own behaviour, which she understood even less.

As if respecting her reluctance to speak, Robert had

never pressed her to converse with him—they had travelled in silence most of the time—until now. Today, he seemed unusually talkative.

"I was wondering whether you had a particular destination in mind," he said, "and if so, would you care to share where we're going? Because wherever that is, I'd rather we arrived sooner than later. This journey is becoming somewhat tedious, wouldn't you agree?"

To this, Louisa had no response.

"She still doesn't want to talk, apparently," Robert continued in a persistent monologue. "One supposes one can count oneself fortunate to have a wife who is as taciturn as a sphinx, not as chatty as a magpie. There is one thing that keeps me curious, however. Why me?"

She looked up briefly. She understood immediately what he meant, and she supposed he deserved an answer. "Why not you?"

He frowned. "Surely that cannot be your answer. Surely, it is anything but natural for a lady of Quality like you to choose one like me to marry. You could've found some rum duke to marry, some nob or nabob with well-lined pockets. Some titled toff with a manor. Don't you think I have a right to know why you chose someone as me?"

She shrugged. "They bore me."

"They bore you," he echoed in disbelief. "In all earnestness? That is your answer?"

She shrugged.

"You turned down suitor after suitor after suitor, mocking them, humiliating them, because they bore you?"

"Why not?"

The sudden flare of fury in his eyes took her aback. But perhaps she had imagined it, as he quickly hooded his gaze and looked at her as placidly as ever.

He shrugged. "So, it is true what they say."

"What, pray, do they say?" She drew herself up proudly. Truth be told, she did not really want him to answer. After all, she'd read the gossip sheets.

"That you're as proud as a goddess and colder than a glacier. A heart of ice. Hence, the Ice Damsel."

This was not new to her, but it still stung. She would not comment on it with more than a derisive smile playing about her lips.

"Hundreds of suitors, rejected on a whim. Princes, dukes, and earls. Wellington himself, I heard. Tsar Alexander when he was here last month. I suppose he doesn't count because he flirts with all the ladies, they say. But they all bore you." There was a stern glint in his eyes. "You'd reject the king personally if he were to propose. Mind you, not that I'd blame you," he added hastily, "him being mad as Bedlam and all."

"That's an exaggeration. Not hundreds of suitors, but merely one hundred." She pleated the soft fabric of her dress with her fingers.

He barked an incredulous laugh. "Merely one hundred! Jove's beard."

"Wellington and the Tsar are both married. As is King George. I fail to see how I could have possibly accepted a suit from them if they had offered. Which, I emphatically insist, they did not. And no prince has ever proposed." She thought for a moment before adding, "At least I don't think so." She thought a moment longer. "Not that I can remember." She chewed on her bottom lip. Who knows, maybe a prince had proposed, and it had slipped her mind. Hadn't there been that German aristocrat? Tall, blond, in uniform. He might have been a prince. Or he could also have been some other military man. The truth was that the faces of all her suitors had melted to a single mass of unidentifiable features, like wax figures left out in the sun too long, indistinct and lacking in any memorable character.

"I didn't meet a single man who interested me. Not even one who was different. For me, such men are, undoubtedly, a bore."

"Is that why you humiliated them the way you did?"

She shrugged again, refusing to comment.

"Did you enjoy it?" His eyes pierced hers. "Did you obtain some perverse sense of power from putting them into their place?"

She threw her hair back. "Of course. They asked for it."

"They wanted to woo you, and you say, 'they asked for it'?" he scoffed.

She whirled around to him with a hiss. "Yes, they did. What do you know? And how dare you judge me for something you don't understand, will never understand? I fail to see why you find it so preposterous that a lady turns down her suitors because she doesn't want them. She has a right to do so, regardless of her motivation. These men, they're all alike. They're impossible to keep apart. They look the same, dress the same, behave the same, and their motivation is, undoubtedly, the same. Many even bear the same name. Whether it's Lord Lexington or Lord Whatsington, they're all after one thing only: my fortune." She threw him a speaking look. "Including yourself, if I might add."

Not one of them had really cared about her, about who she was, or what her desires, dreams and intentions were. Not one of them had asked, ever. No one had wanted to truly get to know her. She must be remarkably unlovable to attract so many suitors, and none of them, not a single one, had ever expressed the slightest curiosity about her person. She'd never admitted it to herself, but the thought hurt deeply.

He scratched the back of his neck. "Well, if you put it like that..."

"Indeed."

"And yet you'd rather spend the rest of your life with a humble costermonger. Sleeping on the hard ground and eating poor man's bread. Because he's the only one who doesn't bore you."

It was true. Robert was many things: rumpled, grimy and unshaven, ill-smelling, a boor and probably illiterate to boot, but he certainly wasn't boring.

"You'd rather give yourself a life sentence of living in poverty than in boredom," he mused aloud. "That boggles the mind. It really is quite something." He continued to shake his head in disbelief.

That was certainly one way of putting it.

"Or," he continued, just when she thought they'd ended the conversation, turning to her with a level, knowing gaze. "Or this could all be about something else entirely."

"I am fairly agog to learn what conclusion you reach next."

"This could all just be an excellent way to punish your father."

She sat up as if she'd been stung.

He snapped his fingers, then pointed his index finger at her. "That's it, isn't it? Except why you would punish yourself to a lifelong sentence of poverty just to get back at your father, is a bit beyond me. But"—he shrugged—"what do I know about the intricate workings of the female mind?"

She stared at him, speechless that he had been able to place his finger exactly on her open wound. Was she that transparent?

And was what he said true? That this was all about her punishing her father?

She licked her dry lips.

"I'm right, aren't I?" he pressed.

"Possibly. What matters most to me is that I made this decision on my own. I chose you as my husband. Not my father. Not society. Consider yourself the lucky winner."

"So, you did. You chose me, and I am indeed a blastedly lucky man." Once more that mocking look. He was infuriating! "This journey hasn't been easy. You have certainly been heroic so far. Let us see how you fare in your new surroundings once reality sets in, Damsel."

"Reality? What do you mean?"

"The reality of a hungry belly. Of hardship, scarcity,

and hard labour. But you need not be daunted." He flashed his white teeth at her. "For we have each other, do we not? Shouldn't that suffice?" He put an arm about her shoulder and squeezed.

Queasy, she shook his arm off and moved aside, then clung to the seat to keep from falling off.

His voice was deep as he chuckled.

That look, it confused her. It made her blush. Angry at him, but even more at herself, she pulled herself up and lifted her chin.

That made him smile even more.

She couldn't help the feeling that he was doing this on purpose. To rattle her.

Her cheeks burned.

He smirked. "Hiyup," he told the donkey, lifting the ribbons.

As they travelled along the road, the landscape became increasingly familiar with its gentle slopes and vales, and excitement gripped her when they crossed the River Frome. A little further south, and they would reach it: the town she'd had in mind.

The town of her childhood.

AT A CROSSROADS, Robert pulled the cart to a halt. He turned to her as if he had made up his mind.

"Louisa," he said suddenly, "this has gone on long enough. Let's end this."

"We're almost there," she replied. "Look. Piddleton's at the bottom of the hill, over there. Let's find a cottage.

Somewhere on the edge of town, but not too isolated, either. Maybe up by the mill."

He huffed a sigh that seemed to come from the depths of his soul. "So, you can play house? Are you certain you want this?"

"Well, we have to stay somewhere, don't we? Let's rent a cottage. Like this one." She pointed to a lovely stone cottage with a straw-thatched roof by the wayside. "This one would be perfect."

He stared at it with a frown. Then he looked at her. "It's not the manor you're used to."

"I know. I'm no fool. We can't afford a manor. I want this one."

"Very well," he murmured. "If that's what she wants."

SHE WAITED by the cart with the donkey tethered beside her while he made enquiries about the town. The town was quaint and picturesque, its streets lined with charming, whitewashed thatched cottages. Oh, how familiar they were, the narrow, cobbled streets that wound their way to the heart of the town at the central square, where a Norman-style church stood next to the stone vicarage. How was it possible that nothing about this place had changed?

The rhythmic clang of the blacksmith's hammer echoed through the streets, and the enticing aroma of bread fresh from the baker's oven filled the air.

Memories overwhelmed her.

A rush of hot tears shot into her eyes.

She looked up, expecting to see Will's awkward figure hurtling around the corner, his footsteps slapping the cobblestone, his long, unruly hair tucked into a cap, loaves of freshly baked bread under his arms. She heard his bright, cheerful voice calling out as clearly as if he were here now. "Lulu, wait for me! Race you to the old mill, whoever loses is a lazy mule!" And as a punishment, the loser would have to be the mule and carry the winner piggyback all the way home. Louisa usually won, for she'd had long legs and was an astonishingly fast runner. Will, who was a head smaller than her but sturdy and strong, had had to carry her on his back all the way back and up the hill to Meryfell Hall like a sack of flour.

It was time to face the truth, time to face the ghosts of the past.

She'd come here for him, hadn't she?

She'd made Robert drive all the way to Dorset—because of Will.

Before Louisa was aware of what she was doing, her feet moved of their own accord in the direction of the bakery. She came to a stop when Robert interrupted her reverie as he emerged from the vicarage. "Alas, the cottage you had your heart set on is currently not available, and the landlord is absent. But we're in luck. The vicar says there's a small cottage just beyond the town's edge, atop yonder hill that we can rent. Shall we have a look?" He paused. "Louisa?"

She hastily brushed away her tears and managed a nod. "Yes, let's have a look."

"Are you certain?" He looked at her steadily.

Now that she was here, she suddenly knew with crystal clarity what she wanted.

She wanted to live in that cottage and have the kind of simple life she would have had if her fate had been different. She wanted to see what life would have been like ... if she had married Will.

"Yes," she heard herself reply. "I am certain."

Chapter Six

The term 'cottage' was a euphemism. Shed was more like it.

It looked picturesque enough from the outside, with its grey stone and thatched roof. Rose brambles crept up the walls and there was a rickety bench under the small window—the only window in the entire hut.

Robert forced the jammed door open with his shoulder. "Welcome home, madam wife." He held the door open for her with a mock bow.

Louisa stepped inside and remained speechless. She'd been prepared for the worst, but not in her wildest imagination had she expected to see anything like this.

It was a squalid, dark room with low beams, the walls sooty and black, the floor littered with hay and animal excrement, a pile of half-cut wood stacked in the fireplace. Scattered around were bits of furniture and fragments of half-broken crockery. Robert picked up a chair that had fallen over and attempted to set it upright, only for it to topple over due to one leg missing. There was a rough wooden table, more broken chairs, and along one wall, something that might have been a bed. The frame consisted only of a simple wooden platform with a lumpy mattress on top.

"Charming." Robert strolled over to the bed, sat down to test the mattress, and when the bed's frame didn't collapse, he threw himself on top of it in one fell swoop. It gave off a gigantic puff of dust. He looked up at her with a rakish grin. "Luxurious and comfortable, and just big enough for the both of us. Join me, wife." He patted the mattress beside him in an invitation for her to lie down.

Louisa shook her head. "It's infested with vermin."

"Most likely," he agreed. "Still, it's a thousand times more comfortable than many a bedstead I've had in the —" he broke off, pulled his hat over his eyes, propped one boot on top of the other, and sighed contentedly as if he were reposing in a luxurious canopy bed in the royal bedchamber.

Louisa watched him with a frown. "In the what?" What had he been about to say?

Robert didn't reply.

She surveyed the room, a feeling of exhaustion and despair sweeping over her. This was intolerable. She couldn't possibly stay here. It was too dirty, too dilapidated, too poor. Too, too—everything.

"You don't, in all earnestness, intend for us to live here? This isn't a proper abode for people. It's more of an animal pen, a pigsty. It must have been used to house chickens, pigs, and goats at one time or another." Louisa wrinkled her nose in disgust at the foul stench that permeated the room.

"There's nothing wrong with this place," her husband replied, his eyes still closed. "It's more than many people in our class can expect." He emphasised the word '*our*'. "You can't imagine in what squalor and misery some people live. This is nothing in comparison to what they endure." There was a faint patronising reproach in his tone, as if she were an overindulged princess who knew nothing of the world and the reality of the lives of the people of the lower classes, which, of course, happened to be entirely true.

But that realisation didn't improve her mood. It rankled. When she'd thought of a cottage where they could live, she'd imagined a small, dainty cottage, romantically situated at the edge of a forest. It would be a simple, modest abode, yes, but clean. She had completely forgotten that such a place didn't come with footmen, maids, and butlers to clean, cook, and maintain the household.

She rubbed her forehead. It dawned on her that this wouldn't happen on its own, and that she would have to lend a hand herself to get things done. Fetching the water, throwing out the slops, washing, cooking, and cleaning.

As if he knew what she was thinking, her husband said, "Well, wife, commence the cleaning operation." He yawned. "Driving the cart for four days was hard work, and I deserve some rest now."

She looked at him, aghast. "You want me to clean?"

He pushed back the hat and opened one eye. "Who else? This place certainly won't get clean on its own. We don't have any servants to do it, and we can't afford any, either."

She'd never, in her entire life, even touched a broom. "But I don't know how to—" she began, then bit on her lip when she saw his eyebrow rise.

This was exactly what he wanted, wasn't it? Him and her father.

To take her down a peg.

To teach her a lesson.

To prove to her that she was nothing more than a sugar princess who would break at the first challenge.

Robert, seemingly oblivious to her inner struggle, closed his eyes once more. His breathing steadied and after a while he began to snore.

Louisa watched him in amazement, unable to comprehend how he could find rest on such a filthy mattress, likely crawling with lice.

It struck her as a deliberate provocation, a silent challenge, as if he had thrown down the gauntlet and dared her to pick it up.

She stared at his sleeping form with narrowed eyes, her hands clenched into fists.

What on earth should she do now? Capitulate?

She took in the overwhelming chaos of the room, and she closed her eyes in despair.

Back at her father's house in London, he'd called her a useless china doll. She'd been proud of herself for surviving the arduous journey on the costermonger's cart.

Miss Louisa's Final Waltz

She'd proved her resilience by sleeping on the cold, hard ground for three nights without a word of complaint. She'd begun to think she could handle anything life threw at her—but this? Was she ready to admit defeat on her first day in her new abode?

Homesickness washed over her. She wanted nothing more than to return to her safe, warm house in London. But if she stayed here, she could not only prove her mettle, but she could also learn more about Will.

The mere thought of him infused her with an unexpected surge of strength and determination.

"You can do it, Lulu," Will would have said with that wry, cheeky smile of his. "I know you can."

Clenching her jaw, she carried the dilapidated chairs outside. She picked up the broom that lay atop a pile of rubble and began to sweep the floor.

She could do this.

After an hour's rest, Robert propped himself up on one elbow and watched her sweep the floor with grim determination. He cleared his throat. "It might be easier if you made one big pile of dirt, instead of just sweeping it back and forth from one end of the room to the other, spreading it all over." When she gave him death's stare, he raised both hands in defence. "Otherwise, it appears you're doing a rum job for someone who's never even touched a broom, so I suppose I'll hold my tongue." But after all her efforts, she merely succeeded in casting the entire room in a thick cloud of dust, coughing helplessly. He took the broom from her hand without a word and swept the room himself. Within minutes, the floor was cleared of the dirt.

Then he hoisted the mattress onto his shoulder and carried it outside.

Louisa thought he'd taken it into the yard to be cleaned, but when she went outside, she found him gone.

Fine. She was better off doing this on her own, anyway, without having someone looking over her shoulder and criticising her every move.

What now? Her eyes travelled from the rickety bedstead to the crooked shelves on the wall, then ended at the fireplace.

An iron hook hung inside it, along with a black iron cauldron that was filled with logs. Having cleared that away, she took the cauldron out and stared at it in dismay. It was heavily encrusted with rust and dirt, so much so that she preferred to not know what exactly it was.

She took it out, poured water from the well into it and dabbed at it with a rag. An hour later it still looked just as it had before, except that the water was now black, and strange things were swimming in it.

Robert returned with the mattress, whistling. "I went to the neighbouring farmer and had it restuffed with horsehair. It's free of vermin now." He'd also obtained some fresh linen sheets and a basket of food. He took the basket into the house, then sat down in front of the bench with the mattress, pulled out a needle and thread, and began to sew.

She watched in astonishment. "What are you doing?"

"I have to secure the edge of the mattress, to prevent

the contents from spilling out." His fingers moved quickly, each stitch precise and orderly.

Louisa was at a loss for words. "You can sew?"

"It's one of my many accomplishments. But yes. I can sew rather well. If I had to choose another trade, tailoring might well have been my calling." He grinned.

When he had finished sewing, he carried the mattress inside and placed it on the bed frame. Then he set about repairing the broken chairs, hammering the loose legs back into place.

Meanwhile, Louisa persisted with the cauldron, her efforts undiminished.

Robert put down the chair he was working on and shook his head. "That won't work. You need sand and a proper fire."

She looked at him in confusion. "Whatever for? And where would we get sand?"

"From the bank of the river, over there." He pointed to the nearby stream. He took the cauldron, emptied its contents and, after scraping the remains out with a stick, scouring it thoroughly. Then he filled it with sand again.

He expertly built another fire and hung the cauldron directly above the flames. "Leave it there for a few hours. Perhaps even overnight. Tomorrow, it'll be spotless. In the meantime, fetch the basket, sit down, and eat."

Louisa did as he suggested, savouring the stew, fresh bread, and cheese while keeping her eyes on him.

"Now that we've finished the journey, we can't afford to buy food every day," Robert said in between two bites of cheese. "You must start cooking for yourself. Starting from tomorrow, you'll cook me pottage and porridge."

"But I don't know how to cook pottage and porridge."

"You cannot clean, you cannot cook." He threw up his arms. "Is there anything at all you can do?"

"I can embroider. I can make pretty watercolours. I can read Latin, speak Italian, French and a smattering of German, play the pianoforte and the harp and sing."

"None of which is in the least useful to us. Can you at least make baskets?"

She shook her head.

"Use the loom? A spindle? I suppose you have no idea how to work in the fields either, or how to make butter and cheese." He sighed. "Truly, I've condemned myself to a hard fate by marrying you."

"I can learn to do all that," she told him, but he merely looked at her sceptically. "And you? Now that the cart is empty and all the fruit and vegetables have been sold, how will you earn your keep? Will you idle away the entire day by sleeping?" Suddenly a profound feeling of unease assailed her. Summer would turn to autumn, soon, and then winter would come. How would they survive, indeed?

But he seemed unconcerned about that. "Never fear, I always find a way to earn my keep," he said, but wouldn't elaborate further.

He pulled off his boots and socks and stretched out his bare feet, wiggling his toes. He tossed one sock into her lap and handed her thread and needle.

"Since the only useful ability you seem to have is that of wielding a needle, you can start your wifely duties by darning my socks."

Louisa was about to lash out at him and tell him to

darn his own stinking socks, particularly since he'd bragged earlier that he was good at sewing. Then she changed her mind, recognising this as yet another one of his challenges.

"Very well." She stifled a shudder as she picked up the foul-smelling sock with two fingers and inspected the hole in it.

It was undoubtedly the largest sock she'd ever seen. The man's feet were massive. And that hole was a disgrace.

Several hours later, she handed him the sock, neatly folded into a small rectangular packet.

He unfolded the sock and stared. "What the deuce is that?"

"A ladybird. Isn't it pretty?"

"A ladybird! On my sock?"

"It is a particularly hideous sock. Not to mention the stench." She pinched her nose. "I thought I would improve its coarse appearance, so I added a ladybird. And if you turn it over, you'll find a pretty butterfly," she said. "Along with some flowers and leaves." She'd embroidered an entire garland of tulips and daisies winding themselves around the ankle. "It would have been prettier if I'd had colours other than white."

The look on his face was priceless.

Louisa bit on the inside of her cheeks to keep herself from bursting into laughter.

"Would you like me to darn your other sock as well, so they're matching?" she offered in dulcet tones.

"No, thank you," he said hastily, moving his socks out of her reach.

"What about that hole in your shirt?" She pointed at his linen shirt, which sported a hole at the elbow. "It is my wifely duty to fix that, I believe."

"Thank you, but I'll fix this one myself. Otherwise, you'll turn it into a dandy's embroidered waistcoat or some such nonsense," he muttered under his breath.

Louisa repressed a grin. "Any other wifely duty you'd like me to perform?" she said without thinking.

"Wifely duty? Let's see." A wicked smile spread over his face. "I could think of something," he drawled. He leaned back on his arms, and his gaze slowly trailed down her neck, over her decollete, paused by her chest, and swept further down. The air between them was suddenly thick and dense, charged with something she didn't quite understand.

He extended a hand and gently stroked a stray curl out of her face that had escaped from her bun. His fingers touched the skin of her jaw, leaving behind a blazing trail of heat.

Her skin prickled all over, and she held her breath as it flushed through her entire body down to the tips of her toes. She became aware of how close he was, tall and masculine, radiating heat like a furnace.

She tore her gaze away. "I mean for the h-household," she stammered, wishing she had her ballroom fan so she could fan herself.

He dropped his hand. "Of course. For the household." His voice was husky. Rising, he cleared his throat and said, "You can tend to the cauldron over the fire. Tonight, the responsibility of standing watch falls on you."

Louisa nodded, simultaneously relieved and disappointed as she watched him move away. What on earth had that been about?

She picked up a stick and poked it into the fire, stirring up some embers. It was rather cold now that he had left, even though she was sitting right beside the fire.

Chapter Seven

In the end she'd fallen asleep by the fire, snuggled up in her shawl. When she awoke the next morning, she was lying on the freshly stuffed mattress, wrapped in blankets and shawls. She'd slept soundly all night, something she rarely did.

But how did she end up here? He must have picked her up and carried her, but she didn't remember it at all. Her cheeks flushed.

And him? Where had he slept?

She sat up and looked around. On the other side of the room was a simple straw pallet that hadn't been there before. The hut was empty and there was no sign of him anywhere. Once more there was that feeling of simultaneous relief and disappointment. She felt that when he was here, he took up the entire space of the hut and the air with it. But when he wasn't here, there was an odd emptiness, and she found herself looking for him. It was most irksome.

Louisa shook herself and rose from the bed. On the

table, she found a loaf of coarse brown bread along with a jar of milk. That would have to be her breakfast.

After she ate, she put on a cotton dress from the previous day and briefly wondered what to do about the laundry. Where did one wash laundry? And more importantly, how? Could she hire a laundry maid to do it? She quickly dismissed the idea. No, she'd have to do it herself. Water she had aplenty in the river behind the hut. But where did one obtain lye? Or carbolic soap. Or whatever else it was that one used to wash one's clothes.

Overwhelmed by these questions, she decided that she had done enough work the previous day. Today, she would devote herself to her purpose of finding Will.

She washed her face in the ice-cold water outside, bitterly regretting that she'd left her precious Pears soap at home. Little did she know how precious and rare a commodity perfumed soap was, something only the upper classes could afford. Where could she get another bar? And what did most people use to wash themselves with, if not Pears soap?

She put on her bonnet and headed for the village, walking briskly down the mud-packed street towards the central market square. The smell of freshly baked bread led the way.

Large multi-pane windows displayed an array of baked goods. The sturdy door was open to let out the heat, and a wooden sign hung above it. It depicted a bundle of wheat and the words Brooks' Bakery.

Louisa's heart began to hammer wildly as she entered the shop.

Warmth and the fragrant smell of vanilla, cinnamon,

cloves and the rich, yeasty fragrance of loaves fresh from the oven greeted her. A variety of breads, pastries, and cakes were displayed on shelves behind the wooden counter.

"How can I help you, ma'am?" asked a woman standing behind it. She was large with child and wore a white cap over her dark brown hair and an apron over her swollen stomach. Her face was red due to the warmth. For a moment, Louisa looked at her in surprise. "Is Mr Brooks here?" She tried to peer into the adjoining room of the bakehouse, where Mr Brooks usually baked.

"Mr Brooks? Oh, no. He's long gone."

"When will he be back?"

"He's passed on," the woman clarified. "Dead. Choked on a fish bone. But that was about"—she calculated—"five years ago? Six, maybe?"

"Oh!" Louisa looked at her, stricken. "I didn't know." Of course, how would she? She hadn't talked to Mr Brooks for over a decade.

"Did you know him?" The woman gave her a curious look. "I haven't seen you here before."

"Yes. I used to come here regularly when Mr Brooks was alive."

"I can't seem to remember seeing you here, though," the woman said, looking at Louisa closely.

"It's been a long time." Louisa hesitated. "Is ...Will still here?"

The woman took loaves of bread from a basket and arranged them on the counter. "No."

Her shoulders slumped. Of course he wouldn't be here. Not after all this time.

"Well, then." Fighting her disappointment, Louisa fumbled with her reticule for some coins and handed them to her. "I'll take a loaf of this bread."

The woman studied her from top to bottom, taking in her fine dress and shawl. "Who's asking?"

"Miss Louisa High—that is, of course, Mrs Louisa Jones." Must remember her new name now that she was married.

"Are you of the Quality?" The woman knit her forehead together. Louisa's cotton dress, though wrinkled, was fashionable and of the finest cut.

She hesitated for a moment, then shook her head. She supposed that being married to a costermonger no longer made her a member of Quality. "We only arrived yesterday, my husband and I."

"Newly arrived, are you? You must be the ones who rented the cottage on the hill." The woman wrapped the bread in an old newspaper.

Louisa nodded. "News still spreads fast in this town, I see."

"Oh aye. There's nothing a body can do without the entire town knowing it the next day."

Little had changed then, in that regard.

"He's out all day delivering bread," the woman said as she handed the loaf to Louisa. "I keep telling him it's time to take on an apprentice, but he's not taking on anyone, only wants the best." The woman sighed. "But no one wants to be a baker's apprentice these days. 'Tis hard times."

Louisa's fingers froze as she reached out for the loaf. "Excuse me?"

"I was sayin' he needs an apprentice—"

"I mean, what you said before. He is out?" Suddenly, she was out of breath. "Will?"

"Aye. He's delivering bread and returning late. And tomorrow he's out all day in Dorchester. It's market day. If it's urgent and you want to talk to him, you'll have to go to Dorchester."

"Th-thank you." Louisa's heart leapt and pounded in a fast rhythm as she left the shop.

Will was still here. Will was still here. Will was still here. The phrase repeated in her mind in an endless loop.

Her dear friend Will was still here, and he'd become a baker, just as he'd always wanted.

A surge of pure joy shot through her and suddenly, the sun was shining, the sky was blue, and life was wonderful.

With a spring in her step, Louisa hurried back to the cottage.

Chapter Eight

The day Louisa met Will eleven years ago had been a summer's day, with a light mist hovering over the meadows like an embroidered veil.

She'd run away from Meryfell Hall, weeping. Her father had just announced that he was to remarry a Miss Sarah Ballard, a pretty girl of eighteen who had more feathers in her head than sense, but who otherwise possessed a kind and sweet disposition. Louisa was devastated. Her mother had died of consumption only two months before. She'd been close to her mother, who'd taught her to love nature, good books, and a good laugh. "You have to laugh at least once a day," she'd told her, "because the world is serious enough as it is." The day her mother died, Louisa was certain she'd never laugh again.

Meryfell Hall and the surrounding estate belonged to a friend of her father, Lord Simon Milford, a red-faced, boisterous man. Sarah, her future stepmother, was his cousin. Her father and Lord Milford were good friends who enjoyed various sports together, including hunting and horse racing. To Louisa's chagrin, it had become almost a tradition for them to spend the late summer months at Meryfell Hall. She just couldn't get on with Lord Milford's children, George and Celeste. George, two years her senior, was devilishly handsome, but his angelic blond locks hid a malevolent disposition. Louisa feared his tantrums and was grateful when he ignored her, but when he didn't, he pulled her hair, tripped her deliberately, and once even decapitated her doll with a homemade guillotine. George was never punished for what he'd done. He was a terrible boy, and she'd tried to avoid him as much as possible.

She barely remembered his sister Celeste, other than that she was three years younger, cried easily, and was altogether too juvenile to be Louisa's companion.

Louisa felt isolated during those summer months. Her governess had resigned, and they hadn't found a replacement. So, she escaped and wandered alone through woods and fields and learned to keep her own company. No one seemed to notice. No one seemed to care.

It was that summer when she turned thirteen, shortly after her mother's death and her father's remarriage, that her life took a decisive turn.

That day, she'd run away sobbing to a nearby lake, when she'd sat on the shore, staring out at the milky green water, wishing she were far, far away.

Her attention was drawn to a small fishing boat manned by a lone boy. Louisa watched him dispassionately for a while. He made frantic movements, and the boat rocked, and before she knew what was happening, he lost his balance. There was a big splash—and the boat was empty.

He was flailing about in the water.

Surely the boy could swim, she thought. But then his head went under, and he was gone.

Louisa jumped to her feet, and without thinking, plunged into the water and swam to the boat. She was a strong swimmer, having been taught how to swim by the stableboy, after she'd pestered him to do so for three whole days.

She swam to the boat with sure strokes, dived under the surface, grabbed the boy's arm, and managed to pull him safely to shore. He lay there pale and lifeless. Just when she thought he was dead, he twitched and coughed up water.

"I thought you'd drowned," she gasped.

The boy sat up, spluttering. He was plumpish and short, with dark, shoulder-length hair plastered to his pale round face, full lips and wide eyes framed by long, dark lashes. He was the prettiest boy she'd ever seen. One could easily mistake him for a girl, Louisa thought. He wore a rough linen shirt, a vest, and a pair of breeches. He'd lost a shoe.

"You really should learn to swim." Louisa's body shivered from the icy water.

"I would if I could, but I hate the water," he said through chattering teeth.

"Then you really shouldn't be out there fishing alone." She rubbed her hands over her arms to warm them. "This lake belongs to Lord Milford. If he catches you poaching, you'll be severely punished. They transport poachers to the colonies." She'd overheard the servants gossiping about a poor farmer who'd been caught hunting on Lord Milford's land. He was transported within a week.

"I wasn't fishing." Rivulets of water ran from his hair down his face. He wiped his eyes. "And I would never poach. I might be poor, but I don't steal. Never. Word of honour."

"Then what were you doing in that boat?"

"I was trying to get to Glubbdubdrib." He pointed to the small island in the middle of the lake.

"What's Glubbdubdrib?"

"A magical island." He leaned forward to whisper. "It's full of sorcerers and magicians."

"That's a bag of moonshine," Louisa scoffed.

"It isn't! Can't you feel the magic there?"

Both children stared at the island in the middle of the lake. It was verdant, densely covered with alder, willow, and birch trees. Mist hung between the trees, giving it a mysterious aura.

Louisa tilted her head to one side. "How do you know it's a magical island?"

"I'm certain it's Glubbdubdrib. According to Lemuel Gulliver, its inhabitants are capable of using magic."

"Gulliver! I haven't read it. My governess wouldn't let me. She says it's too agitating for the female mind."

He snorted. "Now that's a bag of moonshine for sure!"

Louisa agreed with him, for she firmly believed the

female mind was no different from the male mind. "Why are you so certain it's Glubbdubdrib?"

"Why are you so certain it's not?" he countered. "Have you ever been there yourself?"

She had no answer to that. "One would have to investigate," she grudgingly asserted.

"Exactly what I think. What do you think I've been doing? How's that for a lark?" He grinned, and a dimple appeared in his right cheek. His hazel eyes lit up and tiny flecks of gold danced in their depths.

"What is your name?"

"I'm Will."

"Louisa." She looked down at the boy, being a full head taller. She'd had a growth spurt and was lanky, long-limbed, and tall for her age. Her governess had complained that she was growing too much too fast, and that the maids couldn't keep up with lengthening the hems of her gowns.

The boy studied her. "I know who you are. You're the young lady who comes every summer to stay with the swells up at the grand house. They call you a proud hothouse flower because you're so beautiful." He tilted his head sideways. "But they have you all wrong."

"You don't think I'm beautiful?" Louisa asked, more intrigued than put off.

"I daresay you're a prime article all right. But I don't think you're a proud hothouse flower. You're more like that birch tree over there." He pointed at a tall, elegant, silvery tree standing in the distance. "Tall and graceful."

"Don't be cheeky." She raised her chin haughtily. "And you're like a drowned rat."

His sudden chuckle was bubbly, cheerful, and infectious. It made her want to laugh too. "I suppose that's true."

"Can I come with you next time?" The words were out before she'd had time to think about them. "To the island."

The boy was wringing out the water out of his trousers. "Sure. As soon as I've fixed the boat. It seems to be leaking." He stared at the boat out on the water. "Once I get it back." He scratched the back of his head and watched the lonely boat drifting on the lake. "I wonder how I'll get it back?"

"Easy. Swim out and get it back."

He looked at her with big eyes. "Would you—could you do that?"

Louisa could. And she did. She swam out again, grabbed the rope that hung from the boat, and hauled it back.

Will watched her in awe. Then he helped her pull the boat ashore.

She wrung out the water in her dress clinging to her legs. She'd have to sneak into the house through the kitchen and secretly ask a maid to find her a dry dress. Hopefully, no one would see her, least of all George.

Will glanced at the sun. "Thunder an' turf! I'd better return. There'll be the devil to pay if Reverend Graham doesn't find me at home when he returns. I'm supposed to be translating Cicero this afternoon, but I've decided it's more exciting to go on an adventure. There's nothing more boring than having to learn Greek and Latin. I don't see the point of it if I'm going to be a baker. I want to bake bread, not translate texts from dead languages." He kicked a stone into the water.

"Why does Reverend Graham want you to learn Latin if you're going to be a baker?"

"He's my godfather." He took off his shoe and poured out the water. "My father was a gentleman, and Reverend Graham doesn't want me to learn a trade, 'cos that's not what proper gentlemen do'. He wants me to go to Oxford to study theology. But I'd rather be a baker. I want to start an apprenticeship with Mr Brooks in the bakery. I figure it's better for my belly." He patted his stomach. "I'm always so hungry, you see."

"What happened to your parents?"

"They're both dead." A stark expression crossed his face. "My mother died when I was born. My father followed her three years ago." He stared at his shoes. "He had a terrible fever that couldn't be cured. Then Reverend Graham took me in. He's good to me if you overlook the fact that he makes me learn the classics." He pulled a face.

Louisa's heart went out to him. "My mother died, too. Two months ago. And Papa wants to marry again." Her eyes burned and she blinked quickly. "Soon."

The look he gave her was sympathetic. "Figures. That would explain this blue-devilled look hanging about you. You have the saddest eyes a person could have."

She swallowed bravely. "Do you know the feeling of being under a bell jar? That's how it is for me."

Will nodded. "You're inside the bell jar and everyone else is outside. You keep knocking on the glass, but no one sees or hears you."

"Yes."

The tears spilled over. Louisa sniffed and wiped her cheeks with her hands, for she had no handkerchief.

He looked away, pretending to be preoccupied with his shoe, giving her time to gain control of her emotions. Then she felt his warm hand slip into hers. Somehow that comforted her, and she no longer felt like she was the only person in the bell jar. Will was there with her.

"Thank you for fetching my boat and saving my life, Louisa Highworth." He leaned forward and planted a kiss on her wet cheek.

Louisa blushed crimson. "What did you do that for?"

Now Will flushed. "I wanted to. It was the right thing to do. Next time I will save your life, Louisa Highworth. I promise."

Will was wrong. The next time, Louisa would save his life—again.

Lost in thought, she followed the forest leading to the lake. Everything was so familiar, yet it had been so long since she'd been here.

She reached the shore of the lake and marvelled at its unchanged beauty. The small island before her looked exactly as it had when she was younger, perhaps even more untamed, its undergrowth thicker, looking wilder and more enchanting than it had back then.

Will had taken her to Glubbdubdrib in the days after they'd met. He'd rowed her across and taken her hand as they explored the island together. She knew there was nothing much there, just trees and bushes. But to them, it had been a place of magic.

Louisa gazed at the small island, lost in memory. Then, settling by the water's edge, she sat down and pulled the shoes and stockings from her feet. With a swift motion, she pulled the dress over her head, leaving her in nothing but a simple cotton shift.

For a moment, she stood as still as a Greek statue, listening to the birds and the buzzing of the insects in the undergrowth. Then she took a step forward, plunged into the cold water and swam with strong, determined strokes towards the island of Glubbdubdrib.

There was nothing on the island, really, just a dense vegetation of trees, shrubs, bushes, rocks, and moss. In the centre of the island, they'd built a circle of stones for a fire. Sometimes, Will brought fresh bread dough from the bakery in a clay bowl, which they wound around long sticks and baked over the fire. It was the best bread she had ever eaten, crispy and smoky on the outside and soft on the inside. It was a mouthful of goodness, of fire and nature, of magic. Nothing she had ever eaten in the most expensive ton suppers had ever tasted so divine. She loved it because Will had made it. She loved it because they had baked it together over the fire on their very own island.

Louisa stepped gingerly over the roots, pushing aside the branches of the bushes and trees, and found the stone circle now overgrown with moss.

This was where they'd eaten their bread, reading from *Gulliver's Travels*, telling themselves versions of even more fantastic stories. Over there, on that stone,

Will had hunched over a piece of wood as he carved his figures.

A tight, sad smile played on her lips as she remembered all the memories that rushed back at her, memories she hadn't thought about in all these years. Memories she'd been willing to forget because she could never have them back.

Why was she torturing herself like this? Why had she come here? She returned to the shore, took off her wet shift and slipped into her dry dress. She squeezed the water out of the shift before laying it out on the grass to dry. At least she'd had a bath, Louisa thought, soapless though it was. And her shift, now freshly rinsed, was somewhat cleaner. She had still not found a solution to the problem of washing laundry. She wondered if Mary from the bakery would lend her some soap.

Her stomach rumbled.

She was hungry.

Chapter Nine

Louisa was cooking.

Her plan was to surprise her husband with a sumptuous three-course meal. She was going to prove to him that Louisa Highworth could do it; that she was not a simpering, useless china doll, too squeamish to put her hands to good use. She might have been brought up to be a lady, but she could work when life demanded it, and life demanded it now.

She tied a wide linen apron around her dress, put her hands on her hips and pursed her lips as she looked at the ingredients at her disposal, which she'd placed on the rickety table.

Flour.
Oat flakes.
Bran.
Salt.
Lard.

Robert had placed them on the table earlier, with the cryptic comment that they'd have to make do with this until he could procure better fare. Somehow, she'd have to make a soup, a main course, and a dessert from this bounty. At least they had real bread from the bakery; the entire loaf that she'd bought earlier.

"Right. Soup." One required some sort of liquid to make soup. She'd brought a bucket of fresh water from the well and poured it into the cauldron that hung over the fireplace. Robert had been right; after scouring it with sand, it was reasonably clean. Thinking back to all the different soups she'd had in her life, there had been pea soup, carrot soup, beetroot soup, parsnip soup, or a soup with all of them in it. The problem was that none of these ingredients were available. How vexatious! Wasn't her husband a costermonger? Shouldn't he be sitting on vegetables galore? She looked around. Where were his goods? Certainly not in the cottage, nor outside, either. Not a single carrot or onion in sight. For a moment, she wondered where on earth he got his produce if he didn't grow it himself.

The fire crackled.

The water bubbled over and splashed into the fire, almost putting it out. She cursed under her breath, took some liquid out with a cup, then more and more ... Was that enough? Maybe a little more? She poured the water back into the bucket and wondered what to do with it now. Robert would probably know. Where was the man? He'd left early this morning, claiming to be "going to work". She wondered if he was truly standing by the side of the road with his cart, sorting cabbages or calling out in his loud, hoarse voice: "Cherries! Sweet cherries! A penny a score!" or "Ho, ho hii! Here's your turnips!" Not that she'd seen any cherries or turnips in his vicinity lately. And the only carrot she'd seen in the cottage had been fed to the donkey.

What did he do all day?

And since she was thinking about Robert, it had occurred to her once or twice earlier that something was off with him. She couldn't quite put her finger on it. Was it the way he spoke, perhaps? It seemed different, as if he'd changed his accent at one point during their journey; he dropped in and out of it and went through long phases during which he seemed to forget to speak it altogether. But then, maybe he'd always spoken like that, and she hadn't realised.

Louisa held the ladle in the air, thinking how he didn't seem to be quite the man she'd first thought he was. Then she shook her head. What did she really know about costermongers? She decided to solve that mystery later. She had to concentrate on her soup. She decided she wanted to cook white soup, her favourite, which was usually served at the balls at supper. Unless she was mistaken, it contained milk and mutton. She had neither. No matter, the flour would surely make the soup white.

Then, she supposed, something had to be added to give the water flavour, otherwise it would taste like nothing. She looked at the ingredients and her eyes fell on the salt. Of course! She dumped in two cups, and just to be on the safe side, a third. Then she stared at the remaining ingredients, her teeth worrying her lower lip. Then, having made up her mind, she doled out a generous cupful of the flour, the bran and the oat flakes into the water.

"Will that be enough?" she wondered. "It looks grey, not white. Just for good measure, for the colour, let's add some more flour." She added the rest of the bag. After a moment of consideration, she added the remaining bags of the bran and oats as well.

And then she stirred. Oh my! And how she stirred.

She hadn't realised that cooking required such physical effort. Beads of sweat formed on her forehead as she wielded the long, wooden ladle with both hands.

A feeling of elation filled her. Today was indeed a good day. Not only was she cooking, but Will was still living in town. She would meet him soon. She would talk to him. She would rekindle a dear childhood friendship. How she was looking forward to it!

THE SECOND TIME she'd met Will had been in town. She'd gone there with her maid to buy some ribbon for her bonnet. Louisa bought a roll of velvet ribbon at the haberdasher's and forgot her reticule there. While her maid went back to the shop to fetch it, she waited by the fountain in the market square.

She bent down to tie her boot, and just at that moment, she noticed a scuffle in the side streets. Curious, she went to see what it was about.

She immediately recognised Will's short, chubby figure. He was bravely facing three tall, lanky boys who were taunting him, his hands clenched in fists in front of his face. Then, as if on command, all three pounced on him, hitting, punching, and kicking him. Will fought back bravely, but he was no match for them. She recognised the blond locks of the tallest boy at once.

"George Cooper-Wiles!" Louisa cried. "For shame! I'll tell your father that his son is no better than a common gutter rat, ganging up with other street urchins to fight boys who are smaller and younger than you!"

For a moment she thought he hadn't heard, but as she turned to go fetch help, he stopped and ran after her. "Louisa, don't you dare tattle on me!" George pulled her back by the arm and slammed her against the wall of the house.

Louisa took a swing and smashed her fist into his face. He staggered back. The other two boys stopped beating up Will and gaped.

"Run, Will!" she shouted.

Will didn't need to be told twice. He scrambled to his feet and limped off towards the bakery for refuge.

Linda, the maid, came running and took Louisa home, scolding her the entire way. George and his friends had run off like lightning and were nowhere to be seen.

By dinnertime, he had a black eye. When asked what had happened, he said he'd fallen off his horse. He glared at Louisa the entire time, daring her to contradict him. She did not. They had an unspoken agreement that neither of them would reveal what had happened. George would die with humiliation if anyone were ever to discover he'd been hit by a girl, and Louisa would be confined to her room for the rest of her life if they found out she had involved herself in a street fight. They both sat at the dinner table, eating their soup in silence.

From that day on, Will worshipped her.

. . .

Robert returned later that day, a cheerful whistle on his lips.

"I've returned, madam wife. Mrs Gary sends this." He placed a bundle on the chair. "With best regards."

"Who is Mrs Gary?" She wiped her forehead.

"She lives on a farm nearby. She's elderly and half blind and dependent on outside help. I've been helping in return for food as payment." He set down a box overflowing with fruit and vegetables.

"What is this?" Louisa lifted a high-waisted brown linen dress from the bundle, the kind worn by working women. Suitable and sturdy without any adornment. Her hand slid over the fabric. It was faded and coarsely woven, but clean. There was also a simple white shawl and an apron. She picked up the cap that married women wore. It was not a frilly lace cap like her stepmother wore, but one of sturdy white linen. She stared at the clothes as the full implication hit her that these were the clothes of lower-class commoners. She was no longer a lady. She was a working-class peasant. A costermonger's wife. She had to dress like one. The thought stung.

"Clothes. She has no need for them and thought you might find them useful."

"I suppose it's useful." Her own muslin and cotton robes were too delicate for the kind of life she led now. She'd already torn a hole into one of them when it got caught on a nail in the doorway. She would have to put it aside and wear the rougher dresses, thereby erasing any indication of her lineage and breeding.

He stretched and rolled his shoulders back as if to ease a strain. Louisa noticed how broad and muscular he was. He filled the room with his presence, taking up all the space, making her feel small and vulnerable, even though she was anything but small. She looked away hastily.

"Mrs Gary asked me to sell her fruit and vegetables at the market in Dorchester." Robert had brought in several crates and placed them on the table. He tossed a carrot in the air, caught it, and bit into it with gusto.

Louisa perked up. "The market in Dorchester?"

"I'm going there tomorrow." He finished the carrot in three bites and threw the remains to the donkey, who was tethered outside the open door.

"I'd like to go with you if you're going to the market at Dorchester. I—I could help. With the selling." Her heart pounded against her ribcage at the thought of seeing Will as early as tomorrow.

"Certainly. Two hands are better than one. Hm. What do I smell?" He sniffed and wrinkled his nose.

She pointed proudly with the wooden spoon at the cauldron hanging in the fireplace. "White soup. I have decided to cook dinner, you see."

"Did you, now? I'm a lucky man; my wife has finally decided to cook for me. I'm a lucky man ind—" He approached the cauldron and stared into an indefinable greyish mass. "White soup, you say? It looks, er, dangerou —I mean, delicious."

"You must be hungry." She handed him a bowl. "Help yourself."

Robert attempted to lift the ladle out, but it was stuck. "Did you say it was soup?"

"Hm. Yes. The consistency is debatable, but it is definitely meant to be soup."

He set the bowl down and pulled at the ladle with both hands. "Highly solid, this soup," he commented, giving the ladle another strong tug. "Extraordinarily solid." Another tug, and he lifted the cauldron off the hook. "I'm impressed. What sturdy consistency, quite commendable, really. Have you ever seen anything so strong? It won't fall off even now." He carried it halfway across the room. "Like dried paste." He lifted it up to his nose and sniffed. "Or plaster. No, I have it! It's a lime-based mortar, used for binding stones together in construction." He lifted it up and down. "Houses built with this powerful adhesive are indestructible. It'll withstand the onslaught of an entire French artillery regiment, including an entire battery of Gibreauval 12-pounders."

"Gibreau-what?"

"The heaviest cannon of the French field artillery reserves. It fires rounds at distant targets; its rate of fire is about one round per minute, with a range up to 1700 yards. Although during the Peninsular Campaign they preferred the lighter 8-pounders, because fortunately for us, the challenging Spanish terrain hindered the movement of heavier artillery like the 12-pounder."

She blinked at him. "Ah."

He knocked at the side of the cauldron, which gave off a dull clank. "My point being, when the end of the world comes and the day of reckoning is near, when the angel's trumpets sound to herald the last day of civilization, Mrs Jones's house will be the only one left standing on the face of the earth, steadfast and strong, thanks to this miraculous adhesive, I mean, of course, soup."

Louisa dropped into a chair, shading her eyes with her hand. Her shoulders shook.

"As for the taste I can't say since it refuses to come out." He stuck a finger in, smelled it and licked it carefully. "Hm. Generously seasoned with salt. And it must be mortar since now my teeth are glued together. Gnn!" He bared his teeth. He used a branch to pry them apart in mock desperation.

She could no longer hold it in any longer and burst out laughing. She laughed until her sides ached and tears streamed down her face. She couldn't remember ever laughing so much. Certainly not since she'd been an adult.

He grinned at her. "Ah, she is laughing. That is good, indeed."

There'd only ever been one person who'd been able to make her laugh, and that was Will. The thought of him sobered her.

She mopped up her tears. "This is my first attempt at cooking. I dare say neither of us would survive if we were to eat it. What shall we do now?"

He set the cauldron down. "I'm afraid you have destroyed the cauldron for good. And I'd rather keep my teeth." He crouched down beside the cauldron. "We could try to sell this paste at the market tomorrow. Mrs

Jones's miracle mortar! Or we could sell it to the army. That's it! Let's do it. I daresay we'll be rich in a jiffy."

Louisa laughed again. She threw her handkerchief at him. "Be quiet. You have made your point; you need not expound upon it. I shall, henceforth, never attempt to cook for you again."

"Ah. But 'tis only the first attempt. 'Practice is everything,' says Periander."

A slight smile played on her lips. "Indeed. One supposes the Greeks must have known what they were talking about. So, you've read Periander?"

"Not willingly," he confessed.

She studied him thoughtfully as he continued to try to pull the ladle out of the cauldron. "Removing Excalibur from the stone would have been easier," he grunted. Finally, the spoon came out, and the cauldron fell to the ground with a clatter. "There. We'll have to buy another cauldron and ladle at the market tomorrow."

"But what now? I'm famished."

He picked up a bundle that he'd dropped by the door. "Let's eat this." He unwrapped it to reveal a partridge.

"It's a dead bird." Louisa crossed her arms. "It still has feathers. You can't possibly eat that."

"Yes, it is a dead bird. And correctly observed, it still has feathers. And I absolutely mean to eat it. Because one commonly eats birds without feathers."

"How?"

Robert heaved a sigh that came from the bottom of his heart. "I suppose it would be too much to ask you to pluck the bird. You wouldn't know how. Let me show you. Watch carefully, wife."

As Louisa watched Robert prepare their meal, a single thought took hold in her: if he was a costermonger, she was the queen masquerading as a milkmaid.

Chapter Ten

Louisa Highworth was no fool. She was as certain as the compass pointing north that Robert was a gentleman. She'd suspected something was off with her husband as early as London, even though she might not have been fully aware of it then. There had been a thousand signs. If she hadn't been as aware of them as she should have been, it was because she'd been distracted by her tumultuous thoughts and emotions.

She occasionally suspected that beneath his frequently cheerful façade simmered a hidden resentment or grudge. The brooding looks he gave her in unguarded moments reminded her that despite all they'd been through, he harboured some aversion towards her, or the class she represented. She couldn't understand why it bothered her so much to think that he didn't like her.

Certainly, Louisa could sometimes be absent-minded and oblivious to her surroundings. She had a tendency for wool-gathering, even in the middle of a ball or a cotillon. She was terrible at remembering faces and made no great effort at remembering names. More than once, she confused her suitors. What could one do? These men all looked the same, sometimes even had the same name, and there simply were too many to count.

Once she even mistook the great George Bryan "Beau" Brummel for another Pink of the ton, Lord George Brandon. They'd worn the same clothes, the same cravat knotted in the Oriental style, had the same windswept brown hair, the same burgundy coat. They were even called the same.

It had been an unforgivable mistake. Brummel had been deadly offended and declared that her nickname of Ice Damsel was more than appropriate. But maybe he'd already lost his grip over society by then, for instead of his proclamation making her a social outcast, it had heightened her fame even further.

Yet, regarding Robert, she ought to have noticed the signs earlier. There had been so many details, a random gesture; hands that were meticulously clean and fingernails trimmed; the way he pulled out his pocket watch and flicked it open with one hand. Hadn't she seen the same movement a thousand times in the drawing room? He'd continuously lapsed into refined speech until he dropped the cockney dialect altogether. She could not recall the precise time and place, but he may have done so as early as London. Then there was his posture. When he forgot to stoop, he carried himself with quiet confidence, standing tall and erect, and when he forgot to drag his feet, his step was firm and precise.

He had a penetrating gaze, and little escaped him as

he surveyed his surroundings. And when he focused on her, it was with an intensity that she found both thrilling and unsettling.

Robert Jones was a gentleman, all right. There was no doubt.

A gentleman gifted with acting, a gentleman pretending to be a lower-class commoner.

Had her father known?

Surely he must have. Why else would he have facilitated this marriage in the way he had? Did either of them truly think they could hoodwink her for long? They must have hatched this plan together. There was no doubt in her mind that this was what it was; they must have cleared the roads around her house and placed him in that strategic position, together with the cart and the donkey, so that she'd immediately notice him and head in his direction.

Her father and he, they'd certainly put on a jolly good show. They'd managed to deceive her completely. But not for long.

A flash of anger shot through her, but then a resolution formed in her mind.

Very well, if that is what they wanted, she could play this game, too.

She'd leave them in the belief that she'd married a costermonger, and she'd lead the life of the costermonger's wife with all its hardships and privations.

Her smile was cold and hard.

Which of the two would yield first? Which of them would tire of the game first? After all, he too was accustomed to the comforts of upper-class life and would find it increasingly difficult to maintain a lower-class lifestyle for longer than, she estimated, a fortnight.

Yes, she'd give him a fortnight.

In the meantime, she would try to find Will.

WILL HAD LIKED to wait for her under the three birch trees, usually with a bundle of bread rolls, saffron cakes, or hard eggs, which they ate by the lake. He also fed her hot buns, misshapen loaves he'd made himself that smelled divinely of nutmeg, cloves, and mace.

Louisa, who ate only morsels at the table, devoured his food like the sun would never rise again.

He gave her little wooden figurines that he'd carved and painted himself. Wizards and sorcerers from Glubbdubdrib, he said. A particularly dainty one, which he'd made in her image. "The Princess of Glubbdubdrib," he told her. It was her favourite.

His eye bruise was a scintillating blue; after several days it turned green, then yellow. He wore it with pride. "You're my guardian angel, Lulu," he told her. "I'm sure they would've killed me if you hadn't come when you did. I'm rubbish at fighting, and I'm not as fast a runner as you are."

"Stay away from him, Will," she urged. "I don't know why George hates you so, but it's best if you stay out of his way."

"It's because I delivered a bun spiced with chilli to the house, specifically for him, you know." A mischievous gleam danced in his eyes.

"Will! How excessively silly of you! What if Lord Milford had eaten it instead?"

"I attached a note saying it was meant for George." He grinned. "He hates me, which is fine, because I hate him, too. He can beat me up all he wants, but I'm smarter than him. I'll get my revenge one day. I can be very, very patient. And when he's forgotten all about it, when he least expects it, I'll strike."

Will found his opportunity one sunny day when Mrs and Reverend Graham invited them to the vicarage for a garden party, with the purpose of raising funds for repairing the church. Louisa came with her father, Lord and Lady Milford, and George. They were having afternoon tea at delicately set tables in the shade of the trees. This was the moment Will had been waiting for. He slid an inflated pig's bladder under George's seat just before he sat down. The honk it emitted to simulate flatulence was wet and loud.

The entire tea party froze in embarrassed silence.

George's face turned deep red.

Louisa choked and nearly spat out her tea.

"Good heavens!" Reverend Graham exclaimed.

Lady Milford smiled painfully and apologised for him.

Mrs Graham immediately offered some fennel and aniseed tea to calm down his digestive tract.

She watched how Will skulked away, collapse against the wall of the house, holding his side, and nearly dying with laughter.

Oh, how happy he was that he'd finally had his revenge on George! From that day on, that was the only kind of tea George was given at teatime. Each cup was a reminder that Will had bested him.

A smile flitted over her face.

They spent many hours on the island reading. Will lent her his tattered copy of *Gulliver's Travels*, which they took turns reading aloud. She hid the copy of his book under a floorboard in her room, along with the wooden figurines Will had carved for her, extracting an oath that she would keep them as her greatest treasure. In return, she taught him how to swim.

She also helped him to translate Cicero. She had only been taught the basics by her governess, but she was a fast learner and grasped the Latin declensions faster than he did.

"It's easy, Will. Look: 'Nor is there anyone who loves, pursues, or desires pain itself because it is pain ...' Dolor means pain. You add an -em to it to make the accusative case, so it must be 'dolorem'."

"Dolor, dolores, dolorem, bah, it's all the same to me." He tugged at his hair in frustration. "And it's so depressingly morbid! Let's do something fun, Louisa. Let's row over to the island and have a rollicking adventure."

She liked to tease him, too. "You don't know how to swim, you don't know how to fight, you can't run particularly fast, either. You don't know any Latin. What *do* you know how to do, little Will?"

Will grinned, and the golden flecks in his hazel eyes lit up. "I know how to bake the best buns in England. I can carve the smallest wooden figures with my knife, and I know how to make my Lulu laugh."

That he certainly did.

He had a cheerful personality and a positive outlook on life, despite the harsh cards that life had dealt him. He was always cracking jokes and was full of mischief and nonsense.

"What would you do without me, little Will?" She ruffled his hair.

He pulled away.

"I'm not that little," he replied with dignity.

Louisa had looked down at him with a smirk.

"Someday," he told her, "I'm going to marry you, Louisa. I think it would be fabulous. You and me. Don't you think?"

She'd agreed.

But Louisa hadn't married him. And now she never would.

Chapter Eleven

THE MARKETPLACE WAS TEEMING WITH PEOPLE AND among carts and stalls. It was a hive of activity, a bustle of people, animals, sounds, and smells that were overwhelming.

Robert drove his cart into the middle of the square at a walking pace, and then got off the cart and led the donkey on foot.

"Make way!" he commanded in a loud voice. "Stand aside." He stopped the cart between two stalls. "This will do," he said and immediately began shouting at the top of his voice: "Fine cabbages, fresh cabbages! New potatoes, rhubarb, radishes, peas, and turnips galore!"

Louisa watched him for a while, almost admiring him, thinking he was doing a rather good job at selling his goods. Almost as if he were a real costermonger. He must have had some practice earlier. She was wearing the clothes Mrs Gary had given her, with a cap on her head and a linen apron tied around her waist. She looked just like one of them.

"How much for this?" A woman had approached, holding up a cabbage head.

Louisa had no idea. She'd never sold anything in her entire life. How on earth would she know how much to charge for a head of cabbage?

"Well?" The woman shifted a heavy bundle from one arm to the other. She had a burlap sack in one hand and a crying child clinging to her skirt. "I ain't got all day, missus."

Louisa looked over at Robert, who was busy haggling with a burly looking man who wanted to buy a sack of potatoes.

"Er. A shilling."

The woman stared at her with eyes so wide they looked like they might pop out of her face. Was that too much? Too little?

"A shilling?" the woman shrieked. "Are ye out of yer bleedin' mind?"

It was obviously too much.

"Is the cabbage studded with gold? Is it stuffed with diamonds? Has our king, Farmer George, harvested the bloody cabbage himself? Is it not enough that they have raised the prices of flour and bread? Are they now raising the price of ordinary vegetables as well? What do they expect us to eat? Dirt? They want us to starve, they do! Yer nothing but a highway woman in market clothes!" The woman spat on the ground in front of her.

Louisa pulled herself up proudly. "I beg your pardon. *What* did you say I am?"

Several people stopped to stare.

"Look at her puttin' on airs when she's nothing but a daylight robber. A shilling indeed!"

Louisa's temper flared. "I'm a *what*? And who do you think you are—"

A pair of iron hands clasped her shoulders. "Our valued customer, of course." Robert lifted the cabbage. "It's a mere penny a pound, ma'am."

The woman sniffed. "That's more like it. She said a shilling for one cabbage." She jerked her chin at Louisa.

"A misunderstanding." Robert smiled charmingly at her. "She meant a penny, didn't you, darling?" He leaned over to the woman and whispered conspiratorially with a wink. "It's her first day here. She's out of her depth."

"Oh. Aye." The woman shot her a mistrustful look. "Be more careful who you employ, mister." She fished a penny out of her pocket and handed it to him. "She'll ruin yer business."

Robert handed her the cabbage and offered the child a handful of cherries. "No harm done, eh? Here's some for you, too. They're fresh and sweet. Good day to you, ma'am."

When the woman had gone, Louisa dropped on a box to sit, exhausted from the interchange.

Robert crossed his arms. "Careful, wife. You nearly started a riot here. Don't trifle with food prices. These are hard times, and people here can barely afford the basic cost of their daily bread. They depend on our vegetables to remain cheap."

"I-I ... How should I know how much cabbage costs? I've never sold any in my entire life. Our cook usually goes to the market for us. I've never set foot in a place like this before."

He looked at her with a stern, brooding gaze. "Indeed. How is a drawing room princess to know how much cabbage costs? Here is your assignment: reconnoitre the marketplace. Your objectives are threefold: first, how do the merchants behave? Second, what do they say when they sell their goods? Third, how do they price their goods? You will report back in an hour with your findings. Forward, march."

He gave her a gentle shove to send her on her way.

It wasn't the worst idea, Louisa thought. Now she could try to see if she could find Will. Where would he be? There were endless stalls and carts selling produce, dairy, meat, and poultry. Other stalls sold pottery, baskets, glassware, brooms, and tools.

The sweet smell of lavender filled her nostrils. One stall was selling small bags of it. Louisa picked up one. They were delicately embroidered with dainty flowers and butterflies, not unlike the ones she used to embroider in the drawing room, and easily of the same quality. A wave of homesickness swept over her.

"What beautiful embroidery." Louisa ran a finger over the delicate stitches.

"Only a penny a bag," said a girl, who looked less than ten years old.

"Only a penny!" That was as much as the cabbage head cost. Surely it was worth more.

"Yes, ma'am. These are the last ones. My mum made

them but she ain't making more. Her eyes are too weak. I've been trying to embroider myself, but mine aren't as nice, and no one wants them." She sniffed. "We need the money to buy her medicine."

Louisa pulled out a coin, hesitated, then pressed it into the girl's hand.

"But, ma'am, I have no change," the girl cried.

"It's what I'm paying you. Keep it. It's worth it."

She'd given her a shilling.

"Thank you, ma'am. You're too generous, ma'am!" the girl stammered, unable to believe her fortune.

"Do you know where I could buy some soap?"

"Yes, ma'am. Over there." She pointed with her finger to the end of the row.

The stall did sell soap, but it looked like brown jelly stored in barrels that was scooped into smaller containers with a ladle. It smelled pungent and unpleasant. Next to the soft soap were coarse blocks of lye soap. These were cut into smaller bars before they were sold and did not look at all like the kind she was used to, which smelled of roses, lavender, violets, and myrtle.

"Don't you sell any Pears soap?" she asked the merchant.

"Pears soap? Are ye the Prince Regent to be able to spend such a fortune?" he scoffed. "That soap is a luxury item found only on Bond Street, not in this here market."

He cut a slab of soap off the longer block. "This is the best we have here. Solid, good soap." He slapped it down on the table in front of her. "Cleans as well as any Pears soap, if not better."

Louisa sighed. She had learned her lesson for the day

and would not argue back. "Very well. I'll take it." Any soap was better than no soap at all.

"Where would I find the baker's stalls?" she asked the man after she'd paid for it.

He jerked his head to the right. "Over there."

Indeed, there were stalls selling bread, rolls, pastries, pies, and biscuits.

"Fresh bread! Rolls, loaves, and sweet buns, all ready for your table! This is pure, good bread of the finest quality!" a hoarse voice shouted.

Louisa's heart thumped so loudly it drowned out all the noise from the market.

She drew closer and stopped, her hands clasped over her chest as if in prayer.

There he stood.

He'd grown, of course. He was much taller, and much wider, and his belly had grown into a round paunch. He wore a long white apron and a wine-red waistcoat with his shirt sleeves rolled up. His dark hair was long. He'd really turned into a burly baker.

"Fresh bread, pure, good bread!" He caught Louisa staring at him. "Good day, ma'am. Care for some bread?" He lifted a loaf.

"Will," she whispered. Her voice cracked.

He lowered the loaf. "Ma'am?"

"Don't you know me, Will?"

He stared at her uneasily. "Have we met before, ma'am?"

He didn't recognise her. Of course. So much time had passed. Eleven years? She'd barely recognised him. How much had she herself changed?

His stare intensified and something in his gaze shifted as recognition set in. "Miss—Miss Louisa?"

She smiled. Tears shot into her eyes. "Will."

"Louisa." His mouth fell open. "Zounds. I hardly recognised you. It's been so long. Is it indeed you?"

"Yes. How are you, Will?"

"I am well. Thank you, miss. And yourself?"

He stared at her.

"I am fine, too." She twisted the corner of her shawl around her hands.

A customer interrupted, wanting to buy a loaf of bread. Will turned to him, collected the payment, and handed him the loaf before turning back to her.

"Look at you. All grown up. You've become a lady." He looked at her reverently.

"Yes, well. And look at you. You're a baker now. You always wanted to be a baker."

"Yes, indeed I did."

An uncomfortable silence fell between them.

Don't you remember? Have you forgotten? The summer days we spent together in the forest and by the lake. I taught you to swim and you taught me how to accept myself ...

"But ... why are you here? Aren't you in London?" He waved his hand. "In some ballroom. Or at the manor house?"

"I live here now. At Piddleton." She took a big breath. "I'm married."

He smiled at her politely. "Congratulations. That's wonderful news."

She let go of her shawl and fiddled with the string of the pouch bag that was attached to her apron. "Yes."

"So am I."

"I beg your pardon?"

"Married. To my Mary. Expecting our first child in the spring." He beamed at her proudly.

Louisa's mouth suddenly went dry, and she ran her tongue over her lips. "This is wonderful. It really is. Felicitations." Why did it feel as if all the noise of the marketplace had fallen away? And why did she suddenly feel so wretchedly hollow inside?

Do you remember the kiss you gave me when I turned fifteen? It was my first and only real kiss ... you asked me to wait for you ... no, you didn't ask, you demanded ...

Will was speaking and she had trouble focusing on what he was saying.

"Of course, times could be better, especially for us bakers. It's not a good time for our trade." Will nodded at another customer, collected a coin, and handed over another loaf of bread.

"Horrendous price for a loaf," the man growled. "Where will it end?"

"Yes, I know, the price of a good loaf of bread is dear. But my bread is good and pure and unadulterated. I do not add any chalk or alum to my bread, if you please. You have my word of honour. Here, try some, sir." He held out a plate with bread pieces. "Louisa, you too. Try my bread."

She took a piece and chewed on it. "It's wonderful." She barely registered the taste.

"I bake the best bread in all of England, I do," he boasted.

"That you do." She smiled. "You always said you would."

"What with the Corn Laws driving up the price of flour, we've had to raise our prices as well. It led to the recent riots in Bridport when they broke into the bakeries." He shook his head. "I feel sorry for the people, but what can I do when wheat is so dear? I also need to make some profit. I also need to feed my family. They say we bakers are greedy and dishonest, but we're just trying to make a living ourselves. We're doing the best we can."

She nodded but hadn't understood a word he'd said. "I've always loved your bread."

I've always loved you, Will.

"I should be returning to my husband."

He looked up quickly. "He is here?"

"Yes. My husband is a costermonger and he's selling his produce here."

Will tilted his head aside and furrowed his brows. "You married a costermonger?"

She nodded.

"Why?" Then he flushed. "I beg your pardon. You need not answer that. It is, of course, none of my business whatsoever who you decide to marry."

In an attempt to change the topic, Will started talking about his job, about working in the bakery, about Mary, about the plans they had to extend the back part of the bakery and add on several more rooms. "For the little ones," he added with a smirk.

Louisa felt a pang of jealousy but kept on smiling and nodding as she listened to him.

Then he asked her how much they charged for a loaf of bread in London (she had no idea); whether the bakers in London were as affected by the Corn Laws as they were here (she supposed they were but couldn't say for sure), and whether there had been riots in London as well (if there were, she hadn't heard of it).

After that, an awkward silence fell between them.

"Will," Louisa started up after a while, whisking the breadcrumbs from her shawl. "I went to Glubbdubdrib the other day. It hasn't changed at all; it still has the same magic. But it was odd to see it all through different eyes, the eyes of an adult. It's so full of memories there it's almost unbearable. Have you gone to the island lately?"

He stared at her.

"Have you?" she repeated.

He shook his head slowly. "Louisa—" He looked at a loss at what to say. Then he shrugged. "I wouldn't have time for that."

"O-of course not." Something pressed down on her chest again; a familiar old, heavy feeling. She jumped up. "Never mind. It was silly of me to bring up our old childhood silliness. There are more important things to think about. Like customers who are waiting for you. I shan't keep you any longer."

Will nodded. "Mary would be happy to have you for tea. That is, if you would like."

"Of course. Nothing would be more delightful." She smiled at him brightly. "I'd better return to my husband. He's waiting for me."

"Aye. You'll drop by our shop soon, yes? I'd like you to meet my Mary."

She nodded. She'd already met Mary at the bakery, big with Will's child.

Lucky Mary.

"I will come."

"Splendid. Fresh bread! Rolls, loaves, sweet buns ..."

Good-bye, Will.

She made her way back between the stalls, her vision blurred with tears.

He'd forgotten.

Will had forgotten the magic of Glubbdubdrib.

Louisa walked through the stalls, barely hearing the clamour of the market as it receded to the background. She really ought to let go of it all. Let go of Will. He was married. As was she. Let go of her childhood. It was long over.

Let go of Glubbdubdrib.

She stopped between the stalls and rubbed her eyebrow. Why was a childhood dream so difficult to let go of? Of course, they'd only been children then.

It had only been puppy love. First love always was puppy love, was it not? As painful and soul-crushing as it had been, it had consumed her completely, and she'd been convinced she'd never love anyone as she'd loved Will, before or after.

Or ever again.

Cheeky, cheerful, Will; pudgy and clumsy but endearingly sweet, full of dreams and mischief and endlessly loyal to those he loved. He'd grown into a big, burly bear of a man, firmly rooted in reality.

Memories fade, of course, and it was clear that he barely remembered their time together. Life had run roughshod over it. He was married and about to be a father soon. What a lucky woman his wife was.

Of course, the promises one made to each other then had little meaning now. They were promises made by children. She could hardly hold him to them now.

He'd broken his promise to her.

And she'd broken hers too, hadn't she? She'd stopped waiting for him long, long ago. Louisa shivered. In fact, she'd probably broken her promise long before he had.

Then, in a fit of anger, she'd married the first man off the street that came along. A complete stranger: hard, rugged, and the opposite of Will in every respect.

Theirs had been a childhood romance, nothing more. A fairytale love as magical and ephemeral as the mists of Glubbdubdrib.

Chapter Twelve

"You've been crying," Robert said as soon as she reached their cart. He lifted her chin with a finger and examined her face. "Was it that bad having to interact with the farmers and merchants at the local market?" That hard, mocking smile was on his lips again.

Louisa pulled away. "One of the farmers was burning wood in a stove, and the smoke irritated my eyes. Nothing more." She rubbed her cheeks and sniffed.

"Well then, if it's nothing else. I've sold all of Mrs Gary's fruit and vegetables. She'll be happy. Look, I've bought us a new cauldron." He lifted a shiny black kettle. "Is there anything else you'd like? We have some blunt now that we can spend."

"Yes, in fact, there is. I'd like to have a sewing kit. With colourful threads. If you please."

He nodded. "I've seen them sell something like it over there. Follow me."

They bought her a basket filled with threads of all

colours, needles, and scissors. None of it was as good as the ones she commonly used. But it would do.

"I'd like to return to the market again with you tomorrow," she informed him on their way home. "I have observed how people sell their wares. I think I understand how to do it now."

"Very well. If that is your wish." He didn't sound enthusiastic about the prospect. Louisa repressed a smile.

It was, of course, entirely unnecessary. But she wanted to keep up the pretence just a little longer.

Back at their hut, she pulled out her muslin dress and spread it out on the rickety table. She pulled out a pair of shears, and with a big breath, started cutting the dress into small squares.

Then she threaded a needle and began to embroider.

THE NEXT DAY, she helped Robert sell the fruit and vegetables. She let him interact with the customers while she rearranged the fruit, weighed them on the scale, and folded the stack of old newspapers into cones, filling them with cherries. They made a good team. If it turned out she'd been mistaken, and he was truly a costermonger after all, they might make their living in this fashion after all.

Toward noontime, when the rush of buyers eased, she picked up her basket and told Robert that she would take a turn about the market.

She avoided the baker's stalls this time, even though she felt the pull, the yearning to see Will again. But she would not. She couldn't bear facing him again. Not when he'd forgotten all that they'd shared.

"Good day again, ma'am," a small voice said next to her. It was the girl who'd sold her the lavender bag.

Louisa smiled at the barefoot girl who stood in front of her, wearing a patched dress. "Just the person I was looking for. Look what I have for you." She opened her basket and showed her the little embroidered pouches she'd made from her muslin dress the night before.

The girl gasped. "They're even more beautiful than the ones my mum makes!"

"If you have some dried lavender, you can fill them, tie them up with a ribbon and sell them." She leaned down and whispered, "But they are worth more than a penny."

The girl looked at her with bright eyes. "I have dried lavender here. And there's some ribbon left. Will you help me sell them?"

Louisa hesitated for a moment, then shrugged. "Why not?"

THEY SOLD THEM ALL. Whether it was the superior quality of her embroidery, or the delicate muslin of the bags, or that a beautiful woman and a pretty girl together made an irresistible duo when selling their wares, or whether she had finally lost her fear of interacting with people and discovered her inborn talent for negotiating, for she wheedled and haggled with more passion than a fishmonger—or a combination of all of them—they sold their wares and the money flowed in.

After they'd sold the last lavender bag, she heard a soft laugh.

Leaning against the barrel of a neighbouring stall with his arms crossed was Robert, who'd been watching her for a while with clear amusement. "I see business is going well," he said.

She beamed at him. "Yes. Somehow, it is easier to sell things when it is not for myself. Let's count the coins, Anna." She helped the girl count.

"I've never made so much," the girl said, her eyes shining. "It will pay for my mother's medicine." Then she hesitated, split the coins in half, and pushed one pile towards Louisa. "For you. It was my lavender, but you made the pouches."

Louisa shook her head. "No. It is all yours. This was important to me in a way you won't understand. I have already received my due payment. Thank you," she told the girl, who was beside herself with joy.

"God bless you, ma'am," she cried after her when she turned to leave.

The sense of satisfaction and accomplishment and pride was unlike anything she'd ever experienced before.

"Shall we go home, then?" Robert took her arm. And for the first time, she felt a sense of gladness that her husband was Robert, and that they had a home to return to, even if it was only a small, rickety hut.

He helped her onto the cart and steered it out of town.

The road back to Piddleton was clogged with vehicles. The donkey plodded along at a snail's speed. At this rate, they would not arrive until well after dark.

Robert gave her a sideways glance. "You did a good thing there."

"And you didn't think I had it in me," she replied.

"I confess I did not."

"I didn't know it could feel so good to sell one's own creation. It makes me feel quite accomplished. I had a good day ... mostly." She fell silent. The memory of her conversation with Will surfaced again.

"Are you certain there is nothing more? You seem somewhat sad."

"No, nothing more." Louisa shook herself. She would have to pull herself out of the doldrums as best as she could, forget Will, forget the past, and focus on her life now. She would have to stop running around with her head in the clouds and become more aware, more observant of what was happening around her.

Including her husband, who was still watching her with sharp, piercing eyes.

"I'm aware that I haven't been quite myself these past few days, I suppose. I've been wool-gathering and distracted and oblivious to my surroundings. I'm not usually like that."

He arched an eyebrow at her but refrained from commenting.

"Nor am I unintelligent or uninformed. I do care. About people, I mean." It sounded defiant.

"I've never doubted that," he drawled.

"Reading about laws and politics in the papers and discussing them in the drawing rooms is one thing, but actually seeing how they affect people is quite another. I admit I've been naïve." She tilted her nose up and sat as if an iron rod had been implanted in her spine.

"Would you like to explain what exactly you're referring to?"

"The Corn Laws. I've heard Papa talk about them. I've also read about them in the newspapers. But I confess I've never really thought about how it might affect ordinary people. How it might impact their lives." She thought for a moment. "I never really thought about what it means to be poor and what it means for a family with four or five children to not be able to buy bread because it's become too expensive."

"I'm not surprised. It isn't generally expected of ladies to be conversant about the Corn Laws, if I may say so. And they're not expected to have an opinion about it, either. So, you needn't belabour the point too much. It is quite acceptable for a society damsel to not know about the Corn Laws. It wouldn't do to exhibit too much interest in politics and social affairs, would it?"

His patronising, sarcastic tone irritated her. "But it bothers me. And I'd rather you didn't lump me in with other feather-brained society ladies who are like that. You seem to enjoy hammering home the notion that I'm a rich, spoilt heiress who is incapable of forming a coherent thought on such matters, never having set foot in the marketplace." She disregarded the fact that that was exactly what she was.

"Oh my. I'm impressed. In other words, the Ice Damsel has learned something about life."

"I wish you would stop calling me that." She looked at him crossly.

"Then why did you do it?"

"Do what?"

"Act like you are the Ice Damsel, when you're anything but." He leaned his arms on his knees, his body turned to her.

When her eyes flew up to meet his, he held them in a steady gaze. She was silent for a long time. Robert, no doubt, must have thought she'd never reply, but she did. "It's because ... they expected me to. None of them would ever see me as I really was." Not a single person had ever attempted to see beyond the beautiful façade of Miss Louisa Highworth, heiress. It was as if her true self was of no interest to anyone. It was as though the truth of who she was simply wasn't enough.

"Who are you, then, truly?" His voice was soft.

"What I like and what I'm truly interested in is not compatible with the image of Miss Louisa Highworth."

"For example?" he probed.

She took a deep breath before continuing. "I enjoy reading. I suppose one could call me a bluestocking. My favourite writer is Jonathan Swift, *Gulliver's Travels,* in particular. If I could have been a man, I would have gone to university to study The Classics. I love the smell of bread. I like coarse brown bread more than the soft white one. But the best bread is the kind you bake over an open fire. I also like caraway cakes and orange preserves. I don't like dancing and balls; I never did. I enjoy swimming in the sea or ocean. Papa takes me—took me—to Brighton to the seaside every summer. When I was younger, I used to think I might have made a better boy than a girl." She shrugged. "This is who I am. But people will always see me as Miss Louisa Highworth, heiress, worth twenty-thousand pounds per annum."

"It must have been hard for you," he said quietly. "Never being seen for who you really are."

A lump formed in her throat. Zounds. Why did he suddenly appear to understand her as if he truly saw her? She was about to weep again. She shook her head impatiently and tried to deflect from her emotional state by posing him the question. "And you? Who are you truly, Robert Jones? What are your interests?" *Other than running around in disguise, attempting to fool all and sundry.*

He shrugged. "The opposite. Aside from a book or two that I enjoy, I read little. Hate to dance, hate the water, and am not particular about food. I eat whatever I can get my hands on as long as it fills my stomach. I don't like confined, dark spaces. My ideal day consists of sleeping, preferably outside. Give me a hammock under the trees, and I'm a happy man. That's it."

She looked at him sharply. "Do you crave sleep during the day because you do not get enough at night?" She'd been awakened several times by muttered, thrashing sounds. He was sleeping on the straw pallet on the other side of the room, and she'd noticed his sleep was fitful and disturbed by nightmares. He'd usually awaken with a start and leave the hut to spend the remaining night outside. She wondered what had given him those nightmares.

As if she had hit a raw nerve, he frowned. "I simply

feel the walls of the cottage close in on me, especially at night. I don't like it."

She wanted to press further and enquire why that was the case, but they had reached a crossroads, and Robert pulled the plodding donkey to a halt. Just in time, too, for a curricle came smashing around the curve with great velocity. The driver, unable to rein in the horses, gave a shout of alarm before the vehicle ploughed into a stagecoach that was on its way to Bournemouth. There was a tremendous crash, wood splintering, horses neighing, and people screaming as the stagecoach overturned into the ditch. The curricle flew through the air before coming to a stop on the ground shortly before their cart, burying the driver underneath the splintered, broken wood. A lone wheel bumped off into the field.

Louisa screamed, hiding her face in both her hands. She pressed against Robert, who'd instinctively thrown himself over her to shield her from the flying debris.

"Are you hurt?" he asked after pulling away. His hands cupped her face, checking to see if she was unharmed.

She shook her head. "I'm fine."

A general hubbub of panic broke out as people cried and shouted. "There's blood!" cried one woman.

"The horses have run off!" cried another.

Cries of "Fred? Where is Fred?" and "Mary, are you all right?" were drowned out by groans and cries for help.

"Attention! Everyone, remain calm!" A steely voice cut through the commotion. "Don't panic, shout, and dissolve into hysterics. Keep your wits about you and let us assess the situation." Robert had released Louisa and climbed onto his seat to address everyone. He pointed to a man. "You there, swiftly check the coach and help the people out. Louisa, help him get the people off the road to safety, and look after the women and the injured. You three over there." He pointed to a group of men who'd approached cautiously. "Instruct all approaching vehicles to halt at a safe distance. And you, boy, go to the nearest farm to fetch cotton cloths and bandages. Posthaste. There are casualties."

"Aye, aye, sir!" The boy set off in a jiffy.

"Rally to me, men. We need to lift the curricle first for the people trapped beneath. Form teams of four, one on each corner. On the count of four, we lift."

The men did as he said, and together they lifted the curricle. Underneath it lay both the hapless driver and his tiger, who was unconscious.

Robert continued to bark out rapid orders.

Louisa, together with the man Robert had singled out, helped the people out of the stagecoach and led them to the side of the road. They all seemed unhurt, save for some bumps and bruises.

A girl with a straw bonnet was weeping silently. "It was such a loud crash," she sobbed, "and it happened so suddenly. One moment I was sitting in my seat, the next I was flying through the carriage. I thought we were all going to die."

Louisa soothed her as best as she could. "You are in shock. Come and sit here on this stone and take some deep breaths."

The girl did as she said, and Louisa helped her untie

the mangled bonnet. She had light blonde hair and big blue eyes that swam with tears.

Louisa stared at her face.

The girl, too, stared back. "But I know you," she said slowly. "Why do I know you? You're, you're ... Louisa Highworth!" Recognition dawned on her small heart-shaped face.

Louisa frowned at her.

"I'm Miss Celeste Cooper-Wiles. Don't you remember me?"

Louisa stared at the face she'd last seen as a child. "Celeste. Of course." She was terrible at remembering faces. But the light blonde hair, the blue eyes, the pretty face were uncannily like the girl who'd been Lord Milford's daughter at Meryfell Hall.

"What strange circumstances under which we meet again." Celeste gave her a strained smile. The girl self-consciously plaited her dress, which Louisa noticed was not only dusty but also washed out and of a simple cut.

"It is strange, indeed. How fortunate that you are unhurt. Let's see to the other passengers before we talk further, shall we?"

Celeste nodded and helped Louisa tend to the other passengers.

In the meantime, Robert and a group of men had pulled the curricle aside and were concentrating on returning the coach to an upright position. He issued orders on how to best accomplish this.

"How efficient he is," Celeste whispered to Louisa. "So commanding. Everyone jumps at his orders. Did you see? He has the entire situation under control. He must have been an experienced army officer, someone higher in the ranks, don't you think?"

Louisa stared at Celeste as the light dawned upon her. "Of course," she replied in a monotone voice. "How excessively foolish of me. I don't know why I didn't see it earlier."

"And he's enormously handsome. Do you think he might still be a bachelor?"

Louisa smiled at her wryly. "Alas, he's married. To me."

Celeste stared at her, mouth agape. "Oh! But they said you'd have no one—none of the suitors—but of course it must have been merely rumours," she added hastily. "How long have you been married?"

It felt like an eternity since she'd dragged the grubby costermonger from the street into their drawing room and declared that she would marry him. Yet it had hardly been ... "About a week."

"Felicitations!" Celeste beamed at her.

Louisa wiped her hands on her apron. "Yes. Well. I suppose. I married a costermonger."

Celeste looked at her, confused. "Indeed?" Then she took in Louisa's simple cotton dress and apron, as if seeing her clothes for the first time. "I see." But it was clear on her face that she had a thousand questions, the uppermost of which would be why would a rich heiress marry a costermonger and traipse about the country in a farmer woman's clothes? But she was too polite to ask.

"And you? You haven't married?" Louisa tried to steer the conversation in another direction.

A look of sadness crossed her face. "No. Oh, no. You

haven't heard, have you?" She wrapped the string of her tattered bonnet around her finger. "Mother died a year after your last visit. Father passed away three years ago, and George inherited. Except ..." She bit on her lips and sighed.

"Except he didn't take good care of his inheritance?" Louisa guessed. She hadn't yet visited Meryfell Hall. The thought of doing so had crossed her mind several times, but something had stopped her.

Celeste nodded. "He gambled most of it away and sold the house and the estate to cover his debts. Meryfell Hall is gone. We've lost our home, George and I."

Knowing George and what he'd been like in his youth, Louisa wasn't really surprised. But he'd dragged his poor sister down with him. Her prospects were ruined, and it would be unlikely for her to find a suitable match in the future. Louisa took her hands and squeezed them. "I'm truly sorry to hear that. Where are you staying now?"

"I am staying with my aunts in a village near Bournemouth. In fact, I am on my way to them right now. George is—" she waved her hand around. "Who knows where. He drifts around. He stays with friends or at inns. Most of the time I don't know where he is. He never writes. I have no prospects at all. I have never had a Season. I would have liked to go to London, but as you can see"—she lifted her dress—"with this outfit I am rather unsuitably attired to be seen in any kind of society. So I suppose I shall spend my remaining days looking after my aunts." She sounded resigned to her fate.

"I'm terribly sorry, Celeste. I did not know." Her

father might have mentioned Lord Milford's death, but she couldn't remember the exact circumstances. As for George running wild, that did not surprise her in the least. "We're staying at Piddleton," she began, then interrupted herself. She was about to issue an invitation for Celeste to call on them for tea, then remembered she could hardly entertain her in the rickety hut where they were staying. And she certainly had no drawing room in which to host guests. And even if she had a drawing room, she had no tea to offer. Least of all a teapot or cups in which to serve it. Louisa sighed. "Yes, well." She smiled helplessly at Celeste.

The men had finished cleaning up the scene of the accident and turned to the two injured men lying by the side of the road. The tiger had now regained consciousness. He appeared dazed and was bleeding profusely, but Robert declared it was a mere scratch.

The culprit of the accident was a tulip dressed in the latest fashion, a whipster who'd underestimated his ability to drive a curricle-and-two. Robert was in the process of giving him a sharp tongue-lashing, the gist of which was that he had no business driving such a vehicle if he could not control it, and that these roads were not suitable for racing.

"But I am injured!" the man replied with a whimper. He pointed to his leg, which, indeed, seemed to be at an unnatural angle.

"You'll live," Robert replied curtly.

"But my leg!" the man moaned. "It hurts like the very devil."

Robert crouched down beside him. "Let me have a

look. Yes, it does look bad. With injuries like that, the best course of action is to just cut off the offending limb altogether. Where's the surgeon?"

The man screamed. "Don't you dare!"

Robert lifted a lazy eyebrow.

He whimpered, "Don't let him touch my leg."

Robert looked at him contemptuously. "What a lily-livered milksop. Fashion a stretcher and carry him on it. He'll have to wait here until the doctor and the constable arrive. Let this be a lesson to you not to use this road for racing."

Traffic gradually resumed on the now-cleared road. A surgeon had arrived and was tending to the injured. Celeste had walked over to Robert and exchanged a few words with him. It appeared she was thanking him, but he brushed her away. The travellers on the stagecoach were instructed to wait until another coach arrived.

"I hope we meet again soon," Louisa told Celeste before they parted.

Celeste merely gave her a wan smile.

Several people came up to Robert to express their gratitude for his help. Afterwards, he walked over to Louisa and nodded. "Things are under control. Let us resume our journey home."

TACITURN and deep in her thoughts, Louisa returned with Robert to their hut. Once arrived, she climbed down from the cart and stared at their rickety hut as it dawned on her how unnecessary it all was.

She knew now that all she had to do was say the word

and they would sleep that night in a feathered bed with silken sheets, and a butler who would serve her tea in her very own drawing room.

Should she challenge him on the matter?

Or should she continue the game?

If so, why? And for how long? Why was she resistant to ending it?

She was so very tired.

"You are rather efficient in dealing with emergencies," she commented, but refrained from saying more.

He merely grunted. "Don't forget to feed the donkey," he said brusquely before he walked away.

Louisa stared after him. Then she took some carrots and held them out to the donkey, who ate them gratefully.

A single question remained uppermost in her mind: Which one of her hundred rejected suitors was Robert Jones?

Chapter Thirteen

"There's no need for you to accompany me to the market today," Robert told her the next morning as he fastened several crates filled with vegetables to the cart. "Instead, I'd like you to go to Mrs Gary's and help her on the farm. I promised to help in return for a pail of milk and a dozen eggs."

Louisa frowned. "What kind of help does she need?" She'd intended to spend some time at the lake thinking through this entire situation with Robert—the costermonger-who-wasn't-really-a-costermonger—and coming up with a suitable plan of action. Whoever he really was, she must have humiliated him terribly for him to take his revenge to such extraordinary lengths.

There was no doubt in her mind that this was what it was all about: revenge.

How much had she humiliated him? And when?

She suspected it must have been quite bad if he'd gone through the trouble of disguising himself just to get back at her. It was not just his elaborate disguise. There had been the long journey in the donkey cart. The uncomfortable nights sleeping on the ground. The poor cottage. The trip to the market. It had all been carefully planned to teach her but one thing: humility. And now, to drive the point home, he wanted her to do manual labour on a farm.

At best, he wanted to show her what life was like for the lower classes, and then to pull back the curtain to reveal the truth, saying, "Aren't you relieved that I'm not a costermonger, but one of your former suitors? Aren't you glad to have escaped such drudgery? Aren't you glad to be married to a gentleman of good breeding after all, madam wife?"

How magnanimous he would appear, like a *deus ex machina* rescuing her from impecunity, offering her a luxurious home, wealth, perhaps even a title, which she would, of course, accept with grateful humility. Spared a life of drudgery, sweat, and toil. What a relief!

A wave of anger shot through her, but she held her emotions in check. She was still deciding on whether to deal with the matter head on, or to continue playing along and hatching her own plan of revenge. Let him think he'd had her hoodwinked, then turn the tables on him and surprise him with—with what? She did not know. She needed time to think.

However, this would mean feigning ignorance and enduring this situation for a little while longer. It would mean to continue living in the ramshackle hut, wearing coarse clothes, and eating poorly cooked food with no possibility of taking a hot bath. It would mean going to this Mrs Gary and helping her with the farm.

"She mentioned she needed help with the vegetable garden as her back aches and her eyesight is poor. Both her sons died within a week of each other at Waterloo, and the farmhand broke his leg, so he's no use to her. The woman is entirely on her own. I have promised her help for the remaining week. After that, her daughter will return with her family to take over the farm."

Louisa felt a pang of sympathy for the woman. "Poor woman, to have lost both her sons at the same time. This is a hard fate to bear."

"It is, indeed. Will you help her?" He picked up the ribbons but waited for her answer.

She had made up her mind. Regardless of Robert's true motives for helping Mrs Gary, she would help out of her own good will. Simply because she wanted to.

"Very well, Robert. I'll go see Mrs Gary."

He gave a curt nod, lifted the reins, and led the donkey along the road to Dorchester.

Mrs Gary's farm consisted of a stone building with a thatched roof, a barn, a stable, a chicken coop, and a vegetable garden. Surrounding the farmstead were fields and pastures.

Louisa knocked hesitantly at the door and waited until she heard a voice call. "Who is it?"

"Miss Louisa High—that is, Mrs Louisa Jones, of course. My husband has sent me to help you."

She heard some dragging footsteps, then the door opened.

Mrs Gary was a small but wiry woman, her grey hair

tucked under a cotton cap. She was hunched over with grief or hard work over the years, possibly both. Her wizened face looked tired. Her eyes were not focused.

She was blind.

"I'm here to help," Louisa repeated, wondering how on earth the woman could cope if she couldn't see.

"So, you came, did you? I didn't think you would. But Robert is a man of his word, a man you can rely on. Came every day to help me pick the vegetables and milk Bessie."

The stark, direct words took her aback. "Robert milked a cow?" Louisa repeated.

"Aye, that he did. He's a man worth his weight in gold. Remains to be seen if you're worthy of him."

Before she could think of a suitable reply, the woman took her by the arm and marched her to the stable. "Open the door."

After some awkward fumbling, she managed to pull back the bolt that locked the shed.

The sharp, pungent smell of animals and dung enveloped her. Louisa gagged.

"Exactly," the woman said. "The manure needs to be removed. The animals are lying in their own excrement. And Bessie needs milking. I would've done it myself in the morning, but my back is giving me trouble and I can't for the life of me sit on that low stool."

Louisa's mouth dropped open. "You want me to clear out the manure? And milk a cow?"

"That's what I said."

Louisa crossed her arms. "I've never done either."

"Good for you, missy, because now you'll learn how

to do it. Get the cow, the goat, and the horse out of the shed and tie them to the fence. Then take the pitchfork and scoop up the manure. Throw it on the wheelbarrow and take it to the pile behind the barn. Sweep the floor and spread fresh straw. Then milk the cow. The bucket is in the corner. That's all there is to it." As if everything she'd just said was crystal clear, the woman simply turned and walked back to the house. Having lived on the farm for decades, she apparently knew her way around, even if she could no longer see.

Louisa stared after her in shock. She was to shovel manure?

She, the Incomparable, the queen of London's most glamorous balls? She, who had danced with dukes and princes? Who had received one hundred proposals of marriage from the pinks of the ton?

Her nostrils flared.

Surely not.

AN HOUR LATER, Louisa's dress was soaked with sweat, her hair was in disarray, and she smelled from head to toe of the substance she was shovelling. Earlier, she'd slipped on a warm, mushy pile of excrement and landed bottom first in the wheelbarrow—filled with even more manure.

She had not allowed herself to burst into tears. Instead, she'd pulled herself up and wiped off her dress as best as she could, but it was hopeless. She looked worse than the night soil man, and likely smelled even worse than him, too.

With every dig into the manure pile, she imagined it

was Robert's face and cursed herself for ever having laid her eyes on him.

But give up?

Never!

She would show him. She would do a better job than he had. She would finish sweeping that stable and it would be so clean one could eat one's supper off its bare floor.

After another hour of heaving the manure onto the pile behind the barn, she decided the stable was clean enough. She swept the floor and spread the fresh straw as Mrs Gary had instructed. Then she stared at her hands. A lump formed in her throat. Blisters and calloused hands were the mark of the labouring class. Her hands had always been manicured, soft and white, and in her entire twenty-six years of existence, she'd never even touched any tool that belonged to the working class.

How could Robert do it with such little effort? Selling things in the market. Harvesting vegetables. Milking a cow. She cast a disheartened glance at Bessie, still tethered to the fence, waiting to be milked. It seemed incongruous with the image of her suitors. It seemed impossible to her that a gentleman of her acquaintance would know how to do such a thing.

Louisa rubbed her aching hands on her dress as she rested on the milking stool.

Who was he, then?

Celeste had pointed out that he might have been an army officer. His behaviour and ability to take command of a situation where everyone else was panicking certainly suggested it.

But officers were gentlemen. Was Robert truly a gentleman? If he was, or had been, a soldier, that narrowed down the list of suitors somewhat, but there were still a considerable number of gentlemen who might fit the bill. After all, many of the gentlemen of Quality who'd courted her had been officers who'd returned from the Continent to take part in the victory celebrations in London. She'd danced with countless officers. The drawing rooms had been full of uniforms, and to Louisa, who couldn't tell the difference between a major and a colonel, they all looked the same in their scarlet regimental regalia.

She could rule out that hero—Twiddlepoops—because the gossip sheets had announced that he'd found solace with someone else and had married less than a week after she'd turned him down so spectacularly. It was almost insulting how quickly he'd found his happiness with someone else.

Nor was he Carrothair, unless ... Louisa gasped. Robert might have dyed his ginger hair black. Zounds! He hadn't, had he? Could he have gone to such lengths to hide his identity by dyeing his hair? She shifted uncomfortably as she remembered how badly she'd humiliated him. She'd slapped him, then dashed a glass of ratafia in his face. He'd been furious, furious ...

She wrung her hands. Heavens, Robert might really turn out to be Carrothair. What would she do if he was?

The problem was that for the life of her, she couldn't recall what Robert—ruggedly tall and broad, with his beard and shaggy hair—would have looked like in the ballroom, in full evening dress, clean-shaven, styled hair, and in a perfectly tailored suit—or rather, a uniform.

If not Carrothair, could he be the Corinthian in disguise? The nonpareil who'd bored her to tears. What was his name again? Lord something-or-other. She'd called him Frippery Fop. He'd also been tall and athletic. He'd been perfect in every way. Louisa chewed on her lower lip. No doubt she'd made no secret of the fact that she'd found him a bore. She'd probably made fun of him. Since he'd been the catch of the Season, no doubt she must have hurt his pride by rejecting him.

One incident with Lord Frippery Fop made her cringe.

Like any gentleman, he'd conversed with her father, asked to be introduced, and then he'd asked her to stand up with him in a set. It had been the supper dance. Afterwards, he'd led her to supper and arduously tried to charm her. The problem was that she'd been uninterested ... and simply bored. And he'd been oblivious, talking on and on, well, about what? It could have been about horses and horse racing. Or had it been some military campaign he'd been involved in? Some action he'd seen during the wars, for he'd been an officer before he'd sold out.

The next day, as true as clockwork, like they all did, he'd turned up with a bouquet and a request to talk to her.

This was the moment she hated the most, the moment of the proposal. It was intensely embarrassing, and nothing about it had ever been romantic. They all got down on their knees as if she was some kind of goddess they worshipped. Why did they do that? All she wanted to do was to run away. Then, they would stammer out something in the nature of, "You would make me the happiest man in the world ..." and that was always followed by a conditional clause: "if you would marry me/give me your hand in matrimony/become my wife." There were not many varieties thereof.

Frippery Fop had been more suave than others. But in the end, he'd uttered the same clichéd proposal.

"No." Short and to the point, she believed, was always the best answer.

He had still looked at her expectantly, as if he hadn't heard or believed that she could possibly turn him down.

She'd huffed impatiently and left the room, leaving him kneeling on the floor like a fool.

Alas, she'd left the door to the drawing room wide open, so her father's visitors had a good look at Frippery Fop on his knee.

"Did you just refuse him, Miss Highworth?"

"Naturally," Louisa had answered. "I couldn't imagine being married to a tulip."

"Dash it, I just lost a wager," complained another.

The entire group had burst into commentary, and he'd pushed past them, his ears burning red with such a look of hurt and anger in his eyes that she'd felt a pang of discomfort.

She pursed her lips. If Robert was Sir Frippery Fop, he certainly had reason to be angry with her. He certainly had reason to want revenge.

"What are you doing sitting there, staring a hole in the air?" Mrs Gary called out.

Louisa jumped. How on earth did the old woman know that she was sitting on the stool, doing nothing?

"Have you milked Bessie yet?"

"Er, no." Louisa looked nervously at the cow.

"Then do so. I promised your husband a good pail of milk and a dozen eggs. You'll have to fetch those eggs yourself, of course."

Louisa groaned. What more must she do?

"I promised it to him," Mrs Gary continued. "And what would you like?"

"I beg your pardon?"

"I asked what you'd like as payment for your hard work."

"You mean you will give me something in return for the work I have done?"

"Of course. I am fair with my payment."

"I thought the milk and eggs would be sufficient payment."

"I asked what *you* wanted."

Louisa didn't have to think twice. "A bath," she blurted out. "With soap. Real soap."

"Very well. I happen to have some real soap. Milk the cow first. I'll heat the water."

Louisa almost fell off her stool. Then, with renewed determination, she turned to Bessie the cow.

"I can do this," she said, as she reached out to touch the cow's teats.

LOUISA RETURNED TO HER HUT, pleased with herself. She had blisters on her hands and been covered from head to toe with substances too horrible to mention. She'd shovelled manure, swept the stable, and milked the cow. The first few tries she'd squirted milk everywhere but where it was supposed to go. It ended up on her face, her clothes, and the floor. Then Mrs Gary had shouted some instructions and with grim determination, Louisa had done it. She'd milked a cow.

Dazed by this achievement, she felt she could do anything. She'd even crawled into the henhouse to collect eggs, which she now proudly carried home in a basket.

She'd had a bath.

True to her word, Mrs Gary had prepared a steaming bath for her in the kitchen, and there had been a bar of soap! It hadn't been Pears soap, but neither had it been that coarse stuff they'd sold at the market. It was homemade lavender soap made with goat's milk, Mrs Gary had explained. Louisa had loved it.

She'd soaked in the bath until her skin was wrinkled like a prune. She couldn't recall ever having enjoyed a bath more in her entire life than the one she took in Mrs Gary's kitchen.

Then she'd washed her hair, dried it, and plaited it into a long braid.

She felt reborn.

Mrs Gary gave her a fresh linen dress and tucked the soap in the basket she'd prepared for her. Inside was mutton pie, cheese, butter, a pint of fresh milk, and the eggs.

"My daughter doesn't fit into these clothes anymore. It is best that you wear them. They are good and sturdy.

Now, carry this basket carefully and don't drop it, or you'll break the eggs," she advised.

"Thank you," Louisa said, speaking from the heart.

"Hush. It's not easy for a lone woman like me to get everything done around here. But there is no one else. All my men are all gone." She sniffed. "My Gregory died too young. And my two sons died in the war. It's always the women who are left behind. Always us women who must survive and be strong." She groped for Louisa's hand and patted it. "You're a good one, too. A proud exterior that hides a heart of gold. Your worth isn't in your status or in what they say you are. That is a lie. Therefore, listen to what I'm telling you now. Learn to fend for yourself. Don't rely on men to take care of you. Learn how to do it yourself. Mark my words, there is nothing dishonourable about it. Only fools say it is. And never forget your true worth."

It was unlike anything anyone had ever told her. In fact, she'd been raised to believe the opposite. A warmth filled her chest. "Thank you, Mrs Gary. You're too generous. Both with your gifts and your advice."

As she carried the heavy basket home, she thought about Mrs Gary's words. How everything had turned out differently.

She felt proud of herself.

While her parents would surely be horrified to learn that she'd spent the entire morning shovelling manure, she felt oddly ... accomplished. She'd done this on her own, without anyone's help. She'd milked a cow and collected eggs from the henhouse.

She'd learned to fend for herself.

She set the basket down on the table in their cottage and looked around for Robert.

Where was he? The donkey cart was in the yard, therefore he had returned. Louisa walked around the back of the cottage to the river. There he was, motionless on the edge of the bank. She hid in the shade of the apple tree, watching him.

This was no polished gentleman of the drawing room. This was a rough, rugged figure. The problem was his overgrown facial hair, which obscured his features and gave him an air of neglect.

But—good heavens, what was he doing now? He took off his shirt, tossed it aside, and then proceeded to remove his trousers. Louisa stifled a gasp and covered her eyes with her hands. She peered through her fingers and saw him in the middle of the stream, the water up to his hips.

He was washing himself with the soap she'd bought at the market.

She couldn't tear her eyes away.

He was beautiful, like one of the Greek statues she'd seen, the Elgin Marbles come to life. A hard male body with narrow hips flaring out to broad, wide shoulders, rippling with muscle. Several thick welts, some red, some white, curved along his back. They were terrible scars.

Louisa forgot to breathe.

He turned around, and she saw it was the same on the front part of his body, though not quite as many.

"You might as well hand me that towel," his voice rang out.

Louisa jumped. He knew she'd been watching him the whole time.

She met Robert's intense gaze. A slight smile played across his lips as if he knew exactly what she was thinking. Louisa turned and ran away as fast as her legs would carry her.

Out of breath, hot, and with her mind whirling, she ran.

Past their cottage, past Mrs Gary's farmhouse.

Without thinking twice, she ran up the familiar path across the meadow that led to Meryfell Hall.

Chapter Fourteen

THE WIDE-OPEN HOUSE BUSTLED WITH ACTIVITY. The persistent sounds of hammering and sawing suggested the roof was under repair. In the meadow in front of the house, a pair of maids vigorously beat carpets. Workers were inside, painting the wooden banister.

Meryfell Hall had been sold, Celeste had told her. That would explain why it was being extensively restored. The new owner evidently had ordered it.

The park surrounding the manor house had transformed dramatically. The once neatly trimmed lawn and flower beds adorning the estate were gone. In their place, long grass and unruly bushes had overgrown the area, and the formerly well-trimmed trees were now shrouded in wild undergrowth.

Come to think of it, the land and the tenants in the nearby cottages did not seem to thrive, either. George had badly neglected them. Would the new owner do anything to improve their situation?

Louisa walked hesitantly up to the entrance with the heavy oak door.

A maid rushed out of the house and said, "Make haste, we are to help clear out the library shelves. We need every pair of hands we can get with those thousands of books!" The girl had evidently mistaken her for a housemaid.

How low I have fallen, she thought wryly. But who could blame her? She was still wearing the simple, threadbare cotton dress of a peasant with a dusty and wrinkled apron tied around her waist, and a lopsided cap hanging off her head. Louisa adjusted herself and with a big breath, stepped through the main door.

Meryfell Hall was an old Elizabethan manor house that had been in the possession of the lords of Milford for many generations. There were dark wood, panelled walls, and heavy marble fireplaces everywhere. The tapestries were faded and the carpets, she noted, had been rolled up and put aside.

At first glance, the house had lost much of the splendour that it had when she'd visited as a girl. Cobwebs hung in the corners, and a musty, mouldy smell clung to the walls as if the rooms hadn't been aired in a long time.

Two maids were waxing the floor, two more were taking down the curtains, and several footmen were carrying boxes of linen and other contents down the stairs. No one noticed or cared that she was there; those who saw her assumed she was part of the household staff.

With light steps, Louisa went up the stairs, turned right, walked down the corridor, and after a quick look to the right and left to make sure no one was around, she slipped into the room and closed the door.

This had been her room when she stayed at Meryfell Hall whenever they visited. It was half bare of furniture; the bed had no mattress, and no curtains hung on the windows. She ran her hand over the wooden windowsill.

W and L were engraved there, intertwined.

Will had done that after she'd smuggled him into her room to show him her collection of books. George had nearly caught him; he'd burst into her room without knocking. "Where is he? I know he's here!"

"Get out of my room at once, George. You have no right to be here," Louisa had snapped.

"I know the cur is hiding somewhere." He lay down on the floor to look under the bed. Then, seeing that no one was there, rushed over to her wardrobe and pulled the door open.

At that moment, her mother had fortunately appeared, scolding him for entering a girl's bedroom, and George retreated with a scowl and a barely muttered apology.

Will, meanwhile, was hanging on for dear life outside the window. Then his foot slipped, and he'd fallen headlong into a bush. He'd hobbled away with nothing worse than a bruised ankle.

A smile flitted over Louisa's face as her fingers traced the engraving.

W and L.

A door slammed outside. Footsteps sounded. Her head snapped up, and she held her breath.

"We must make haste. The bedrooms are to be

finished within the next two days," a male voice said. "He'll come to inspect them in person."

"All the bedrooms?"

"All of them."

"Heaven have mercy, this is impossible! The walls are completely damp. And the roof is leaking! How are we to repair it all within this short time?" The voice that answered was filled with despair.

"The word impossible is not a part of our vocabulary. An order is an order. It is to be done with immediate effect without ifs or buts."

"But …"

The voices faded, and no one entered the room.

When the footsteps receded, she walked over to the fireplace and felt for the shelf in the chimney. She pushed aside the loose brick, then fished out a small package and held it reverently in her hands.

She unwrapped the flannel cloth to reveal a tin box. She blew away the ashes and soot and lifted the lid.

Inside was the book of Gulliver. She turned it over in her hands. It was a leather volume; dirty and somewhat faded, but still in good condition.

Then she lifted out a tiny figure, that of the Princess of Glubbdubdrib, which Will had carved for her.

Wrapping the box back in the flannel, she picked up a pile of curtains lying on the floor and hid it underneath. Lowering her head, she left the room and walked purposefully down the corridor to join the other maids. Once outside, she dropped the pile of cloth on a heap and scurried off into the forest.

She hesitated in the clearing, wondering if she should

go to the lake. She remained undecided until she saw a flash of blue between the trees.

Someone was coming.

Ready to flee, Louisa picked up her skirts, then stopped. Coming through the trees was none other than Celeste Cooper-Wiles.

"Louisa!" Her hand fluttered to her chest. "I did not expect to see you here. It appears you've caught me trespassing."

"If you were trespassing, then what of me? I thought you were in Bournemouth."

Celeste stepped over a fallen log and walked towards her. "Yes, that was the plan. Shortly after you'd left, Mrs Browning's carriage pulled up, and she offered me the chance to stay with her at the vicarage for a while to keep her company. I gladly accepted."

"Mrs Browning?"

"You never met her, did you? She's the wife of the new vicar. She has always been very kind to me, and I am more than happy to stay here for a little longer, even though I know I will eventually have to leave for my aunts in Bournemouth." She gestured to the path on the right that would lead deeper into the forest. "Shall we walk together for a while? I have always enjoyed this part of the forest."

Louisa agreed.

Celeste looked at her with a smile. "I always admired you when I was younger, you know, when you spent the summer here with your parents. George was so horrid, wasn't he? He was not much of a brother to me." This was certainly still the case. "And then, in the summer, you would come and bring all the glamour of the ton with you. I was too shy to talk to you."

"I remember that every time I tried to talk to you, you would run away and hide."

Celeste grimaced. "I was young and timid. I would have loved nothing more than to talk to you and to try on some of your wonderful dresses." She laughed. "Well, I can be honest now, I suppose. I used to follow you around secretly."

"You did?"

"Yes. You spent a lot of time here in the forest." She held up her hand. "And by the lake."

Louisa did not answer.

"With that boy." Celeste smirked.

Louisa's eyes shot up to meet hers. "Will?"

"That was his name, wasn't it? Look, we have reached the clearing of the birches. Shall we sit here? The tree stumps here make a nice spot."

This was the clearing where she'd always waited for Will. "I did not know that you knew Will. Or that you were following us." Louisa frowned.

"Yes. I hid in the bushes, and I was good at covering my tracks. One learns to do that when one has a brother like George." She said it matter-of-factly.

"You should have shown yourself. We would have accepted you as a playmate." Or maybe not. Truth was that Louisa would have been too possessive of Will's company to share him with anyone.

"I enjoyed being invisible and watching you from my hiding place." She chuckled. "I hope you'll forgive me. That last summer. It was so romantic."

Louisa's eyes widened, and she covered her cheeks with her hands. "Oh dear. Oh no!"

Celeste laughed. "Oh yes! I saw you kissing." She looked so cheeky it was impossible to be angry. "You kissed a lot that summer."

Louisa buried her face in her hands with a groan.

"Never fear, it was nothing indecent! Will was always such a gentleman, and I saw nothing indecorous, just two young people madly in love. I was so charmed that I vowed that one day, I, too, would find someone with whom to experience something like that. True love." Her fingers toyed with the fabric of her skirt, no doubt as she realised that her prospects of doing so had disappeared.

Louisa's cheeks still burned. "I feel terrible that I never really noticed you. I thought you were too young. You must have been very lonely."

"The advantage of being ignored is that nobody pays any attention to what you're doing. And if George didn't pay any attention to me, so much the better. He'd only come up with nonsensical ideas—"

"Like cutting off the heads of all your dolls," Louisa interjected.

Celeste laughed. "He did that to you too, didn't he? Horrible boy. To avoid him, I roamed about the forest and played by the lake. I had a tranquil childhood, Louisa. Yes, it was lonely, but I was content."

And now she'd lost her home. Life wasn't fair to women.

"Will lived in the vicarage then, didn't he? I think they gave me his old room." Celeste gave a short laugh.

"He must have hated studying there, for the desk is still full of marks and inscriptions. Instead of learning his Latin, he carved figures into the wood. One of them says 'May Cicero rot in hell.'" She giggled. "He has it carved in the drawer where no one can see it."

"He hated Latin with a passion," Louisa said softly. "But the vicar pushed him to study because he wanted him to go to a boarding school. He wanted him to study theology eventually. But Will never wanted that."

"It was the old vicar, Reverend Graham. I can barely remember him. He was the one who'd taken care of Will, right?"

Louisa nodded. "Will always wanted to be a baker. He makes the best bread in England." She smiled sadly. "He's achieved his dream, hasn't he?" She should be happy for her old friend. Then why was she feeling so maudlin?

Celeste tilted her head. "What do you mean?"

"Will becoming a baker, I mean. Now that he's taken over Mr Brooks' bakery, I dare say he's achieved his dream."

Celeste looked at her strangely. "Louisa. Will didn't take over Brooks' bakery."

Louisa jerked her head up. "What do you mean? Of course he did. I met him only yesterday."

Celeste blinked, looking confused. "Will? Are you certain?"

"Yes, at the market in Dorchester. He was selling his bread. He was telling me about life as a baker, how he'd taken over Brooks' bakery, and—and how his wife Mary was expecting a child."

"Oh." Celeste exhaled.

"We talked for a while. Life isn't easy for a baker these days."

"Louisa."

"I met his wife Mary in the bakery the other day when I was buying bread. I didn't know she was Will's wife."

"Wilbur."

"I beg your pardon?"

"The man you spoke to at the market was Wilbur. He was also an apprentice to Mr Brooks at about the same time as Will. Will was never an official apprentice. Don't you remember Wilbur?"

Louisa stared into Celeste's earnest face. "I don't understand what you're saying. Will—but of course he was an apprentice."

Celeste shook her head. "Reverend Graham was emphatically against it."

"You mean that was Wilbur? I spoke to Wilbur?" Louisa massaged her temples as if that would help her understand more quickly.

"Wilbur was Mr Brooks' apprentice. He took over the bakery when Mr Brooks died, and then he married Mary. They're expecting a baby now. As far as I know, but not for certain since I was very young, your Will was allowed to spend time in the bakery because Mr Brooks had a soft spot for him. He probably taught him some rudimentary baking skills. He may have wanted to take him on as a second apprentice as well. I'm not sure, I just know that he never formally did. Reverend Graham had other plans for Will."

Louisa nodded. "Yes, Will always spoke in conditional terms. 'If Mr Brooks takes me on as an apprentice'—but he talked about it as if it was a fact that it would happen." She frowned deeply, her hand absentmindedly touching her temple. "I just can't believe I've been talking to Wilbur all this time, thinking he was Will. How excessively stupid of me to have confused the two." It would explain his strange behaviour towards her. He'd recognised her, but he'd remained distant and formal. He hadn't remembered Glubbdubdrib. Louisa barely remembered Wilbur. A vague memory of an older boy at Mr Brooks' bakery hovering in the background, carrying heavy sacks of flour, pounding in the trough, rose in her mind. He'd been older, bigger, burlier than Will. "He's like my older brother," Will once told her. "He's a good sort of fellow and I am fond of him."

Wilbur would have known her, of course, since she'd visited the bakery quite often. They would have talked.

"How silly of me to mix them up." She rubbed her hand on the bark underneath her, agitated.

"I suppose it's easy to do. They have similar names, and so much time has passed. And we have all grown up. I suppose we all look different from what we used to look like back then."

"And Will? What happened to him? Do you know where he is?"

Celeste looked at her with her big blue eyes. "Oh. You wouldn't know, would you? You returned to London rather quickly that summer."

"What happened? Tell me." A sense of dread inexplicably overcame her, and her heartbeat quickened.

Celeste bit her lip and looked away.

"Tell me. He must have gone to that boarding school Reverend Graham recommended. Did he study theology at Oxford? Maybe he is a clergyman now, like his father?"

Oh, please, God, please ...

But Celeste shook her head slowly, and tears swam in her eyes. "They never told you, did they? Of course not. They wouldn't."

"Celeste. Please." Louisa's voice shook.

"They threw him into Dorchester prison. He was sentenced to transportation for burglary."

All the blood drained from her face.

Celeste took a deep breath. "They say he died less than a month later."

Chapter Fifteen

"Impossible," Louisa breathed. She swayed slightly as a sudden wave of dizziness washed over her. Her cheerful, cheeky Will wasn't dead. It was inconceivable.

"I'm terribly sorry. I had no idea you didn't know. It happened so long ago, you know. But for you ..."

"It can't be true. They threw him into prison?"

"Dorchester."

"But he wasn't a criminal!" Louisa stood up.

Celeste grimaced. "I'm sure he wasn't. Someone like Will could never be, for sure. But ..." she sighed. "My father had him arrested for burglary and robbery. Apparently, there was evidence. It was the word of a poor boy against that of a lord. I'd like to believe that my father was a good man at heart, and that he always tried to do his best according to his conscience, but sometimes he was unnecessarily hard and stubborn. He truly believed that Will had broken into the house and that he had been caught red-handed."

"A prisoner. Transported." Dead. A sob rose inside her, but never found its way out. Instead, she kept staring at Celeste with burning eyes. "They never told me."

They wouldn't have, of course.

She'd been packed up and sent back to London. She'd written letters. He'd never answered.

She was told to forget him. She knew they had no future together. A baker and a gentleman's daughter, an heiress. It was an impossibility. It could never be.

The pain of losing him had been immense. Where her heart had been now lay a gaping hole.

"Promise you'll wait for me!" he'd cried.

She had done so. She'd waited. Oh, how she'd waited! Until one day, she decided to stop waiting and yielded to her parents' insistence that she had a Season.

And then the suitors came.

CELESTE PLACED her hand on Louisa's arm. "I am so sorry to be the bearer of this terrible news. Let us walk back to the village together." She continued talking the entire way, but Louisa's mind was numb, and she took in nothing more.

"Thank you, Celeste." Louisa ran her tongue over her dry lips. She gripped both her hands. Her own were ice cold.

Celeste looked at her with concern. "You've gone completely white, Louisa. I'm worried. Please take care of yourself."

Louisa nodded mechanically.

"Do call on me tomorrow, at the vicarage. Will you?" she pressed.

Louisa nodded again.

They parted at the entrance to the village, with Celeste impressing on her once more the promise that she would call on her. Louisa made her way back to her cottage.

Robert was repairing one of the rickety chairs when she arrived. He put down his hammer.

"I'm tired. I'm going to bed," she announced, crawling into the rickety bed with the lumpy mattress and pulling the blanket over her head.

"I'll be away all day tomorrow. There's important business to do."

Louisa didn't have the energy to ask if he was selling produce at the market in Dorchester again, or whether it was some kind of other business altogether. It occurred to her he probably wasn't selling any produce at all. There was no need, was there?

Was there any need at all for them to keep up this sham of a charade?

She should tell him it was no longer necessary to do so. It was no longer necessary to pretend. But she was too exhausted to address the matter.

"I'm staying here," she said through the blanket.

"Very well. As you wish." He paused. "I have something to discuss with you. But since you're tired, we can have our talk when I get back."

"Yes, yes."

The last thing she wanted to do now was argue with Robert. She knew she needed to confront him about his identity as Lord Frippery Fop, confound the man, but she felt a profound indifference now.

For now, all she wanted was to be left alone.

THE NEXT MORNING, she awoke early to find Robert already gone with the donkey and the cart. Truth be told, she cared little for what he did. She was glad he was gone, for what she needed to do now with great urgency was to go to the bakery and talk to Wilbur.

She dressed quickly, washed her face with cold water, and choked down the hard bread and apple that Robert had left for her.

She tied her hair back, put on a bonnet, and wrapped her shawl around her shoulders. The early morning hours were chilly, and one could feel summer slowly drawing to a close.

Louisa walked briskly to the village bakery.

Drawing in a big breath, she pushed the door open with a jingle and stepped into the shop. The warm, comforting smell of bread engulfed her. She smiled wanly at the woman who stood behind the counter. Mary.

"Good morning, missus." Mary wiped her hands on her apron and smiled as she recognised Louisa. "You're back again. Wilbur told me he met you at the market the other day, Miss Highworth." Her demeanour was more deferential than the day before. The name Highworth was apparently still remembered here.

"Is he here?"

Mary nodded. "One moment." She stepped out of

the room into the adjoining baking room and returned with Wilbur, his face flushed and sweating from the heat of the oven. His face lit up when he saw her.

"Miss Louisa. Good to see you again."

"My name is Louisa Jones now, Wilbur. I'm married, remember?"

"Aye, I believe you said that earlier." He weighed his head back and forth. "Haven't had the pleasure of meeting Mr Jones, though." He frowned. "You're staying at Meryfell Hall, Louisa?"

"No. We don't live at Meryfell Hall."

"Strange." He frowned. "The entire town's been wondering, but the new owner remains elusive. After meeting you, I was sure it must be you who's staying there. The house has been bought, you see, and is being extensively renovated. I must say I'm glad, because Lord Milford, the new one—George, I mean—has not been good for this estate."

"Yes, I heard. But it's not by us, I'm afraid."

"Come," Mary moved to a table where she set down a cup of tea and a plate with pastries. "Wilbur's childhood friends get nothing but the best."

Louisa sat down and gratefully took a cup. It was her first proper cup of tea in goodness, how long? Since she'd left London. What felt like another lifetime.

She turned to Wilbur. "I confess I was labouring under a misapprehension when I sought you out yesterday. I thought you were Will, you see."

Wilbur stared. "Will? But Will is d—"

"I suppose it's a simple mistake to make since I

haven't seen you for nearly eleven years," Louisa rushed on. She didn't want him to say that terrible word.

"Yes, eleven years is a long time. I hardly recognised you myself."

"People change very much over time," Mary put in, rubbing her stomach.

"But Will—" He shook his head. "Who knows what he would have looked like now? Poor sod."

Louisa's fingers cramped around the pastry she was holding. "I heard he was arrested and transported for burglary and theft. They say he d-didn't survive."

Wilbur sighed and shook his head. "It was terribly tragic. It shook us all to the core. At first, I couldn't believe that Will was guilty of such a crime. We knew he had a tendency for mischief and always got himself in a scrape, but outright theft? I don't know." He shook his head. "I still can't believe he had it in him. But he was caught red-handed, wasn't he? With the loot in his hands, they say. The evidence was damning, and Lord Milford had him convicted. The old vicar tried everything he could, and so did Mr Brooks. He avoided the death penalty and was sentenced to transportation instead. Which turned out to be the same, in the end, because the poor sod didn't last a month in the hulks. What an ill-starred wight that boy turned out to be. You really didn't know about any of this?"

The dread that had lodged in her stomach since she'd talked to Celeste turned into a cold lump of sick anguish —and guilt. Wilbur had just confirmed what she had said. There couldn't be any mistake. "No," she whispered. "I didn't know. I didn't know any of this." Her fingers trembled as she dropped her crumbled pastry. "I was taken back to London, and all communication was cut off. I'd sent letters, even to Mr Brooks. Did none of them arrive?"

Wilbur shrugged. "I wouldn't know. I haven't seen any of them for sure. All I know is that Mr Brooks was in shock for a long time; he'd vouched for the boy's honesty. He would've taken him on as an apprentice alongside me, but he always said that Will was a gentleman's son and that he'd be better off studying as the old vicar wanted. He blamed himself, saying that he should have just given him the apprenticeship anyway—because Will wanted it—and kept him so busy with work he wouldn't have had the chance to think of anything foolish like breaking in and robbing the manor."

He shook his head, as if still in disbelief. "Life for a baker's apprentice is quite hard, you know. I didn't have a minute of free time to run around like Will did. I confess I was always a tad jealous of that." He smiled vaguely, then he sobered. "I always thought the law was too harsh. Even if he was guilty, the sentence they gave Will was too hard. The Bloody Code, they call it. You can be hanged for any trivial offence in this beautiful country of ours. And they sentenced Will to be transported to the Colonies." He heaved a sigh. "In the end, it didn't make any difference because he died anyway."

Louisa slumped in her chair. Then she sat up straight as an idea occurred to her. "I need your help with something, Wilbur. Do you think you could do that?"

He exchanged a glance with Mary. "What kind of help do you need, miss?"

She licked her lips. "I need to go to Dorchester. I need to go to the prison there and find out exactly what happened to Will. Would you accompany me?"

He shook his head. "I don't think that will be helpful at all, miss. It was so long ago, see."

"There must be some sort of record left. Or a guard I could talk to. I didn't know any of this had happened." She swallowed. "We were good friends. I should get to the bottom of this. I must do this for Will. Please?"

They were silent for a while, then Mary spoke. "You should do it, Wilbur. You used to be friends, after all, you and Will. And with Miss Louisa here, too." Turning to Louisa, she said, "I remember Mr Brooks saying that he was charmed every time you used to drop by, waiting for Will, eating his bread. Said Miss Highworth appreciates the taste of good bread. Honestly, Louisa, if I may say so, I do not think you will accomplish anything by going to Dorchester gaol. But I think you should support her and accompany her, Wilbur."

He stood up and took off his apron. "Very well. Let's do it for old times' sake. Let's do it for Will. I have a cart in the back. If you'll follow me, Louisa."

Chapter Sixteen

THE DORCHESTER GAOL CONSISTED OF SEVERAL blocks and courtyards, surrounded by a strong grey stone wall. Iron bars covered the windows and the heavy wooden doors had iron spikes. One could easily imagine that whoever entered through these gates would not easily leave. As Louisa and Wilbur approached, she was overcome with doubt. Surely one couldn't just walk into a prison and ask for information about the inmates.

In the end, as they were not visiting a prisoner, they could get no further than the entrance block,

The guard who opened the door was unhelpful and unfriendly.

"I would like to speak to the warden," she insisted.

"Impossible. Ye can't just walk in here and talk to the warden." He pulled out a long knife and picked at his fingernails. "First, ye must make an appointment. Which is difficult enough as it is with his schedule. Might take several months."

"Several months?" Louisa groaned.

Wilbur stepped up close to the guard and pressed a small velvet bag into his hand. "All we need to know is what happened to the inmate Will Cole, who was incarcerated here in June 1804. We need to know his fate. If you could help us, we might procure a second one." He gave him a speaking look.

The guard weighed the bag in his hand. "Will Cole, ye say?" he grumbled and left.

After an eternity, he returned. "The records say there was a Will Cole incarcerated here for theft June 21, 1804. Transportation. Was sent to the galleys the day after he got sentenced."

"Does it say anything about what happened to him afterwards?" Wilbur persisted. "Did he survive?"

The man held out his hand. Wilbur dropped another small bag into his palm.

"Died July 21, 1804. That's all I know." He slammed the door into their faces.

Coldness spread through Louisa. She shivered. Wilbur heaved a sigh. Then he gently led her away from this terrible place.

They didn't speak a word the entire trip back.

When he saw her hut, Wilbur was shocked. "I can't believe you're really staying here," he protested, refusing to leave her there. "There must be some mistake. Let me take you up to Meryfell Hall."

Louisa smiled wearily. "It's quite all right. You can leave me be. I will reimburse you for the money you spent on that guard, of course."

He brushed her away. "Don't mention it, Louisa. It was nothing at all."

When Louisa entered their cottage, Robert was already there, kneeling in front of the fireplace, building a fire. He looked up with a frown.

"Where the deuce were you, madam wife?" he demanded. "Without taking leave or writing a note."

"In Dorchester."

He frowned. "In Dorchester? How did you get there?"

"Wilbur from the bakery gave me a lift."

He scowled. "I don't approve of strange men giving my wife a lift without my permission. The road is dangerous, as you have experienced yourself, and I don't want you out and about on your own."

"For your information, I can do whatever I want, and I need not consult you about every move I make," she told him. It was really the last straw. Was he playing the domineering husband now?

He pulled himself up to his full height, and she found herself at a disadvantage having to look up at him.

His eyes, hard and unyielding, pierced through hers. "You seem to have misunderstood. You will not go off on your own without first informing me of what you intend to do."

"Oh, I understood you perfectly." She took off her bonnet and threw it on the table. "Except I have no mind to listen. The role of an autocratic husband doesn't suit you."

"What were you doing in Dorchester, anyway?"

"None of your business." She was tired and hungry, and all she wanted to do was lie down on her lumpy mattress and sleep.

That was the wrong thing to say.

He stepped up so close to her she felt the heat of his body. "Let me be clear. Everything you do is my business. You are my business. And if my wife goes with a man on a pleasure trip to the next town without telling me, that is very much my business." His words were laced with a chilling anger that sent shivers down her spine. If Louisa hadn't known better, she might have concluded he was jealous. But that was nonsense.

"It wasn't a pleasure trip. We visited the gaol."

"The gaol?" He paused, lifting his eyebrows. "What in all that's good and holy were you doing there?"

"I was looking for some information." She walked to the shelf, looked for a mug, and poured herself some water. Her throat was parched. Was the hut hotter than usual? Yet, she shivered. Robert followed her with every step, scowling down at her.

She wished he would stop following her. She wished he would stop scowling. She wished he would stop being so large. She wished he would envelop her in his powerful arms and help her forget.

"The deuce? What kind of information do you expect to get from a gaol?"

She turned to him. "Robert Jones. Is that even your real name?" He was towering over her. "I suppose not. Or is it Lord—" She closed her eyes, wanting to remember the name. "Lord Richard Pelham? Or Robert Pelham?" She opened her eyes to gaze directly into his. "That was the name, wasn't it? That smart Corinthian with a military past. He did everything perfectly. I called him Lord Frippery Fop.

Seemed to be more appropriate. That was you, wasn't it?"

A cynical glint entered his eyes and his lips twitched. "Ah. Trying to change the topic, I see."

"Was it?" she pressed.

He stared at her with hooded eyes. "Not quite, but you're getting there."

Her head throbbed.

"It might also have been Lord Paget. Is that the name I'm looking for? Something with a P. The one who went on and on about horse breeds and horse races. I was bored out of my mind."

"Upon my word. You really despised your suitors, did you not? Or was it just me?" he asked softly.

She leaned her head against the wall. The bed was on the other side of the room, but it seemed far away. Besides, Robert was in the way.

"Yes," she sighed. "I despised them all. What does it feel like to have won, to have outwitted them all? Are you enjoying your revenge, Lord Robert Pelham? Having reduced the Highworth heiress to living here"—she waved her hand—"in this hovel. No doubt you must've come to some sort of agreement with Papa regarding the inheritance. It must've been such a lark."

The room swam in front of her. He attempted to take her hand, but she pushed him away.

"Louisa."

"Quite clever of you, I must say, to take advantage of my difficulty of remembering faces. But I must confess that I realised there was something wrong with you as early as London. But I wasn't willing to admit it to myself. I ignored it. I just wanted to get away from it all. I wanted the fantasy so badly, you see. To be married to a costermonger. How uncomplicated life must be, I thought. I wanted this particular adventure more than anything else in the world." Her voice hitched.

She closed her eyes and leaned her cheek against the wood. It felt cool and rough. She felt his hand on her forehead.

"Louisa. You're burning up with fever."

"I let you think I didn't know. But you're not a good actor." A strange weakness took hold of her legs, as if they had turned to jelly. She opened her eyes. "Are we on a ship?" she asked. "Because everything is wobbling."

He lifted her in his arms and carried her to the bed. He smelled of smoke, earth, and musk. It was not unpleasant, she decided. She clung onto him because the ship was swaying, and he seemed the only steady, solid thing on the ship.

"I killed him, Robert," she sobbed. "I will never forgive myself."

"By Jove's beard. Who?"

"Will. I killed Will."

Chapter Seventeen

THINGS MIGHT HAVE TURNED OUT DIFFERENTLY IF her father and Lord Milford hadn't concocted the harebrained scheme to betroth her to George. They must have been foxed; there was no other explanation.

The day her father and Lord Milford announced that an engagement between George and herself would unite their families remained vivid in her memory.

At first, she thought it was a joke.

"The idea has merit," her father had said. "We discussed it last evening over a glass of port and concluded that both our families would benefit enormously from such a union." He'd folded his arms and nodded to himself. "It was Milford who first thought of it. And the more I think about it, the more I like the idea."

Louisa laughed. "Papa, dear. You must be joking. We're far too young to get married. I'm not even sixteen!"

"No, it is a serious proposition. True, you're both young; but you and George are about the same age. The marriage itself wouldn't happen until much later, of course. You would make a splendid couple. The two of you together look spectacular. I like the idea."

"But I don't like the idea at all."

"You don't?" He blinked. "Come, give yourself time to at least think about it. I won't force you to do anything you don't want to do, you know."

She rested her head against her father's arm. That she knew. As difficult as her father was sometimes with his explosive, irascible temper, she had to grant him he had never, in her entire life, forced her to do anything she did not want to do. No doubt that was one reason she'd grown up so over-indulged.

"I know, Papa. Which is why I don't have to think about it. I won't have George. He is a terrible person. Spoiled and entitled."

Her father pursed his lips. "One could say the same about you. You'd make a perfect match."

"Papa!"

"I said, think about it. That's all I want from you now."

She'd left it at that, secure knowing that nothing would ever come of it.

George had sneered and merely commented with the tasty analogy that an engagement between them would only happen on the day the worms were feasting on his carcass. Louisa quite agreed. Since neither of them were inclined to cooperate in the matter, she did not think that these plans would amount to anything.

Her father, she knew, would have abandoned the idea had it not been for Lord Milford. To Lord Milford their engagement was a given, for he had much to gain from it. He ran roughshod over any arguments and planned to organise a small engagement ball to which he invited the local gentry.

Louisa's mistake had been to tell Will about it.

They were sitting in their favourite spot by the lake. The water lapped gently against the shore, and a few ducks honked in the distance. She had told him about her father and Lord Milford's harebrained idea of marrying her to George. It was so ridiculous, she'd laughed it off.

Only Will hadn't found it funny at all. He'd jerked back in horror and grabbed her arms. "No, Louisa, no. Don't do it!" There was a stricken look in his hazel eyes. "It's madness!"

She'd done the wrong thing by trying to comfort him. "You're right, of course. I'm too young. We're too young! Nothing will come of it. It's just one of those ridiculous things our fathers dreamed up. It won't mean anything."

Only it did.

And Will knew it, too. He shook his head. "No, Lulu. Please. I won't allow it." It came out as a sob.

Despite her explanations that nothing in the world would ever induce her to marry George, nothing she said could convince him that the engagement might not actually proceed.

"You know I despise George. I'll never go through with it."

He clenched his hands into fists. "Then run away with me. Don't go to that ball. Milford will use the occasion to announce your engagement and then all will be lost. Run away with me."

She shook her head. "You always have the maddest

ideas. We don't have to run away. I'll just talk to them. I'll talk to Papa. He'll listen. He never makes me do anything I don't want to do. I know he won't make me do this, either. Trust me, Will."

"You will find you have rather little to say in the matter. You're an heiress. Of course, Milford wants you. He won't let you out of his clutches." He clenched his fingers into fists. "If only ... if only I could do something about it!"

They'd quarrelled over the matter. Louisa had been annoyed and exasperated over his stubbornness and lack of faith in her; he was peevish and irritated by her naivety and what he interpreted as a shocking lack of resistance. He was certain she would eventually cave in to their demands.

In the end, Louisa had thrown up her hands, called him more stubborn than a mule and more thick-headed than a stone wall and stormed off, not knowing that it would be the last time they were together at the lake.

The next time she saw him, Will was being dragged away by two strong footmen, a wild look of desperation in his eyes.

She was out at sea and the ship was being tossed about by the stormy waves.

Then she was in the desert on Glubbdubdrib, and it was hot.

"You're burning up. You must drink something," a voice said.

"Will," she moaned. She had to get up and find him.

She had something important to tell him. But a firm hand kept pushing her down. She tried to escape the nettlesome hand that was always there, alternately brushing her wet hair away from her forehead, then stroking her cheek. Lifting her head and shoulders and pouring some liquid down her throat.

She coughed and gasped.

Will.

But it was the other one. What was his name again?

"Lord Frippery Fop," she whispered. The proud nonpareil who'd disguised himself as a costermonger out of pure vengefulness.

It was he who cradled her head and poured warm liquid down her throat.

She didn't want him. She wanted Will. She whimpered and thrashed.

Then the desert turned into an ice desert because it was cold, so very cold, and she couldn't stop shivering.

And then someone picked her up and carried her—why were there horses and a carriage at the North Pole? Or maybe she was on the boat again. A rocking boat with horses because there were hooves clattering. She wanted to ask, but not a word crossed her lips. It stopped, and someone was carrying her again.

"Sir, everything is ready, just as you ordered."

"Fetch a physician immediately."

"Yes, Major. Right away, sir."

There was a blasted major in their hut, and she wanted to ask Robert what he was doing there. But her lips were glued shut and she did not have the strength to utter the words.

Instead, she fell into a deep sleep filled with fever dreams, and Will's sweet, round, dimpled face swam before her, and he smiled.

But that day, he hadn't been smiling. His eyes had been filled with despair.

It was the evening of the ball. She'd stood up with George with much distaste, after Lord Milford had suggested they dance together. George had also pulled a face.

Suddenly, a loud commotion erupted outside in the corridor, drawing everyone's attention and interrupting the dance. The guests rushed outside to find Will struggling wildly with the footmen.

"We caught him trespassing and attempting to burgle the house, my lord," one footman said, while the other held out a knapsack stuffed with silverware.

Louisa watched in shock, struggling to understand what was happening. Was this another of Will's pranks? Had he climbed into her room, collecting the silverware as part of a jest?

Doubt flickered in her mind, and she hesitated.

Her fingers had gripped George's arm as they paused the country dance.

To any onlooker, they must have appeared like they were a couple.

"Will?" she'd whispered.

"I didn't trespass. I came to the party. Tell them you invited me, Lulu! Tell them!" Will pleaded.

But Louisa remained silent, transfixed by the silver spilling from the bag.

Lord Milford scowled at Will. "Take him away, we'll deal with him later," he commanded.

"Don't do it, Lulu! Don't do it! Promise you'll wait for me! Promise!" Will shouted, his words ringing in her ears long after he was gone.

As her father and Lord Milford turned to her, pelting her with questions about who that boy was and what her relationship to him was, she froze, overwhelmed by a nauseating sense of dread that if she'd only reacted differently, this could have been prevented.

It would be the last time she ever saw him.

She'd never known that he'd been thrown into prison and died in transportation.

Pain burned through her.

She should have run away with Will when he'd suggested it.

She should have listened to him.

She should have spoken up and defended him.

He might be still alive if she had.

For that had been the root of it all. That was where it had all gone wrong.

It was all her fault he had died.

Chapter Eighteen

THERE WAS A WHIFF OF VINEGAR IN THE AIR, mingled with the sweeter scent of linden blossom and willow bark, and oddly enough, fresh paint.

It took an effort for Louisa to open her leaden eyes, but when she did, she discovered she was surrounded by roses.

Maybe she'd died, she mused. Roses abounded on all sides of her, even on the ceiling. It finally dawned on her they weren't real roses, but a rose pattern embroidery on the canopy and the blanket.

The room was panelled in dark wood, and green velvet curtains were drawn over the window, leaving a slit open. It was an unfamiliar room. An elderly woman sat in the corner near the window, sewing in the weak light that peeked through the curtains.

Her head throbbed, and her throat was dry.

Louisa moaned.

"Good heavens, you're awake!" The woman dropped

her sewing, got to her feet, picked up a cloth and dabbed at her forehead. It was wet and cold.

"Thank heavens. It looks like you pulled through."

"Thirsty," she mouthed, and the woman helped her take a sip from a cup. It was a cold, bitter tea. Louisa grimaced.

"Let me call the major at once," she said. "You mustn't …"

Her eyes fluttered shut as she drifted into a fitful sleep.

The next time she was awakened by male voices.

"The worst is over, sir. I won't bleed her again because she's too weak. The fever's broken, so she won't need any more ice baths. But keep giving her the willow bark tea. And rest. Lots of rest."

"What about Dover's powder? A surgeon in my regiment swears by it and administers it to those with fever."

"Good heavens. Keep away from it. It contains opium and vitriolic tartar to induce sweating, but I don't recommend it. Likely, more of your men have died from that stuff than from the actual fever. I am a firm believer in nature's medicine. Willow bark and linden blossom tea will do the trick. And sleep."

Louisa slept. This time it was a dreamless sleep, deep and healing.

She woke once during the night to find herself tightly held against someone's chest. It was firm and muscular.

"What's happening?" she murmured. "Why are you here?" There was something she needed to do, but she couldn't recall what it was. She struggled to sit up, but someone held her down, firmly, gently.

"Shh. Go back to sleep. You'll be all right. Everything will be fine. I promise."

He kissed her head.

Her ear was pressed against his chest. She heard a rhythmical tum-tum-tum-tum, much like the beating of the heart.

It comforted her.

Maybe he was right. Maybe it would be all right. Somehow, in the end.

She slept.

THE NEXT DAY, Louisa sat up in bed. The fever was gone; she was left feeling dizzy and weak, and ravenously hungry. She'd just gobbled down some thin soup which the maid had brought and found she wanted to eat something with more substance. The maid had curtsied and said she'd tell Mrs Dalton.

Louisa had no idea who Mrs Dalton was. Was she the cook? Or perhaps she was that grey-haired woman who'd been in the room earlier.

This time, the curtains were pulled aside. It was raining and dreary outside, but through the bleak daylight she saw that this must be one of the rooms in Meryfell Hall. Perhaps one of the larger bedrooms of Lord and Lady Milford.

She got out of bed and stumbled to the window. It

was Meryfell Hall, all right. The view opened to the back part of the house, with the lawn and the forest in the distance. Her own bedroom, when she'd stayed here as a guest, had had the same view.

She pulled a woollen shawl over her shoulders and stepped out. The wood creaked under her feet as she walked along the corridor. A sweeping oak staircase led down to the great hall. There seemed to be a lot of commotion on the other side.

She placed her hand on the banister and was about to descend when two men in red uniforms emerged from one of the guest rooms, carrying a long, heavy, rolled carpet.

One of them spotted her standing in the corridor. "Attention, ahead!" he called and came to a halt. His comrade whipped his head round.

"Hounds' teeth. Is that her?" the other man said, shifting the carpet from one shoulder to the other to get a better look.

"Must be. Otherwise, it must be the Faerie Queene, herself."

They stared at her with openmouthed admiration.

"Shut your gob and salute," the other hissed.

They dropped the carpet on the floor with a bang and saluted in military style, their movements coordinated in precise unison.

"Good afternoon, my lady. I am Lieutenant John Carey of His Majesty's First Regiment of Foot, currently serving under the command of Major Sir Robert Ashford as his aide-de-camp, at your service," said one.

"And I am Lieutenant Edward Miller, ma'am, also of

His Majesty's First Regiment of Foot, proudly serving as Major Sir Robert's second aide-de-camp, at your service."

Both remained standing at attention, stiff and straight.

Louisa pressed her hands to her chest and backed away against the banister. She supposed she ought to say something. She cleared her throat. "Er. How do you do?"

What now?

They remained immobile and rooted to the spot like waxworks in Madame Tussaud's cabinet. How to get them to move again?

"At ease," a voice behind her commanded.

She jumped and whirled around. A stranger stood before her. Well-dressed and clean shaven, wearing clean, pressed clothes. There was something familiar in the angular face, the high forehead, and the probing look in his eyes as he regarded her. It took Louisa several moments to comprehend it was Robert.

She gaped.

"Take the carpet below stairs to be cleaned, then see to your uniforms as well. I don't require you to be uniformed while you're here," he said.

"Yes, sir," they said out of one mouth, making her jump again. They moved again in unison to pick up the carpet and carried it downstairs.

He looked thunderous. "And who gave you permission to be out and about?" He scooped her up before she could utter a word.

She squealed. "Put me down!"

But he kicked the door open to the next room and

carried her in. The maids who were busily washing the windows dropped their rags and curtsied.

"You're not wearing shoes, either. Fetch some stockings," he ordered the maids.

They were in the library. She'd spent many hours here. It seemed to be one of the few rooms in the house that had remained unchanged. Like the rest of the house, the furniture was made from dark oak and the walls were lined with bookshelves that reached the ceiling. A fire was burning in the fireplace.

"Put me down," Louisa said.

He placed her gently on one sofa in front of the fireplace.

The maid returned with woollen socks.

"I can do it myself," she said, but he knelt, took her bare foot in his hand, and pulled on the sock.

"What pretty feet you have," he murmured. "Long and slim. And those ankles …" His voice was husky.

He shook his head as if to snap out of his reverie, then pulled the stocking over her lower thigh.

Her cheeks burned with heat.

Then he lifted her legs onto the sofa, wrapped them in a woollen plaid and tucked a pillow behind her back.

She'd never been so embarrassed in her life. Not knowing what to say, she said the first thing that came to mind, which was, of course, completely idiotic. "What happened to your beard?"

"I shaved it off." He remained sitting on the floor, his long legs stretched out in front of him.

That was obvious. He'd cut his hair, too.

She studied his face. She could see now what hadn't

been so clear earlier, when half of it had been covered by shaggy hair. It was a chiselled face, full of hard planes and angles, high cheekbones, a proud nose and forehead, and a firm chin. A slight scar ran from his left jaw to his ear. His dark hair was styled and combed backwards, exposing a high forehead.

He was a completely different person.

In fact, he was ...

... An image of a tall redcoat in the ballroom flashed in her mind. Medals. Honours. Everyone had made much to-do about him ... he was that hero of some place or other. Walpurgia. Valeria. Victoria. Vitoria.

"You're Sir Twiddlepoops." Louisa groaned loudly. "Of course. I should have known."

He flared his nostrils. "Twiddlepoops? By all that's holy, couldn't you at least have chosen something less absurd? Something more, I don't know—" he waved his hand. "Appropriate to the military?"

She folded her hands in front of her. "It seemed appropriate at the time. And I don't know any military nomenclature."

"Clearly," he retorted with a dismissive snort.

She took a big breath. "You were furious about that stupid caricature." She plucked at the frills of her blanket.

Judging by the rigid set of his jaw, he still was.

"Furious?" He gave an unamused laugh. "You turned me into a bloody laughingstock. The entire regiment rolled in the fields with laughter." He pressed his lips into a thin line. "If you think I'd let you get away with it, you're wrong. I still am the butt of their jests. 'Major

Ashford might storm any battlement in Spain and France with aplomb, yet he fails miserably on the domestic front. The only fortress the major has been unable to breach is that of the Incomparable.'" His voice was morose.

She lowered her gaze to her hands. "I s-see." She swallowed. "That is, of c-course, excruciatingly t-tragic."

He stared at her sharply. "I swear, Louisa. If you laugh at me, I will have you court-martialled and executed. This is an exceedingly serious matter."

She tore her eyes wide open. "Heaven forbid. I wouldn't dream of laughing." But then a giggle escaped her.

He uttered an oath and dived, and she, shrieking, brought up her hands up to her face, which he pulled away. He pressed her down onto the sofa, gazing intently into her face.

Her mind barely registered his hazel eyes with golden flecks.

She held her breath.

And then his mouth crashed down on hers.

Chapter Nineteen

THERE WERE KISSES, AND THEN, WELL, THERE WERE kisses.

Louisa hadn't had much experience kissing men; heaven forbid she'd ever allow any of them to get close enough to steal a kiss. One of them—was it Lord Stuttervoice or Sweatyhands? she couldn't remember—had tried. He'd lured her out onto the balcony, and noticing almost too late what he was about to do, she'd turned away at the last moment. He'd ended up planting a wet kiss on the side of her head, which had felt rather ticklish and wet, like a dog licking her ear.

There had been Will's kisses, of course, but they didn't count. They'd been merely two children kissing, innocent and sweet, so long ago she barely remembered it.

No, Louisa found that being kissed by a grown man was very different.

HE CRUSHED her to him with a passion that left no room for doubt. His lips, firm and insistent, conquered hers, demanding a response until she finally gave what he sought.

She trembled and burned; she yielded and returned his kiss with equal fervour.

As the urgency of his kisses softened, they became tender and lingering, softly brushing her lips gently, once, twice. Finally, he cradled her in a firm embrace, his chest rising and falling rapidly as he planted a soft kiss atop her head.

A serene sweetness filled her.

Her hand rested on his chest, her fingers lightly tracing the area where she'd seen a vicious scar.

Remorse filled her.

She'd belittled his heroism in front of others. What had she said, exactly? Something to the effect that she thought these tales of bravery were overly exaggerated. The words echoed painfully in her memory.

He had risked his life for her, for her country. And from what she'd seen, the gruesome scars on his body proved that he'd brushed death more than once. There was no getting around it. What she had said with such careless flippancy had been nothing but cold-hearted and cruel.

She flushed with shame and dropped her head.

"I am sorry," she whispered. "For mocking you in public. It was intolerably thoughtless and cruel of me, and you didn't deserve it. I humbly ask your forgiveness."

His grip tightened for a moment, then he let her go. He cupped her face in his hands and looked down at her swollen lips, brooding. "That was prettily said. I accept your apology. But it doesn't change the fact that you find yourself married to that tin soldier, after all, through deceit and cunning on his part. It must be crushing to your pride."

She sighed wearily. "It appears you have achieved what you wanted. You have done what a hundred other suitors failed to do. You have humbled me thoroughly and even received an apology. It was given honestly, mind you. Consider your revenge complete."

"Not quite. There are still some loose ends. But for now, let's call it a detente." He released her and stood up, walking to the fireplace, where he added another log to the fire. "You've been terribly sad. You were suffering." He gave her a searching look. Louisa averted her eyes. "Then you were ill for three days. It was quite critical for a while, and I thought I'd lose you." He frowned into the fire. "I had to take you away from the draughty hut to Meryfell Hall."

A wary look crossed her face. "Which used to belong to Lord Milford. The younger one. George. Until he sold it."

"Yes. I bought it."

"What?" When did that happen?

He shrugged. "I met the chap in London. He was eager to sell it to pay off his gambling debts, so I bought it at a price far below its true value. It was a bargain impossible to ignore."

Lord George Milford had met Sir Robert in London and sold him his manor house to pay off his gambling debts.

"Major Sir Robert Ashford. The strange thing is that I still can't recall the name."

"You heard it on our wedding day. The minister said my name twice. But for some reason that eludes me entirely, you did not hear a word that was said that day. You were completely distracted. I don't think I've ever met a person in my entire life who is as oblivious to what is going on around her as you. If you were a soldier, you wouldn't last two seconds on the battlefield."

"Thank the heavens, then, that I'm not a soldier," Louisa observed wryly. "Besides, I am terrible at following orders."

"Believe me, I have noticed," he said from the depths of his being. "The thing is, Louisa …" He crouched down on his haunches to be at eye level with her. "I've just received a despatch this morning that I'm to return to my regiment in France within a fortnight. We're preparing for grand-scale manoeuvres with the allies, as well as garrison reinforcements and strategic deployments to fortify the defences—" As if realising that she wasn't following, he cut himself short. "The long and short of it is that there is no time to continue this make-believe play we've been playing, this fantasy farce, diverting as it has been. We need to get this house up to scratch as quickly as possible."

"Why?" Why renovate the house when they were leaving, anyway? That is, Louisa assumed she was to leave with him, following the drum. As an army wife.

Good heavens.

"In exactly a week, we will host a lavish dinner party."

Louisa shot up. "What. Here?"

He nodded. "Here. The invitations are out. It will be a rather, shall we say, elevated affair."

"Who have you invited?"

"Your parents, for one."

Louisa leaned back in her cushions. Ah yes, of course. Wouldn't her father be ecstatic that she hadn't married a costermonger after all, but his favourite war hero?

"Papa was in on it from the very first, wasn't he?" She closed her eyes. "You hatched the plan with him."

"Hm. Yes. Maybe I did."

She opened her eyes to glare at him.

"But let us not change the subject. You asked who was coming to our party. I have invited several people of consequence. You will be introduced to them when the time comes. Some of my men will attend as well."

"It sounds to me like this supper will be dominated by men. We shall need more ladies to balance the numbers."

He shrugged. "Try as I might, I can't conjure up suitable ladies at the snap of my fingers."

"I know one. Miss Celeste Cooper-Wiles."

Robert frowned. "Milford's sister? But that would be awkward, to say the least."

"Perhaps. But I would like for her to join us at the party. Besides, I'm not sure you're aware, but buying this house has put her in a most unhappy predicament. She has no home now."

"That is, of course, unfortunate, but it is not really my problem. It is Milford's. I must confess that I am not overly enthusiastic about having her here. I find myself prejudiced against anyone related to Milford. He is not the most palatable of people."

"George may be a terrible person, or at least he was when he was younger, and he probably hasn't improved with time either, but I guarantee you his sister is not. She's a lovely young woman. If you remember, you even spoke to her at the carriage accident. I'd like her to stay with us for a while and maybe we can help her find a better position, even if George won't move a finger to help her. And knowing him, he won't." Who knows, maybe one gentleman who came to their supper party would develop an interest in her. Louisa would do anything in her power to matchmake. That was the least she could do for her former childhood friend.

Robert shrugged. "Very well. You may do as you please. Invite whom you see fit. Also, within this house, take over the reins and manage it as best you can. They keep asking me things I find impossible to answer. How the deuce should I know whether to hang velvet or brocade curtains in the dining room?" He shook his head. "What, pray, is the difference between violet, lilac, and china rose, and what the devil is coquelicot? When Mrs Dalton asked me to choose one, I was so overwhelmed I told her she should hang the curtains in all those colours. She was horrified. I obviously lack the feminine touch. Please, Louisa, take over command of the household regiment. It will be a great help."

She felt a surge of excitement. Bringing this house up to scratch might be just the assignment she needed right now to take her mind off Will and the leaden sadness that still encased her heart. Ever since she'd recovered from her fever, she'd carefully avoided dwelling on him. It was too unbearably painful to think about. But whenever she found herself unoccupied, she could no longer deny the familiar weight of melancholy and guilt that settled over her. Organising the supper party would provide an excellent distraction.

Chapter Twenty

THREE SOLDIERS STOOD ABOUT IN THE HALL, STARING at her with varying degrees of fascination. One of them, she gathered, had just arrived to deliver a despatch to her husband. He was in uniform and there was dust on his boots. She hadn't seen him before, and his eyes almost bulged out of his head when he looked at her, a fair-skinned fellow who blushed to the roots of his hair when she greeted him. The other two were Robert's aides-de-camp, Lieutenants Carey and Miller. To Louisa's great amusement and annoyance, they followed her everywhere. They seemed to worship the ground she walked on.

"We're waiting for your orders, my lady," they said. "The major said we are to be at your disposal."

They were no longer in their scarlet uniforms, but in civilian clothes. They were both young, handsome, and remarkably talkative.

Lt John Carey was keen to let her know that he'd had

every intention of courting her last year, but to his chagrin, he hadn't been granted leave.

"We were in the middle of a rather important battle, you see," he explained, anxious to make her understand that, had circumstances been different, he'd have stood up to dance with her at Almack's and joined the list of her hapless suitors.

"I see. I wonder what important battle that might have been." She crossed her arms and tapped her foot, and she narrowed her eyes, but Lt Baker was oblivious to it and continued to chat happily.

"It was Waterloo, of course. Rather imperative for me to have been there. And for the major, too. Imagine if he hadn't, that sharpshooter would've shot his bullet straight through the duke's forehead." He pointed a forefinger at his own head. "But the major, with his keen eyesight, noticed skirmishers positioning themselves in the line of trees. It was the glint of the sun on the iron. He threw himself at the duke, pulling him to the ground. Just as he did, a musket ball whizzed past. The course of history might well have been different if he hadn't. Imagine Wellington dead, Boney winning, the Frenchies running roughshod all over England and our children growing up speaking French and singing the Marseillaise." He shuddered. "Inconceivable."

A shiver ran through Louisa. "It doesn't bear thinking about," she admitted. "He seems to have been quite the hero, your major."

That was enough to get them gushing about all the other heroic deeds their major had done throughout the years, not least at the Battle of Vitoria. They clearly worshipped him.

"I confess I haven't heard that story yet," Louisa told them. No doubt her father must have told it to her at one point, but she had paid no attention.

Miller and Carey stared at her in shock. "You haven't heard of it? But, my lady, the story has been all over the newspapers in England."

"I confess I am shockingly ignorant when it comes to keeping up with military stories," she admitted ruefully. "But tell me your version of the event."

Robert had apparently managed, almost single-handedly, to take control of a key bridge over a river near Vitoria during a crucial phase of the battle. The French had intended to blow it up to slow down the Allied advance. He'd done this by swimming across the river at a particularly dangerous point, disarming the explosives the French had attached to the bridge, and securing it for their use.

"It was the most daring, the most brilliant, the most heroic thing I've ever seen anyone do, apart from saving Wellington's life, of course. It was simply incredible. The strength, fearlessness, and courage of the man is inspiring. I've sworn to be loyal to him for the rest of my life." There was an ardent glow in Carey's eyes.

"It's a fair amount of daredevilry to do that," Miller agreed. "And to spit in the face of death. Not everyone has it in them. I confess I don't. But I too, have never met a man with the same heroic qualities as Major Sir Robert. I don't think there is a single man in the army who doesn't worship him. Not to mention the ladies, those Spanish beauties, all of them, how they were constantly after him —" At that point, Carey elbowed him in the side and, remembering who he was talking to, Miller ended his story by coughing and clearing his throat.

"Ah, the ladies." She smiled piquantly. "Of course."

"Yes, well, that is to say, none of them ever surpassed the beauty of our Incomparable, of course." He looked at her with big puppy eyes. "It's almost a shame our major has finally breached that particular fortress, not that I ever doubted he would, for I must say it's been a most splendid sport amongst us to place wagers, ahh—" Carey squashed his elbow into Miller's other side.

"Yes?" She placed her hands against her hips. "I suspect the odds must have been quite against the poor man."

Both men coughed.

"He meant to say, of course, that we are most delighted that the major has finally, after having overcome much hardship and obstacles, managed to marry you. Our most heartfelt felicitations."

"Yes." Miller coughed. "That is, of course, what I meant to say, my lady."

"He was quite downtrodden when you turned down his suit."

"Was he?" This interested Louisa. "What did he do?" She leaned forward in a whisper. "Tell me, in confidence."

"The poor man got roaring drunk," Miller whispered back. "Never seen anyone so blue-devilled and heartbroken. Then he slammed his fist down on the table, smashing it in half, and roared vengeance and that he would conquer the Ice Damsel no matter the cost what may—"

"Carey, Miller!" Speaking of the devil. The major strode into the room, frowning. "Stop this nonsense. You were supposed to be assisting my wife, but I see she has no use for you if you're just standing around gossiping like old dowagers having a tea party. I have work for you."

"Yes, sir." The men stood at attention.

"Carey, see that those despatches are delivered promptly." He handed him several missives. "And you, Miller, help me secure the wall outside, as the front of the house is too accessible for scaling. We need to implement countermeasures to prevent access. And you, Louisa, off to bed. You've been up and about too much and need to rest. Your face looks wan and pale."

"But—"

"This is an order. Forward march." He put a hand on her back and pushed her gently towards the door. When she resisted, he pulled her up into his arms and carried her to her bedroom and put her unceremoniously to bed. "Just rest. If you want, I can send Mrs Dalton up, and you can discuss the menu and other household things while you lie in bed."

It wasn't a bad idea, for suddenly she felt a leaden tiredness take over her body. It was apparent that her body was still recovering from her illness.

"You've become awfully overbearing, and I must say I don't like it. But I shall do as you say. But Robert, don't be too hard on those boys. They were merely telling me in great detail about all your heroic deeds. Is it true that you swam across that river under enemy fire?"

He shrugged. "More or less."

"You really are a hero, then."

"Believe it or not, Louisa, but that means little to me. I merely did what had to be done." With those words, he planted a kiss on the top of her head and left the room, leaving her to ponder on the mystery of her husband. Costermonger, hero, soldier. She couldn't quite get to the bottom of who he really was.

Chapter Twenty-One

THE DAY OF THE SUPPER PARTY WAS APPROACHING, and with Louisa having taken control of household matters, the house was improving. New curtains were hung, the carpets were cleaned, the silverware polished, the cobwebs removed. Nothing could be done about the threadbare tapestries, the creaking floorboards, or the damp, mouldy walls in the northern part of the house, but it was as good as it was going to get.

Robert had inspected the damage the moisture had done to the north wing, and concluded with disgust that the only thing to do was to tear the entire structure down and rebuild it, causing his steward to look at him in horror.

"Fear not, Biggs. That will not happen. But come up with a solution that will get the damp out of the house once and for all." Then he'd left to work with Lieutenants Miller and Carey on securing the parapet outside, which could easily be scaled.

The guest rooms were clean, warm, and habitable,

even if they were not redecorated in the latest style. Louisa had consulted with Mrs Dalton and the cook on the menu, which would be as sumptuous as any served at the London ton parties. As far as she was concerned, this would be as glamorous as the supper parties as she was used to in London.

Robert had said to expect some elevated guests. She wondered who that might be, and why he was so secretive about them. Hosting elevated guests did not intimidate Louisa. She'd been helping her stepmother with hosting social events for years, entertaining some dignitaries who'd come to London for the Victory parade; foreign dignitaries as distinguished as Prince Metternich, the Chancellor of Austria, or Field Marshal Blücher.

They had not continued their previous conversation and layers of unspoken and unresolved issues accumulated, creating a palpable tension between them. Louisa had not yet forgiven him for his deception, and each silent moment seemed to widen the gap, leaving them more estranged than before. He treated her with cautious politeness, and she addressed him with the same haughtiness she reserved for her suitors. Yet, in rare moments of nostalgia, she yearned for the uncomplicated bantering they had shared back when they lived in their little hut. Sometimes, she almost wished she could go back there. Sometimes, she wished he really was a humble costermonger, and she a costermonger's wife.

Having finished her work for the day, Louisa took a walk into the village and called on Celeste at the vicarage. When she first had extended the invitation, Celeste had been excited about the prospect of returning to her former home, even if it was for a single night for a supper party. But now her enthusiasm had waned.

"I won't be able to attend after all," she told Louisa, averting her eyes.

"But you must!" Louisa insisted. "Even if just for my sake. There are not enough ladies attending, and I was looking forward to having you join us."

Celeste fiddled with her reticule. "I am ashamed to have to admit that I don't have anything suitable to wear for the occasion," she eventually whispered.

Of course, Louisa should have thought of that before. "Papa is having my trunks sent from London. I'll lend you one of my own dresses, Celeste. I have so many, I hardly know what to do with them all. And many of them are too small for me; they will suit you to perfection. Oh, do take them!"

Celeste's eyes had lit up at these words. Then she hesitated. "I couldn't possibly impose upon you like this," she began.

"Nonsense," Louisa said breezily. "Let there be no false pride, Celeste. We are not mere acquaintants; we have known each other since we were children. Let me do you this one favour and give you one of my dresses. It would be a pleasure if you could see this not as an act of charity, but a gesture of friendship. Besides, I couldn't possibly ask you not to come. The evening would be entirely dominated by men, with Sarah and I as the only ladies. This cannot be." She gave Celeste a quick hug. "It will be such a joy to have you."

Celeste's fate weighed heavily on her mind, and Louisa wondered what she could do to help the girl. Born the daughter of a baron, she was now living in genteel poverty because of her father's mismanagement and her brother's indifference.

Her thoughts turned gloomy when she thought of George.

George, with his terrible personality.

George, who'd been her first jilted suitor.

Louisa's steps slowed as she approached the bakery. Through the shop window, she saw Wilbur and his wife working inside. Even from this distance, she could see how in love they were. Mary gave him a tremulous smile as he stacked the fresh bread loaves on the shelves, and he tucked a stray hair out of her face. It was a simple but tender gesture. For one moment she considered stepping into the shop to speak to them. Her hand was already at the door handle, but at the last moment she turned away. There was still this painful ache inside her that prevented her from facing Wilbur.

Since she'd been ill, she'd avoided thinking about Will. She'd thrown herself into a whirlwind of household management and preparations to avoid thinking about the past. She understood now that she'd wanted to come back to Piddleton to find some kind of closure. She'd wanted to find Will, and by doing so, some sense of peace. She'd hoped to find some answers, to be able to move on with her life. That hadn't happened. All she'd managed to do so far was to stir up the murky mud of the past and to find more questions than there were answers. She had to find contentment in the thought that maybe she would never find those answers.

And she had to learn to live with guilt.

She stared at Brooks' bakery for a moment longer, then turned her steps back to where she'd come from. She'd told Mrs Dalton to order all the bread and pastries from Wilbur, of course. Brooks' bakery would do the business of the year with their upcoming supper party.

On her way back to Meryfell Hall, she passed by their deserted hut, looking as decrepit as they'd encountered it that first day they arrived at Piddleton. She looked at it with nostalgia. Had she really thought she'd find contentment in being a costermonger's wife? She'd found the challenge exciting. She'd been willing to learn; she would have liked to be her husband's helpmate in building up his business. She could have learned how to make baskets, weave cloth, and sell the products created by her own hands at the market. She'd enjoyed having a sense of purpose, maybe for the first time in her life. But it had turned out to be a mere fantasy. All those plans had disappeared in a puff, leaving her as disoriented as before.

Was she to be a mere wife now? That was the fate of all the women in her class, wasn't it?

Only she would be a soldier's wife, a major's wife.

If she was lucky, maybe one day there would be children.

Was that what she wanted?

With a sigh, she pushed the creaky door open and stepped into the hut. It had been cleared of all her belongings, but no one had found the loose board under the bed where she'd hidden the tin box with her childhood treasures. That was what she'd come for.

On her way back, she paused for a long time at the crossroads in the forest. Instead of returning to Meryfell Hall, she took the path that would lead her to the shore of the lake.

It was time to exorcise those last memories.

Chapter Twenty-Two

Louisa settled down on the shore by the lake under the shade of a tree. She took out her tin box and wondered what to do with it. Whether to bury it or burn it to scatter the ashes; some sort of ceremony was warranted. She held the little wooden figure of the Princess of Glubbdubdrib in her palm and clenched her fingers around it. Her heart quivered inside her rib cage. No, she couldn't burn this darling figure Will had carved with such love. She set the figure aside and picked up the book.

She leaned back, feeling the hard bark of the tree against her. The book's leather felt warm under her fingers, and she opened the book and read.

When she looked up again, the sun was lower on the horizon, and a fresher wind blew. She pulled her shawl over her shoulders and decided with a sigh that it was time to return to the house, as she couldn't bear to get rid of the book and her childhood treasures just yet.

A footstep sounded in the undergrowth. Someone

was approaching. There was the crunch of pebbles crunching under heavy boots, and the rustling of branches as they parted.

"There you are. I wondered where you'd disappeared to."

Robert. He was in shirtsleeves and work trousers. He looked like the costermonger again, only this time without the beard. A dark lock of hair fell across his forehead.

How handsome he looked.

Her heart gave an aching jab against her rib cage.

"I visited the village and then came here. It is a peaceful place." She gestured for him to sit down beside her.

He sat down on his haunches. "Have you been resting?"

"Yes." She closed the book. "I was reading this book and lost track of time."

He reached out for it, and she handed it to him. "I used to love coming here when I was a child. I used to spend many summer afternoons here by the lake, reading. Just like this."

He turned the book over and leafed through the pages. "*Gulliver's Travels.*"

"It used to be my favourite book."

He stared at it for a moment. Then he lowered himself on his stomach beside her, leaning on his elbows, the book in front of him, and began to read. "*My father had a small estate in Nottinghamshire. I was the third of five sons ...*"

She listened to his deep voice as he read, fluently and

rhythmically, soaking in those familiar words. Words that she'd read and heard so many times she'd fairly internalised them.

She closed her eyes and listened to him, feeling as if she were in a dream, a bubble, as if time stood still and reality was suspended. The present and the past became one, and the future did not exist.

She swallowed and swallowed, hot tears streaming into her eyes.

But he read on, unaware of how much his words were affecting her.

She opened her eyes and looked at him through the veil of tears and saw the strong, lean profile of his face, the proud nose, the dark lock of hair that fell across his forehead. He rested his chin on his hand as he read, absorbed, sucked into this world of make-believe they'd so loved.

It was a moment suspended in time.

An image of a sweet, kind boy that floated up from the recesses of her memory and laid itself over the vision of the man in front of her.

It hit her like a lightning bolt, shaking her to the core.

She opened her mouth with great difficulty. Once, twice. Her lips formed the word, but the sound would not come. Then, finally, it did.

"Will?"

"*We set sail from Bristol, May 4, 1699 ...*"

"Will." It sounded like a groan.

"*... and our voyage at first was very prosperous.*"

"Will!" She scrambled to her feet, her hands

clenched into tight fists, her entire body shaking, tears streaming down her face as she stared down at him.

He stopped reading, put the book aside, stood up, and opened his arms.

She threw herself into his embrace, sobbing wildly.

"Jove's beard, Lulu. Sixty-two days! You really went above and beyond," he said much, much later, after she'd cried herself dry and his shirt front was drenched with tears. He still held her, rocking her back and forth like a child. Random dry sobs racked her body, but the worst was over now. Slowly, her thoughts functioned again.

"Sixty-two bloody days." He shook his head in disbelief. "I kept track of it in my journal. One mark for each day."

"I don't understand." She wiped her cheeks with the corner of her shawl, neither of them having brought a handkerchief.

"That's how long it took for you to remember me. I am mortally offended, you know."

She looked at him, stricken. "But I never forgot you."

A mocking smile curled his lips. "And yet I was right in front of you all the time and you did not realise who I was until now. Sixty-two days, Lulu. Really? I confess I am somewhat disappointed."

"Really, Will. I did not forget you! Not for one moment. Not for a s-single day, I swear."

He let out a disbelieving huff. "I was about to tell you myself when you finally saw the light. I've been dropping hints left and right. What a slowtop you are! I must confess, the joke was getting old, the entire situation was getting rather dull, and I was beginning to lose my patience."

"You were laughing at me the entire time."

"Yes."

"You thought it was a great joke."

"Naturally."

"You planned it all to get back at me." She swallowed. "Because I humiliated you at the ball."

"To the letter. It was the perfect revenge. Strategy has always been one of my greatest strengths, you know." He drew her closer and stroked her arms.

She looked up at his face and the firm set of his jaw. "You hated me."

He looked over her head thoughtfully across the lake, his eyes taking on the hue of the blue-green water. "I confess there was a time when I did indeed hate you."

Louisa pulled away, shivering. Her breath came in ragged gasps.

"But I have found that hate and love are decidedly close together, like different sides of the same coin." He pulled out a penny and flipped it between his fingers, watching it pensively.

She sniffed.

"You're not about to cry again, are you?" he asked, alarmed. He pulled her back into his arms.

"Wilbur said—Wilbur said you'd died during transportation," she choked out, clinging to him, afraid that she was dreaming and that he'd vanish into thin air. "We went to Dorchester prison, and they confirmed it."

"Poor record keeping. What can I say? As the French

can easily attest, you'll find that I'm impossibly hard to kill." His hand stroked comfortingly over her back. "And they did their best to transport me six feet under at every opportunity, believe me. All to no avail, for they discovered I don't die that easily."

She pulled away from him to search his face, still not quite believing. "What happened to you?" she whispered. "What happened to the boy you were?" She ran her hand through his thick hair. Traced his cheeks, his nose, his hard jaw. He held still, patiently allowing her to explore his face. "You used to be so small. Even though you're older, I always used to be taller than you, at least a good head taller. I used to look down on you easily. And now ..."

His sweet, round, dimpled face had thinned to the hard, chiselled planes of a man, and his features were harsher, more disciplined, almost ruthless. What had he seen? What had he experienced to give him this world-weary expression in his eyes? Only the colour of his light hazel eyes had remained the same, and Louisa wondered how on earth she hadn't seen it earlier. Other than that, there was nothing left in this face that she'd recognised as belonging to the mischievous, bold boy whom she'd so loved. She wasn't at all certain about what to make of the man. He was too big, too hard, and too muscular. She didn't know what kinds of feelings she had for him, for they were a jumbled mess of heated confusion, agony, and joy. Such joy that it terrified her.

"Well, it appears I've finally outgrown you. Thank heavens. I feared I'd stay a podgy little button forever. Turns out I was merely a late bloomer. I experienced a significant growth spurt after I turned sixteen and suddenly shot up like a tree. The rigorous discipline of military life stripped away any remaining excess padding. One is also guaranteed to lose some weight when one is hanging over the railing of a ship for six weeks, puking one's guts out. By Jove, I hate ships! Then the endless trekking through dense jungle and over mountainous trails under the merciless blaze of the West Indian sun. Makes a boy mature rather fast."

"You were transported after all?"

He shook his head. "I enlisted and was immediately dispatched to the West Indies. After enduring the harsh conditions there, I was redeployed to Portugal to take part in the Peninsular Wars. I suppose even a society damsel like you might have caught wind of what we did there," he remarked, his voice laced with a subtle irony. "Turns out I found my life's vocation in the military, Louisa."

"But you always wanted to be a baker. It was your dream. You said you wanted to bake England's best bread."

"I did, didn't I? What a tranquil life I could have led if that had come to pass. Alas, fate had other plans for me." He studied his hands. "Turns out I had more talent with a Baker rifle than being an actual baker and pounding dough. The only bread I ever baked with any kind of success were the dreadful bran cakes that we roasted over the campfire at night. They're pancakes consisting of flour, bran, and chopped straw. Tasty, I tell you." He paused and looked at her gravely. "While waiting for my trial, I was approached by recruiters. I was given the choice between enlisting or a trial. I didn't have to think twice. I figured my chances of proving that I was not guilty were nil. A trial would've ended in transportation to the penal colonies in New South Wales aboard the prison hulks. So, I took my chance in the army. This might have been a death sentence for me as well, but as you can see, Fortuna was on my side, and I survived."

Louisa looked at him miserably. "And what happened then?"

"The Peninsular War." His face hardened as he continued. "Let me spare you the details."

They sat in silence, gazing across the lake at the island, each engrossed in their own thoughts. An icy wind blew across the lake. Louisa shivered.

Wordlessly, he handed her the shawl, which she draped over her shoulder.

"It is getting dark, and the wind is getting cold," he said at last. "You shouldn't be out here so shortly after having been so ill. We should go back to the house." He helped her gather her things, picking up the little carved figure from the box and turning it between his fingers.

"You still have this." A smile lit up his face. "I used to carve an entire army of them. I buried them on Glubbdubdrib. One day, I will row over and see if the box is still there. One day I want to swim with you across the lake in a race, to see who is faster. But not now. Not tonight. It is too cold. Let us return to the house."

THEY WALKED BACK to the house together without touching. It felt like they had more to say, that they'd merely scratched the surface, but somehow it was too much, and they needed to process everything that had been said first.

"That upcoming soirée," Will finally said as they approached the house, "is rather important to me. Some people who are important to me will be attending."

Louisa threw him a quick look. "Why won't you tell me their names?"

"Because they asked me not to."

Louisa frowned. "I hope it's not the Prince Regent. I care little for him."

He barked a short laugh. "Never fear. It's someone of even greater consequence."

Louisa stopped and clutched her hands to her chest. "Good heavens. Who could it be? I'm beginning to feel the nerves."

"There is no need." He gave her a quick smile. "It's someone you have met before; however, knowing you, you might not remember."

"Well then." They reached the house and looked at each other. There was a sudden awkwardness between them.

"You don't need to worry," she babbled to fill the silence. "About the soiree, I mean. None of your guests will want for anything. I will do my best to be a worthy hostess."

He nodded. "I have no doubt in my mind that you will."

Their exchange was formal. He bowed stiffly, and after they entered the house, he excused himself, for he had much work to do.

Louisa wondered what work that might be. There

was still so much she still did not know about him. So much that had not been said.

Dazed, she went up to her room to lie down.

Louisa had finally found Will. He was alive and safe and not dead at the bottom of the sea. She'd even married him. Wasn't this the fulfilment of one of her biggest childhood dreams? Hadn't she wanted this all her life? She should be rejoicing. And indeed, she was glad. But it felt as if there was a gulf between them as wide as ever. And inside, she felt hollow.

Chapter Twenty-Three

OVER THE NEXT FEW DAYS, NEITHER LOUISA NOR Will broached the subject of their past. Perhaps they were both avoiding it because there were still too many unanswered questions and unaddressed hurts that could widen the chasm between them even further. They both trod around the subject carefully, in a mutual avoidance. It might have been simply because they were both too busy, and there was no proper occasion for a talk—Louisa had thrown herself into the preparations for their upcoming social event, while Will's attention was demanded by the estate.

"It is probably not surprising that the tenant farms are not in the best of conditions," he told her over breakfast one morning, a note of frustration lacing his voice. "They have been grossly neglected. Their housing situation is poor, and there is something missing or to be improved at every turn. The levies are too high, and if I'm not mistaken, the books are in disarray as well." He ran a hand through his hair in irritation, causing it to stick in all directions, which Louisa found charming.

Her own hand itched to do the same, to run it through his thick hair and pat down the recalcitrant curls.

"I do not know what the devil Milford was thinking when he allowed the place to fall into such disrepair. It doesn't help that I have little understanding of these matters myself. I am a soldier, not a farmer. If you asked me, I'd just tear the whole place down and rebuild it from scratch."

"If things are that bad, why not hire a new steward?" Louisa suggested, folding her hands tightly, lest she betrayed herself and reached out to pat his hair.

Will hadn't died! He was sitting across from her, a living, breathing human being, eating, talking, conversing. Her mind was still reeling, struggling to process it all.

How she yearned to touch him to ascertain that he truly was her childhood friend and first love. But her fingers remained cramped together on her lap. Instead, she politely conversed with him as if he were a guest or a stranger who'd called for tea.

"One can assume that all this mismanagement is because of someone's inefficiency," she said. "Yes, Milford is to blame. But don't stop there. I'd take a closer look at the steward who's been working here all this time."

Will gave her an appreciative look. "That is a sharp but accurate assessment. You may be right."

How excessively strange it was to talk to him in that manner about business matters as reasonable, level-headed adults.

Louisa didn't know what to make of him anymore. He was her friend. He was a stranger. He was one of her hundred hated suitors. He was her husband. He was Robert, the costermonger. Will, who was Major Sir Robert William Ashford. He was the boy she'd once loved so dearly. She believed he'd loved her dearly too once, but now she wasn't at all sure.

Could he still love her after all that had happened?

He'd only told her the rudiments of his story, a rough outline without any details. He had not described how he'd fared in prison. It must be a harrowing experience for anyone, but when one was but a boy, half a child, still ... Louisa shuddered. She'd heard terrible stories about what they did to people there. And Will had sat in his cell, thinking the entire world had abandoned him.

Including herself.

She felt ill.

All this time, he must have thought she'd betrayed him. Not just that night, when she hadn't spoken up when she should have, but also much later, when she hadn't recognised him at the ball and made a mockery of him.

Had he forgiven her yet?

She couldn't say, and if he hadn't, she could hardly blame him. Back when he was still the costermonger Robert, there had been unguarded moments when she'd caught him staring at her with a strange expression on his face. Hard, assessing, judging. As if he were sizing her up.

He hadn't liked her at first; he'd been angry.

Oh yes, Will had always been adept at holding grudges. It was likely, then, that he had not forgiven her.

"Louisa?"

She snapped to attention. "I-I beg your pardon."

"Wool-gathering again?" His lips quirked up at the corners.

She blinked. "Did you ask me something?"

"Nothing of importance." He leaned back in his chair, flipping the fork between his fingers as he watched her closely.

Louisa sat rigidly, her back straight, her nose in the air, suddenly feeling self-conscious and strangely shy. She knew her shyness might appear as aloofness as she feigned indifference.

Once more, awkwardness hovered between them, along with a swarm of unexpressed emotions that she could neither understand nor articulate.

It was unbearable. Unbearable!

Abruptly, she pushed her chair back; it screaked loudly against the wooden floor, for the carpets were still being cleaned. She rose to walk towards the sideboard to get another helping of eggs and bacon—not that she was still hungry. For the life of her, she couldn't swallow another morsel; it would turn to dust in her mouth. But neither could she bear sitting across from him, making idle conversation as if they were strangers. As she passed him, in the blink of an eye, he grasped her wrist and pulled her towards him. She landed on his lap, his other hand securing her firmly by the waist.

She froze, surprised.

"There, isn't that better?" he murmured into her ear.

Her heart fluttered wildly, her mouth went dry, and her brain could not, for the life of her, come up with an appropriate response.

"And now, Louisa, tell me what is the matter."

"I, uh, nothing is the matter. I merely wanted to get another helping of eggs," she muttered, her hands clutching the lapels of his waistcoat, resolving that she would never, ever let go.

"You've already had two helpings."

"I want a third."

Heavens, how she loved that half-cocked smile; it lit up his eyes and coaxed from her a smile in return. Holding her breath, she stared at his lips, soft with tenderness, and entirely unaware of what she was doing. She pulled him closer towards her.

And kissed him.

Just then, the door swung open. The butler entered, froze at the sight, and quietly retreated, but neither of them noticed. After a wonderful eternity later, he brushed his lips against hers with featherlight tenderness, and murmured, "You were lying just now."

"Was I?" Her voice was thick with emotion.

"When you said that nothing is the matter." He pulled back slightly to look into her eyes. "You forget I know you all too well. Tell me what's wrong."

"Will, I didn't know," she burst out suddenly, the words emerging from the deepest depths of her being.

There was a pause. Wasn't he going to say anything? Did he understand what she was talking about?

After an eternity, he finally spoke. "I confess I didn't always see it like this, but I understand now that you probably really didn't know. You were just a young girl back then. You wouldn't have known that they dragged me off to prison. I learned only later that your father had whisked you away from Meryfell Hall before either of us could blink."

She closed her eyes in relief. He understood.

"But back then, when they left me to rot in that damp cell, I was a frightened, bewildered boy who didn't know what was happening to him. Some loyal friend you were, I thought. All I knew was that I desperately waited for you to come, but you never did." His jaw was grim. "I confess I felt rather betrayed. I thought you'd gone ahead and married George and forgotten me. That was the darkest moment of my life, Louisa, and I struggled hard not to hate you then."

"Oh, heavens!" She looked like she was about to burst into tears. "If only I had known! I would have come. I would have defended you, given you an alibi, helped you prove your innocence. And if all things had failed, I would have helped you escape from prison single-handedly. I would have done it, too! We would have run away together and, and—"

"I know, Louisa. I know." He took her clenched fists in his hands and pressed a kiss on her knuckles. Then he let out a short laugh. "Oh, what I wouldn't give to have seen you break me out of prison. The guards wouldn't have known what hit them. If there was anyone who could have accomplished this, it would've been you."

"It's not funny. I shall never forgive myself that it went that far. That night, Papa had a vehement row with Lord Milford. It was so bad that their friendship broke forever. We returned to London the next day. We never went back to Meryfell Hall. Papa was so angry that he never mentioned Lord Milford's name again, and he wouldn't talk about what had happened, not a word. He wouldn't let me mention it. He wouldn't let me mention you. I wrote and wrote, and you never wrote back. I wrote to Reverend Graham, but he never wrote back either. No one would tell me a thing. You'd simply disappeared. Father would only tell me to forget you. I waited and waited. And then ..." Her shoulders slumped. "One day I just gave up. I thought Papa was right, and the best thing was to move on with my life. What else was I supposed to do?"

"You did nothing wrong, Louisa. You had to do what you did to get on with your life. As did I. I had to focus on survival, so I put you out of my mind. For a while, that worked. I blocked you out, willed myself to forget. It hurt less that way." He rested his chin on her head, lost in thought.

"But you know, when hell raged around me at its worst, threatening to swallow me completely, it was those memories of you that saved me. Short, clear, colourful flashes of you, here, by the lake. Your clear laugh, with that adorable catch in your voice. You swimming across the lake and how the water made your hair darker and stick to the sides of your face."

He tugged on a curl of her hair. "How you'd sit there, bent over your book, reading. The way your nose crinkled when you laughed." He reached out to touch the tip of her nose. "I haven't forgotten. Not a single memory. And in the end, it was those memories that kept me sane."

"I never forgot you either," she whispered. "Never. Not for one moment. You told me to wait for you. You said you would come. You made me promise." It had been his last words before the footmen had dragged him through the door. "So, I waited. I waited and waited." Then her voice broke into a wail. "I waited so long, Will! But you never came."

"Instead, all these other men came," she continued to babble into his chest. "And I didn't want any of them because they didn't want me. They wanted my fortune. And after a while," she heaved a deep sigh, "I simply gave up hope. And then, when you finally came in all your glory, I didn't recognise you, because I'd firmly cut you out of my mind and heart. At least I tried to do so. It was the only way for me to go on. But you stubbornly refused to leave."

He tightened his hold on her and pressed a kiss on top of her head.

"Will?"

"Hm?"

Her finger traced up and down the lapel of his waistcoat. "I still have so many questions. I think that there's still so much you haven't told me. And I want to know."

He was quiet for a moment, then nodded. "Very well." He paused again, collecting his thoughts. "The Peninsula—do you really want me to expound on the gory details?"

"Yes. I want to know everything." She leaned her head against his chest, listening to the steady tum-tum-tum of his heartbeat.

He sighed and began. At first his voice was halting,

then as the memories surfaced, his narrative grew more fluid. He described what he'd experienced during the wars, and how he had survived.

As Louisa listened, tears filled her eyes. No newspaper story could ever convey the vividness of his account. The suffering, the horrors, but also the camaraderie between the soldiers, their unwavering loyalty, the daily acts of heroism that were never rewarded by any medals. It left her profoundly moved.

"We had no newspapers there, so we had to rely on word of mouth as to what was happening in the world and back at home. Eventually they reached us, the stories from the London ballrooms ... on the battlefields of Talavera and Salamanca, even in the hell of Badajoz. The stories circulated among all the soldiers; they were passed on as we marched. You wouldn't believe how thirsty we were for them, how eagerly we listened: stories about an infinitely beautiful but merciless maiden who turned down suitor after suitor after suitor. We dubbed her *La Belle Dame Sans Merci*. The Ice Damsel. You can't imagine how these stories inspired us, how they spurred us on, how they gave us hope, something to look forward to in the greatest chaos. 'Let us survive so we can return to London to woo *La Belle Dame*'—that became our rallying cry. We were collectively obsessed with you. When your name was finally mentioned, I was so startled I tripped over my own feet and fell into a ditch, nearly impaling myself on my bayonet." He chuckled at the memory, but Louisa could only groan.

"I was delighted at first. So you never married that cur George after all. You were holding off all the other fortune hunting nincompoops with fortitude. Clever Lulu. I was proud of you. Then I was terrified. All the countless men who flattered and worshipped you. All the men who came up to scratch. The names grew grander with every Season. The list simply wouldn't end. Earls, dukes, even princes. I couldn't keep up with them. Surely one day you'd cave and accept one of their suits? You'd be mad not to. Then, as time passed, the stories grew less amusing and progressively worse. Good heavens, Louisa! I could hardly believe it was you they were talking about. Surely you hadn't turned into that insufferably proud, superficial, and cynical creature? Surely you hadn't said and done all those cruel things? Toying with men as if they were disposable playthings? Surely not my Lulu?" He looked at her searchingly.

She hid her face in her hands.

"I no longer knew what to believe," Will continued relentlessly. "Then an officer returned from his leave and brought with him firsthand news. It was all true. He'd danced with the Incomparable and, not surprisingly, been cruelly rejected. It was as if it was all a jest, a cruel game, and the men thought it a great lark. But I grew uneasy and wondered—"

"What?"

"I started to wonder ..." He fell silent, lost in thought. After a while, he continued, "People change. Just look at me. Why wouldn't you have changed, too? What if that was what you'd really become? What if that was what life had made of you?"

Louisa chewed on her lower lip.

"We returned to London for the Great Victory

Parade. I was eager for you to see me in my resplendent glory, even if from afar, even if you didn't yet know who I was. How I'd been working towards this moment. I wanted you and your father to see that the wretched fry that I used to be had become someone with a name. Someone worthy of you. Someone to be proud of." A wry smile touched his lips, as if aware of his folly. "So, I piled all my medals on my chest and rode at the head of the parade."

She had watched the parade from the balcony of her father's townhouse. One of the many officers riding in the parade would have been him. "It's likely I saw you, but—"

"You don't remember. Ahh, how cutting to my pride!" He placed a hand over his heart with a groan. "The day after the parade, I was determined to see you for myself. At a grand ball given by the Duke of Asterley."

Louisa remembered the event only too well. It had been a disaster.

"Poor Will. You survived all those terrible wars and came back a hero, only to discover, to your great shock, that those stories about me were true after all." Louisa's eyes glimmered with a quiet, aching sadness. "Not only did *La Belle Dame Sans Merci* fail to recognise you when you finally appeared in front of her, but she also made a public laughingstock out of you most cruelly. You must have been shocked and furious."

He looked down at her thoughtfully. "I was a fool. I should have expected something like this. But what saddened me was your transformation of character. I was surprised that I hardly recognised you, either."

Suddenly, Louisa felt endlessly tired. "We've both grown up, I suppose. You've been through the wars and seen the worst of horrors and suffering. How could that leave anyone untouched? While I ... I've frittered away my time flirting in the ballrooms, bored by the attentions of fawning men. You're right. I'd turned into a superficial, cynical creature. We have both changed, Will. Neither of us is the innocent child we once were."

She made a movement to get off his lap, but he increased his hold on her, not yet ready to let her go.

"And after all that, you hatched that diabolical plan to get your revenge. You disguised yourself as a costermonger. Why did you choose the name Robert, however?"

"It's my name. Robert William Cole Jones. My ma always called me Will, though, which is why I preferred that when I was younger."

Another thing she hadn't known about him.

"So you've achieved your goal. You've had your laugh. And here we are," Louisa said, bringing their conversation full circle.

He did not contradict her. "And here we are."

A heaviness settled upon her.

Was this the answer she'd been seeking?

Revenge. That was all it had been, it seemed.

A great lark by an ambitious soldier whose pride forbade him to lose. With Will, at least she knew her inheritance had never mattered; he was never one to care about material things.

But what if it had been about pride and honour, about proving a point to his men after losing face?

She was but a grand trophy, the ultimate prize.

"But of course, what else could you be?" Will said flippantly. She jumped. Had she just voiced her thoughts out loud?

It appeared she had, for he continued. "Haven't you understood yet? You are a soldier's most coveted trophy, Louisa. The only reason I married you was that I could put you into a vitrine next to my other medals of honour. I polish them every day so I can bask in their shine of glory and triumph. I stand before them daily, preening, patting my own shoulders, congratulating myself on how cleverly I outmanoeuvre all your other three hundred or so suitors." He was, of course, teasing her.

"They were merely ninety-nine!" Louisa said with outrage, hitting his arm.

"Bad enough." He tugged at a curl.

Louisa pouted.

He chuckled. "In one thing you haven't changed at all, my love."

"Oh. And what would that be?" Her tone was icy, her demeanour haughty. She'd turned into the Ice Damsel once more.

"You overthink, running through the labyrinth of your mind until you hit a dead end, letting your thoughts drag you down. And then you shoulder the blame for everything and the entire world. And you can't lie for the life of you." He tipped his lips up in a smile. "That was three things now, wasn't it?"

She scowled.

"Look at me, Louisa Highworth," he commanded.

She stubbornly looked away. "I'd rather not. In fact, it is time for me to get off your lap. It's growing rather cold and uncomfortable." She squirmed, but his hands tightened about her waist.

"You are such an adorable goose," he murmured, turning her chin toward him with one finger and kissing her again.

Her resistance crumbled. She melted against him, and then, somehow, her heart grew lighter.

She was a goose indeed.

How could she have ever doubted him? This feeling of belonging, of being safe and cherished, was all she ever craved.

LATER, after Will had left to meet the steward to discuss further estate matters, she'd remained sitting in the dining room on her own, with a silly smile on her face.

"Lady Ashford, ma'am." A voice penetrated her thoughts. "Would we be using the plain linen serviettes, or the diamond patterned damask?" Mrs Dalton lifted one of each for her perusal.

She shook herself. Louisa Highworth, gather your wits. There was much work to do to prepare for the supper party. This was no time for wool-gathering.

"The one with the diamond pattern, if you please. We also need to start the flower arrangements. If you could have the flowers brought in now, I would like to do that myself."

"Yes, ma'am. If I may say so, this will be the most lavish supper party this house has ever seen."

"I do hope so, Mrs Dalton."

Several days earlier, trunks and boxes had arrived from London. It contained her wardrobe, all her dresses, ballgowns, shawls and slippers and boots, petticoats and bonnets, gloves and stockings, coats, spencers, pelisses, and redingotes; in short, everything she'd left in London. Another trunk contained the finest of linen and tablecloths, and a third with silverware. Then there were boxes full of ribbons, laces, fans, furs, and jewellery. This was her trousseau, her stepmother Sarah explained in a letter, everything a newly married woman needed, and more. But they would discuss all this when they arrived, for Sarah was to accompany her father to their supper party.

"I must say, I was never so relieved when I realised your husband's true identity, Louisa. I would've had such sleepless nights, imagining you in the rookery! Cruel wretches, both of them, to play such a trick on us! But how glad I am that you have made such a favourable match after all, my dear, to the hero of Vitoria no less ..." Sarah had written.

Celeste arrived from the vicarage later that day.

Louisa had told Celeste that Robert was a knighted officer, but not that he was Will. Will hadn't wanted her to tell anyone about his identity just yet, because he wanted to do that himself. Therefore, she had left out that piece of information. Celeste hadn't been surprised in the least. She'd known by the time of the accident with the carriages on the road that Robert must have been an officer in the military.

Louisa made her try on all her dresses, and they settled on a high-waisted dress of cornflower blue silk, which emphasised the colour of her eyes.

"It's perfect," Louisa proclaimed. "You'll turn the heads of the lieutenants who will join us tonight."

Celeste blushed.

A short time later, a carriage drove up the house, revealing it to be Louisa's parents. Her father's loud voice boomed in the hallway.

Louisa hurried down the stairs with mixed feelings.

"Papa." It sounded reproachful.

"There she is." Her father took off his hat and handed it to the butler. "Come and give me a hug, daughter."

"I'm very cross with you, Papa," she said with a wobbly voice and walked into his arms.

"Come, now, did you really think I'd marry my precious girl off to a horrible costermonger?" He patted her back awkwardly. "You know me better than that."

She had a lump of tears in her throat.

"It was a naughty trick we played on you, daughter, granted. But he was rather insistent, that Sir Robert. He'd overheard me ranting at the club, for I admit I was rather furious then, after that trick you pulled at Almack's and how you'd said you'd marry the first man who'd cross your path. He took me aside and told me not to shout it to the entire world, for then our house would surely be overrun with suitors from the lowest gutter. By Jove, he was right. He proposed a plan to me, a plan I liked. It was daring, yes. But also cheeky. He'd already asked for my permission to pay you his addresses, and I'd given it, and a mull you made of it, you did! Yet I confess of the entire lot of grovelling swells, he'd always been my favourite. A well-decorated major, a knight to boot, with his own inheritance waiting for him, so he had no need of yours; young, handsome, reliable, and brave. He was the son-in-law I wanted. I therefore went along with his plan on the condition that you had to choose him."

He rubbed his hands. "And you did. Things went well, indeed. Like clockwork. Look at you now! I see you are well and healthy. Though why the deuce I am back here in this house, where I swore never to set my foot again, eludes me. Where is he? Our hero of Vitoria?"

Louisa did not know. He'd gone out with his steward to inspect the estate and would no doubt return soon. She greeted Sarah, who drew her into her arms.

"Are you happy, Louisa?" She studied her face carefully while adjusting the shawl on her shoulders.

"Yes. I am," Louisa replied with a gentle smile.

"I believe you are indeed. You radiate a contentment that is entirely new to you. I am glad." Sarah smiled back. Then her gaze swept around the room. "How strange to be back here. The house certainly saw better days when Lord Milford was still alive."

"The house still needs much renovation," Louisa said. "Lord Milford's daughter is here and will join us for the supper," she added as they turned to greet Celeste, who shyly stepped down the stairs. She had been a young girl the last time they'd seen her.

"It's going to be a splendid evening," her father said, rubbing his hands. "I look forward to meeting the other guests."

Louisa wondered for the hundredth time who else might be coming.

Then, as the door opened, Louisa's heart jumped, and she turned with a smile.

Will had returned.

Chapter Twenty-Four

THIS WAS SURELY THE STRANGEST SUPPER PARTY she'd ever experienced, Louisa thought.

It was uneven in numbers, with more gentlemen than ladies—something that did not reflect well on the hostess. It had been a challenge planning this dinner party without exactly knowing who and how many people would be attending. Will had been annoyingly tight-lipped about his guests. At first, it looked as if there would be only her parents and Will's two aides-de-camp, and Celeste.

"We are expecting four more guests at least, two of which I hold in high regard," Will had informed her.

Louisa wondered who they might be, but he refused to tell her. "You said, at least?" she echoed. "Could there be more?"

"It is possible that one of my guests of honour will bring some additional company, yes," he admitted.

"But Will, that is rather vague," she said. "How is a

hostess to plan a supper without knowing the exact number of guests?"

He smiled mysteriously. "We shall make do when the time comes, my love. You will be a splendid hostess, and I am proud to be able to present my wife to the world." He lifted her chin and looked deeply into her eyes, causing her to blush furiously and forget what it was that she had wanted to say.

That hadn't exactly helped.

Louisa had the entire evening planned out, complete with musical performances and card games. There were not enough ladies present for dancing, but one could perform on the piano and sing. Tea, coffee, and light refreshments would be served before a five-course supper, consisting of soup, lobster, a meat dish, and an assortment of cheeses, followed by pudding and post-supper drinks, punch, and negus.

Will wore his dress uniform; a scarlet coat with gold epaulettes and white lace embellishments on the chest, a crimson sash tied around his waist, and white breeches. His tasselled Hessian boots were polished to such a shine that one could see their reflection in them. He looked breathtakingly splendid, and once more Louisa felt a wave of shyness in his presence, which she masked behind a veneer of cool indifference.

She wore a high-waisted forest green dress with a gold embroidered overdress that caught the light with every movement. Her honey-golden hair was elegantly swept up, allowing soft curls to cascade down her neck. She'd never felt more radiant.

Will couldn't seem to help but stare at her. "Tonight,

you truly look like *La Belle Dame Sans Merci*." His voice was tinged with awe. "A veritable siren. I must warn my men to tighten the security around the estate lest you draw a crowd of admirers from far and wide."

"Must I be concerned? I trust you will fend them off one by one," Louise teased, a mischievous sparkle in her eyes. "Men have done all sorts of things to win my affection. Flowers, pralines, silly love poems." She ticked them off on her fingers. "Yet I have never had the thrill to witness someone duel over my affections." She looked at him through her eyelashes. "Do you think such an opportunity shall finally arise tonight?"

Will straightened his posture. "Just say the word and it shall be arranged. Who is the dolt I must call out?"

Their eyes locked, a moment hanging between them charged with unspoken emotion, then her composure broke, and she burst out laughing. "You are the silliest of them all, Sir Robert."

He chuckled. "Aye, it seems I am indeed."

Will seemed to grow increasingly tense as the evening progressed. But when the butler entered and whispered something into his ear, a broad smile broke out over his face.

With swift steps he walked towards the door, where the butler ushered in a tall, stately-looking man in a greatcoat. He had grey hairs at the temple, piercing eyes, and a proud nose. Upon seeing Will, he held out both hands.

"My boy. Finally."

"You have arrived in good time, sir. I am so glad." Will took his hands and pulled him into an embrace.

"It took us a good twenty hours to reach Calais, nonstop riding with a crossing in horrific weather, and another twenty hours from Dover, but we made it, indeed. We had but a quick meal of cold fowl in the carriage and that was it. I wouldn't have it any other way."

Louisa stepped up to him, a polite smile on her lips. Will took her hand and drew her forward.

"Father, I am pleased to finally introduce you to my wife, Louisa, formerly Miss Highworth."

Father? Hadn't his father died when he was still in his leading strings?

The man turned to Louisa with an expression of genuine interest.

"Louisa, this is General Frederick Ashford, Lord Wexham. I have the greatest admiration for him; he's been a guiding light in my life and he's as dear to me as any father could ever be."

Wexham bowed over her hand. "Louisa, at last. What a pleasure to finally meet the woman who has captured William's heart. Welcome to the family, my dear."

"This is a wonderful surprise. Will didn't mention that we were expecting you today, nor did he tell me the story of how he came to have another father. How glad I am, Will. I would like to hear that story."

The man smiled at her with kind eyes. "And so you shall, Louisa. In good time. I may call you daughter, yes?" Turning to Will, he said, "'Pon rep, my boy, the stories were all wrong. She is even more beautiful than they say!"

A rosy flush covered her cheeks.

Will introduced Wexham to her father and stepmother, and when all the introductions had been made, Wexham said, "Pray, forgive me my travel dust. Let me wash and change, and I will join you shortly."

The butler showed him to his room.

Before he left, Will pulled him aside and murmured, "Did he come?"

"Naturally. He wouldn't miss this for the world. What's more, he brought three more men." He nodded at the men lingering in the hall outside. "But let us converse anon."

The drawing room was suddenly filled with officers who greeted Will with a military salute and Louisa with wide-eyed deference as they clicked their heels together. After a quick calculation, she realised she needed more places set at the table.

Then the butler announced someone that Louisa had not expected to see tonight. "The Reverend and Mrs Graham."

"Graham!" Louisa's father boomed, pulling away from the mantel of the fireplace against which he'd been leaning. "Haven't seen you in an eternity. It's been what, ten, twenty years?"

Reverend Graham, looking as she remembered him—distinguished with a balding head but a round, kind face—replied, "It's been nigh eleven years, Highworth," and pumped his hand. He looked about, somewhat bewildered, as if he was wondering what he was doing here. He greeted Will politely but with some distance, as if not quite sure what to make of him.

He doesn't recognise him, Louisa realised. *He doesn't recognise his erstwhile godchild and pupil.*

Will smiled slightly but did not enlighten him. What game was he playing?

His wife, Mrs Graham, was short and cheerful and radiated a motherly air. "Louisa, the last time I saw you, you were a wee girl. Look at you now." She kissed her on both cheeks. She greeted Will, but with a slightly knitted brow.

"Mr and Mrs Daggett," the butler announced next, to Louisa's great surprise, ushering in Wilbur and Mary, who, both dressed in their best Sunday dress, looked most uncomfortable. They looked around, thoroughly overwhelmed and intimidated to find themselves in such elevated company.

"We received an invitation," poor Wilbur stammered, entirely out of his depth.

Sarah lifted her lorgnette and wrinkled her nose slightly, recognising them as not being of their class. But to Louisa's relief, she greeted them graciously.

Louisa rushed forward to greet them. "How wonderful that you are here, Mary, Wilbur." She led Mary to a chair, where she sat gratefully.

Wilbur stood behind her and placed a hand on her shoulder.

"More covers on the table," Louisa discreetly instructed the butler. She had the premonition that the evening was about to turn exceedingly interesting.

. . .

THE NEXT GUEST TO arrive cut the ground from under her feet. Tall, lean, with angelic blond locks and a dissolute and degenerate air about him as he leaned in the doorway with a sneer, he sure knew how to make an entrance.

Louisa gasped. As did Celeste.

Her father recognised him immediately. "Stap me vitals! George Cooper-Wiles, as I live and breathe. Lord Milford now, I s'ppose."

He gave a curt nod. "Highworth. And the delectable Louisa. *La Belle Dame Sans* something or other. I did not expect to see either of you here. And why the devil are you here, Cissy? You're supposed to be with the aunts." He acknowledged his sister, who seemed torn how to greet him, with a simple nod. "Sir Robert. Have you invited half your regiment here?" He waved to the five officers standing around with various degrees of curiosity etched on their faces. "I came as you requested, though the purpose eludes me. If you've done this to rub it in and gloat that I had to sell my inheritance to you, let me tell you it's in vain, for what's done is done and I have neither shame nor regret. I ain't taking it back. I hate this pile of stone and am glad to be rid of it."

Louisa gave him a brittle smile. Before she could greet him, Will stepped up with a firm set of his jaw. "Welcome, Milford. We have been waiting for you."

The expression on Will's face made it clear that George's presence was as welcome as a louse in a wig.

"Have you, indeed?" He waved away the butler, who was trying to offer him tea. "I don't oodle my insides with that stuff. Don't you have anything proper to drink?"

The butler offered him some punch. George pulled a face, then accepted a cup of the warm drink of wine and spices. He threw himself into an empty armchair and crossed his legs and looked expectantly at Will. "Well, Sir Robert. Here I am. Wouldn't dare ignore the summons of the Hero of Vitoria himself," he sneered. "Pray enlighten me as to the purpose of this meeting."

Will smiled thinly. "Yes. Now that we're complete, we can begin. Do have a seat, ladies, and make yourselves comfortable. Gentlemen?"

The gentlemen preferred to stand while the three ladies sat on the sofa. Reverend Graham stood behind his wife, Highworth strolled over to join Wexham, who had rejoined them and was now leaning against the mantelpiece of the fireplace. Louisa offered the fauteuil to Mary and sat in a chair beside her. It appeared that they were not to have tea, music, and card games, as she had planned, as clearly Will had his own agenda, which he had not shared with her. A steep frown creased her forehead. He strolled over to the connecting door of the salon and opened it slightly.

Three redcoats positioned themselves on either side of the door. The adjoining room was dark, and perhaps she was imagining it, but was there a figure moving in the room? She hadn't noticed any other guests arriving. How strange.

Will stood in the middle of the room, legs parted, his hands behind his back.

"Ladies and gentlemen, as Milford so aptly put it, this is no ordinary soiree, and there must be a purpose to this meeting. We have all been introduced, but we do not really know who we all are, do we? Sadly, there are two people missing whose presence would have been beneficial to this meeting. The former Lord Milford being one of them, but he passed away several years ago. And Mr John Brooks, who was the baker before Wilbur Daggett took over." He nodded at Wilbur, who looked at him with considerable confusion. "Mr Brooks also passed away several years ago. As for everyone here, we are all connected to each other. We are comrades at arms"—he nodded at the officers standing around—"or family." He nodded to Highworth and Wexford. "My father and father-in-law." Then he placed a hand on Louisa's shoulder. "My lovely wife."

"Demme. You married the Ice Damsel?" George looked shaken.

"I did, indeed." Will's hands tightened on her shoulders for a moment, then he released her and strolled over to Reverend and Mrs Graham. "You're also family."

The reverend looked embarrassed and puzzled. "It is an honour, of course, to be called family by a person of your stature, but I can't for the life of me—"

Mrs Graham interrupted with a cry, clapping a hand over her mouth. "No. It cannot be." She stood up, shaking her head, tears rushing to her eyes. "Will!"

Reverend Graham's eyes bulged out of his face. "What? Will? But how is this possible? The boy was transported—"

Wilbur jumped out of his chair. "Will! By George. Now I see it, too. But you're supposed to be dead!"

"By George, indeed," George drawled, pale. "What in blazes? Is this a bad joke?"

Highworth looked from one to the other, puzzled. "Why is everybody surprised and calling Sir Robert Will? Who is this Will who's supposed to be dead? Do you know him?"

George laughed sharply. "You've always been a devil of a trickster. Impossible to beat, and, it seems, impossible to kill. Few make it back from transportation. It seems you have. Congratulations on being resurrected from the dead."

"Transportation?" Louisa's father said. "Did he say transportation? You must be mistaken." Turning to Will, he said, "You have got some explaining to do, son."

Will stood before him, a smile playing around his mouth that did not quite reach his eyes. "As the French have no doubt learned the hard way, I don't kick the bucket easily."

George jumped to his feet. "I see. Oh yes, I understand now. Is this all part of some elaborate plot for revenge? I want no part of it. You have the girl, you have the house, you have the honours. Now you must rub it into my face, too?"

"Sit down, George," Will said in the lashing, commanding voice he used on his men, and George promptly obeyed and sat down. "You will listen to what I have to say." He turned to the others. "All of you will."

After silence settled over the room, he continued. "As many of you know, I am of genteel birth and lineage. My father was the youngest son of a baron, and my mother the daughter of a landed gentleman. I grew up estranged from both families, though interestingly, members from both sides of the family who have previously denied any relationship have now come forward to acknowledge their connection to me." He shrugged.

"Leeches," Highworth said. "They want to nibble on your fortune, fame, and glory. I have to deal with them all the time. Best to keep them unacknowledged."

Will ignored his input. "I grew up in humble but happy surroundings. Then both my parents died within a short time of each other. I was an orphan."

Mrs Graham nodded. Will stood next to her, and she took his hand and patted it. "Until Reverend Graham—who was my godfather and a friend of my father's—and his wonderful wife took me in, and I came to live in this town. They gave me a new life, a new home, and an education. I would have been a lost waif without them. You were an anchor in my life when I needed it most. For that, I am humbly grateful."

Reverend Graham's face was stony, but he blinked, clearly overcome by memories. "You were an exceptionally bright, inquisitive, mischievous boy who resisted studying. It hurt me to have to be overly strict, but it was the only way to get you to learn your declinations. Trade was out of the question. The plan was to send you to school, and then to Oxford to follow in your father's footsteps. But you had your own ideas."

Will smiled fondly at him. "Indeed. I had other ideas. For whatever reason my convoluted brain cooked up, I was convinced that I wanted to become a baker." He walked over to Wilbur and placed his hand on his shoulder. "You see, when I had to sit at my desk and work on my Latin, the smell of Mr Brooks' freshly baked bread was carried across the street through the open window of my room. I thought there was no greater pleasure."

Wilbur grinned. "Except Mr Brooks had doubts about taking you on as an apprentice. He didn't want to upset Reverend Graham, but he'd taken a liking to you, so he let you loiter around the bakery and taught you a thing or two about making Wigg bread. But, in the end, he took me on as an apprentice instead. Which still rankles, doesn't it?"

Will laughed. "Hardly. You were always kind and patient with me, Wilbur, when I must have been an annoying pest, forever in your way. Even though I was an orphan, I was blessed with a second family and wonderful friends."

He regarded each of his guests, pausing when he saw Louisa. His eyes softened. "I met the love of my life," he said, extending his hand towards her. "The woman who changed everything for me. Her loyalty and courage exceeds any soldier's." His gaze, filled with sweet tenderness, stole her breath away.

"Well said." A distant murmur drifted through the room, but Louisa barely registered it. In that instant, the world dissolved, leaving only Will. Her Will. Her heart flooded with a warmth so intense, a joy so profound, that it could only be love.

He locked gazes with her for a moment longer, visibly reluctant to break the special moment they shared.

Then he moved on to George. "I also made some enemies."

"Hear, hear," George said in a bored tone. He'd crossed his arms and legs and kept the sneer on his face.

Reverend Graham shook his head in exasperation. "I've never seen such rivalry and unbridled antipathy between two young people. Their enmity was legendary and the whole town talked about it. They couldn't miss an opportunity to taunt and torment each other." He pointed a finger at Will. "You were no innocent bystander, mind you. You were as bad as he was, if not worse." His finger rested on George, who studied his fingernails.

"What did he do?" Lieutenant Carey leaned forward, eager to hear some stories about his hallowed superior.

"They almost killed each other." Mrs Graham shook her head. "I remember the time when Will returned home, beaten to a pulp by this one here." She gave George a disapproving look.

"Yes, the good old days," George said. "You were rather short and chubby and easy to punch. Like a sack of flour." He clenched his hand into a fist and punched it in the air. "You didn't know how to fight then, couldn't run. A fine target. I had to practise my boxing skills with someone. Inconceivable how someone like that ended up as a major. The military must be more corrupt than one thinks."

All five officers jumped to attention but froze when Will lifted his hand.

"Yes, a fine target for you and your gang of boys. You never had the guts to face me alone, did you? It is easy to beat up a boy when it is five against one. But what I lacked in physical strength, I made up for cunning and strategy, which you completely lacked, and I must confess that I enjoyed coming up with the most devious plans of revenge to get back at you. I still wonder how stupid one had to be to step into an awkwardly laid trap in the forest as you did. It screamed for five miles what it was. But cunning wasn't your forte, was it? So naturally, you stepped into it."

George hissed and looked ready to shoot out of his chair. They would have flown at each other if Lieutenant Miller hadn't clamped his hand on his shoulder and pushed him back down.

"You did, indeed. You nearly killed me when you lured me onto a rickety bridge and let me fall into the river."

"You knew how to swim." Will brushed it away.

"And another time when you set that blasted trap for me and left me there until nightfall. If our groom hadn't found me, I would have spent the entire night out there." George scowled.

"It wasn't John who found you," a gentle voice spoke up. Celeste. "It was me. I knew what they were up to, of course, George and Will and Louisa." She nodded at them. "You always thought I was too young and disregarded me. But that night I saw how Will set the trap, and George stepped into it, and it was I who set you free."

"Did you, by Jove?" There was open admiration on Lieutenant Carey's face, which Louisa noted with interest.

"One thing that remains remarkably consistent about George is that he keeps underestimating people. That includes Celeste." Will gave her a curt bow. "I knew you were following us, of course."

Celeste flushed with pleasure.

"This was one scheme that worked out to the dot of the i. Wonderful memories." Will grinned. "It might interest you to know that I later used the same trick in the mountains of Salamanca, and the French fell for it as naively as George did. Turns out you did your country a service by offering yourself as an experimental subject. It worked like a charm."

"Go to blazes." George scowled.

Reverend Graham sighed. "Much as I liked you, Will, you had an overly active imagination and a tendency to run wild and cause much trouble. Would you like to tell us what happened the night you got arrested, and how you survived transportation?"

"I'm thinking that that part of the story would be best told by George," Will said quietly.

"No, thank you. I refuse." George's voice was heavy with boredom.

"Very well, then, I will." Will made several turns around the room and stopped in front of Highworth, who was taking a pinch of snuff from his enamel snuff box. When Will stopped in front of him, he hastily closed the snuff box again. "It was all because of you."

Highworth nearly dropped his snuff box. "By Jove. Was it? What, exactly?"

"You and Milford came up with the grotesque idea of marrying Louisa to George. If you hadn't come up with that harebrained notion, things in my life might well have turned out differently."

"Oh, that." Highworth waved it away. "It was Milford's idea. A mad scheme, to be sure, but Louisa would have none of it. I went along with it at first to humour him, but in time, it became clear that he had only one purpose regarding this union, and that was the financial gain it would bring. Milford and I were friends, yes, but not friends enough to give him my daughter so he could get a hand on my fortune."

"I only wish, Papa, that you'd been as clear about this then as you are now. Much suffering could've been avoided if you had," Louisa said with sorrow in her voice.

"Eh? Didn't I say that from the beginning? That you're my precious little girl and that I would never force you to accept the suit of someone who wasn't welcome? And why would you ever doubt me?"

Louisa sighed.

"All I ever wanted for you was to accept the suit of someone who'd add to our family's consequence. For fortune we have enough. I thought George over there would fit the bill, but I did not know then that his father would leave the estate encumbered with debt."

George did not move a muscle in his face as he drummed his fingers on the armrest of his chair.

"Be that as it may, you agreed to an engagement party." Will's jaw clenched at the memory.

"What engagement party?" Highworth scoffed. "It was to be a nice get-together, rather like this one. Except that Milford had the foolish notion of pushing the engagement between our children. Louisa clearly didn't care for it, and neither did that one"—he pointed with his thumb at George—"so I didn't see the point in pressing the matter. They were children, after all. But Milford was surprisingly mule-headed about it. We had a row, and the next morning we left. The end."

Will's eyebrows rose almost to his hairline. "You have forgotten a considerable chunk of the story, haven't you, Highworth?"

"I don't see what I should have forgotten. Was there something else?"

"The part where Will broke in and stole the silver." George yawned.

Silence fell over the room. Then they all spoke at the same time.

"Tosh and nonsense. Although now that you mention it, I seem to recall there was a commotion outside in the hall that night." Highworth rubbed his eyebrows. "Then the butler came in to tell us that there had been a burglary, but they'd apprehended the thief with the loot. He was taken to the magistrate." Highworth shrugged. "That's all there is to it, as far as I was concerned." A jolt passed through his frame, and he straightened his shoulders as understanding sank in. "Jove's beard. That ill-mannered rascal spewing forth the foulest language, was you?"

"Right on the button," George chimed in.

A flicker of pain crossed Will's face, masked quickly by a scowl. But Louisa saw the look of bleakness flash through his eyes before he hooded them. The confident facade he presented to the room crumbled, replaced by the haunted eyes of a lost boy. He was struggling internally, thrashing in a sea of hostile voices, drowning. In that moment, everything clicked into place. She understood why he was doing this. This wasn't just a supper; it was a desperate attempt to reclaim his honour.

Louisa rose and glided to his side, her hand finding his and pressing it firmly.

"Nonsense. Will never stole any silver," she said in a quiet, firm voice that cut through the room. Then, in barely a whisper, only for him to hear, "I will not let you sink, Will." She used to tell him that when she'd taught him to swim. "Never again."

His head snapped up, his gaze raw with emotion. Tears welled in his eyes. He gave a curt nod and a single, grateful squeeze of his hand, and proceeded cling to it as if she were his lifeline.

"We had an argument about this," Louisa addressed the room, "for Will was worried about me being pressed into an engagement I did not want, but to me, the matter was never up for discussion. So I invited him to see for himself that his worries were entirely unfounded."

"I took her at her word, and showed up on this very doorstep that evening." Will continued, having regained his composure. "As far as I was concerned, Louisa would only get engaged to George over my dead body."

"Hear, hear," George drawled. "Well, you got close. Punishment for a felony is hanging."

"Yes, on looking back, that nearly happened, except—"

"You're notoriously difficult to kill. I believe you've already sufficiently belaboured that point. Our judicial system seems to be rotten to the core if they let someone guilty of burglary and felony off to make a career in the army," he sneered. "Didn't your Field Marshall admit that the common soldier was nothing more than the dregs of society, the 'scum of the earth'? The stories of the atrocities you and your men have committed in Badajoz have reached us as well. All the raping, plundering, and other brutalities. No doubt you set a prime example there and proved his point true."

"How dare you? You lying, perfidious scoundrel!" Will would have thrown himself at George if Louisa hadn't pulled him back.

"He's not worth it, Will. Please." Louisa clung to him.

Instead, Will's aides-de-camp rushed forward, throwing over the coffee table. The petit fours went flying in all directions.

Chaos broke out. Wexham lunged, Highworth leapt back with an oath, and the ladies screamed.

Amid the pandemonium, the door to the antechamber opened, and a cool, crisp voice with a slightly nasal accent said, "I must say. The story has come to a frustrating standstill. I perceive the need to intervene."

Heads turned, and everyone froze.

An elegantly styled gentleman in a blue frock coat and white neckcloth stood in the doorway, surveying the scene.

Louisa's legs gave way as she sank against Will, gasping.

"Stap me vitals," Highworth breathed.

The soldiers, all five of them, including Wexford, fell into a military salute.

One of the officers dropped George, whom he had been holding by the collar.

Will supported Louisa with one arm while saluting with the other. "Your Grace."

The tall, hawk-nosed gentleman nodded, his quizzing glass dangling from his fingers. "Sir Robert. My dear friend. Pray, what is the meaning of all this? You are not about to brawl in front of the ladies, are you? In uniform, too," said the Duke of Wellington as he strode into the drawing room.

Chapter Twenty-Five

Wellington surveyed the room, which had fallen into reverent silence, and his eyes rested on Louisa. "Ah. Our charming Incomparable." He walked over, and Louisa recollected her wits.

"Your Grace," she stammered.

"You have already made my wife's acquaintance, Your Grace?" Will asked.

"Naturally." He bowed. "What a pleasure to meet you again, Lady Ashford. The last time we met, I recall, at the ball shortly after the Victory Parade, you were surrounded by a thick ring of admirers, like an impregnable fortress. To exchange a single word with you, one had to penetrate their ranks and infiltrate like a skilful tactician. I, however, persevered and was able to secure your hand for the Cotillon. A rare feat, indeed!"

Louisa smiled at him politely. She searched her memory, but for the life of her, she couldn't recall dancing with him. She might have, of course. She probably did. Because it had been so long ago, she could not remember the event with any certainty. From the scandalised look on her stepmother's face, she guessed it was rather terrible of her not to remember dancing with the one and only legend of Europe.

"However, it must be said that the ultimate prize of victory has been won by our Sir Robert here." He slapped him on the shoulder. "Finally. I never thought I'd live to see the day. You are the envy of all Englishmen. I congratulate you most heartily on your nuptials, my friend. It was about time."

"Thank you, Your Grace."

The rest of the introductions were made. "Highworth." Wellington nodded to Louisa's father. "We must go hunting again when the opportunity presents itself. My foxhounds are always up for a good hunt, as am I."

"Indeed, Your Grace, any time. It would be an honour," Highworth replied, wiping his forehead with his handkerchief.

Wilbur, Mary, and the Reverend and Mrs Graham first looked at the duke with polite reserve, then with awed wonder as introductions were made and realisation dawned as to who he was. Wilbur's jaw dropped, Reverend Graham's eyes popped, and the ladies blushed as the duke addressed charming words to each of them.

Wellington accepted a cup of tea and sat in a chair near the fireplace, crossing his legs. "But to continue a most thrilling story. You were in the midst of what I assume was an explanation of your innocence, while he" —he pointed at George—"insists that you're a thief and a scoundrel who should be hanged, even quoting my very own words. Indeed, I may have referred to my men as 'scum of the earth' on one or more occasions. It is a fact that most of my men come from less-than-stellar backgrounds. However, I also believe that their military experience has honed them into deadly weapons and moulded them into men of distinction. War, undoubtedly, is a horror that brings out the worst in men. A great regret of mine is that I could not prevent the events in Badajoz. I know for a fact that Sir Robert here made every effort to intervene and prevent the atrocities, but the mob was beyond our control. In Badajoz, we witnessed the worst side of humanity, yet we also saw the best. There was courage, heroism, and unwavering loyalty that surpassed anything I have ever seen. Sir Robert here is a prime example." He nodded at Will. "Sir Robert, I suggest you carry on with the story before we hear the other side. I must ask that there be no interjections until he has finished. Proceed."

Will, still clinging to Louisa's hand, resumed his story.

"I believe I was recounting when I sought admittance to this house. But no matter how much I protested that Miss Highworth had invited me, the butler wouldn't let me in. I slipped in through the servants' entrance."

He let the effect of his words sink in. "Note that I did not break in. Note that on my way in I exchanged a word with the cook, who slipped me a biscuit. The cook's name is Mrs Ellen Marley, and I believe she is still alive and well, living in Dorchester. She can be called as a witness at any time. In the corridor just outside this door"—he pointed to the heavy oak door—"two footmen stopped me. I had the impression that they were waiting for me. A third came and threw a knapsack at my feet, accusing me of stealing the silver in the dining room." He paused. "I had never set foot in that room. I had seen none of the silver. My protests were unheard, and before I knew it, I was being dragged off to Dorchester gaol."

He looked grim, his voice trembling slightly. "I was not guilty, yet unable to prove my innocence. Through a quirk of fate, I seized the chance to enlist, than to face a trial that would undoubtedly convict me of felony. I'd barely turned sixteen when I enlisted. You know the rest, Your Grace."

Wellington nodded.

"I daresay all of us military men do," Wexford spoke up. "But the ladies, I suppose, do not, and neither do the others."

"The long and short of it is that, despite the odds being against me, I survived all adverse circumstances including the raging fever that nearly wiped out an entire regiment, and with the help of Wexford who bought me commissions, I was able to rise swiftly through the ranks until you find me here."

"That is a gross oversimplification. Let me take up the story from the point at which you enlisted," Wexford rubbed his hands, eager to say his part. "That is where I come in. When I was a colonel, Sir Robert, who was a mere shrimp of a boy then, saved my life during a skirmish in Saint Lucia. I was hit and left for dead, even though it was a clean shot through the shoulder. I lost consciousness as I fell and was left buried under a pile of corpses. Undaunted, Robert entered enemy territory to find me. At significant risk to his own life, he dragged me out and into the jungle, where we took cover. We spent three, four days in hiding until we were found. Robert looked after me the entire time. I was deeply impressed by the boy's wit, courage, and spunk. He reminded me much of my own son, whom I lost too soon. I also owed him my life. I therefore had no qualms at all about becoming his mentor, and over time our bond grew as close as that of father and son. He is my heir to everything but my title."

"It was the greatest honour of my life when you bestowed your name on me," Will said, deeply moved.

"I saw the boy's potential and realised he'd be better off in the 95th Rifles. He had all the necessary qualities of quick thinking, independence, and marksmanship that a rifleman needed. I helped him obtain a commission as a lieutenant just as I changed regiments. We returned to Europe just in time for the Peninsular Wars. He rose quickly through the ranks, not only through commissions but also through merit, until he ended up in the Royal Scots, where he is now."

Wellington nodded, tapping a finger on his chin. "He first came to my attention after the Forlorn Hope he'd successfully led at Vimeiro, which was a miracle in and of itself that he survived. This boy unites an interesting blend of daredevilry, unsurpassed bravery, exceptional strategic talent, and keen leadership. I personally made sure he received his promotions because I needed him on my staff. You all know the story of Vitoria?"

"I cannot say that I do, Your Grace. What, exactly, happened at Vitoria?" Reverend Graham spoke up, causing all the men to gasp in outrage.

"He swam across the swollen and impassable river under enemy fire to prevent a bridge from being blown up. Thanks to this extraordinary act of bravery, we crossed the river and cut off the enemy from the coast, which ensured our victory. We wouldn't have done it without this extraordinary act of bravery. Hence, the Hero of Vitoria."

"Although, it must be said, the actual hero is here." Will placed his arm around Louisa's shoulders. "For she is the one who taught me to swim. Without Louisa, this never would have happened."

"I commend you for that, my lady. You have done your country a great service." Wellington bowed to her.

Louisa frowned. "No, no, it was John. John, the groom, taught me to swim. And then I taught Will. If we are to dole out medals of praise, he is the one who should receive one."

"That is indeed a splendid idea. Is the fellow around?" Wellington asked.

"John may have retired in the meantime," Will said. "One would have to look for him."

"Do that." Wellington nodded. "Now, to finish the story. By the time Waterloo rolled around, Sir Robert had made himself indispensable to me as an officer on my staff, and I relied on him for accurate assessments of tactics and strategy that greatly contributed to our victory. Sir Robert is not only a highly respected officer, but has become a reliable friend. He's rather like me in that he refuses the prospect of defeat, and as far as we know, he's only ever lost a private battle, once." He coughed discreetly into his hand and glanced at Louisa, who blushed. "But here, too, after overcoming some difficulties, he eventually succeeded."

Someone clapped slowly.

"Hail to the conquering heroes," George said wearily. "Note the plural. I am quite overwhelmed by all this heroism. The presence of His Grace, legendary as he is, isn't enough, it seems. Will's heroism must be pressed upon us as well. I gather you've successfully driven the point home, and the long and short of it, judging by the way you speak, Your Grace, that if it weren't for Will, we'd all have gone to Hades and lost the war miserably."

"Indeed, Milford." The duke turned to him and crossed his arms over his chest. "Do carry on."

"Ah, it's my turn now, yes? As to how I kicked him down the path of heroism? Very well." He stood with a grin that resembled more of a leer. Louisa remembered with sorrow what a handsome boy he'd once been. Now his face was bloated with dissipation, and the lustre of his hair had dulled.

"Yes, tell us, finally, why you have such a problem with me," Will bit out.

George shook his head. "I have no problem with you." He paused. "I just don't like your face. Never have. Doubt I ever will."

Will shrugged. "That's mutual."

"I didn't like that he'd caught my father's attention, prompting him to spout nonsense about paying him a scholarship to Eton."

Reverend Graham sat up. "Yes, he did, indeed. I'd approached him about it. I did not have the financial means to pay for his studies myself, and it was becoming increasingly clear that I was reaching my limits when it came to teaching the boy. I thought it would be best if he went to school. I approached your father to see if he would be willing to be a patron. He met the boy, was impressed, and agreed. In the end nothing came of it, because Milford got himself into financial difficulties and needed the money himself."

"I don't know what it is about you that all the men you meet want to become your patron," George scoffed. "But I didn't like the fact that the scant attention my father gave me was now completely withdrawn and given to that chubby little rat."

"Ah. I see," Will said softly. "Jealousy. That explains some things."

"You were an insufferable know-it-all, an insolent big mouth, and a good-for-nothing cur."

"You therefore had to bully and beat me up regularly."

"That goes without saying."

"Which you were fairly good at in those days, because you were physically superior. Note the past tense." Will stood tall and strong in front of him to show that their roles had now changed. "And I would retaliate a tit for a tat."

George brushed him off. "Most of your capers were rather juvenile and only shocked the ladies at the tea table ..."

"... with the pig's bladder." His lips twitched into a half-smile. "The look on their faces was beyond anything one could ever have imagined."

A vague answering smile tugged at the corners of

George's lips. "Or the time when you put a dead mouse in my boot."

"A servant left them outside the door to dry and I couldn't resist."

"Except that one went awry, and it was the boots of my father's valet. We had the same boot size. He shrieked like a girl."

George and Will grinned at each other.

Wellington took out his pocket watch and consulted it demonstratively.

"But that last trick of yours was a mean one, and it nearly cost me my life." Will looked grim. "Come, George. The time has come to confess. Why did you set me up?"

A sneer passed over George's face, and it did not appear, at first, as though he would speak. Then he shrugged. "Very well. The truth? You stole my girl, and you needed to be punished."

Will's head snapped up. "I did what?"

Louisa frowned. "I beg your pardon, but I was never your girl."

George looked at her as if he were seeing her for the first time. "In my mind, you were. Both our fathers even agreed that we should marry."

"Now, see here," Highworth began, but George raised a hand.

"You never even exchanged a single kind word with me," Louisa said. "When you weren't ignoring me, you were horrid to me, pulling my hair and making me fall. You broke my dolls. You said you'd marry me over my dead body. Not that it mattered, because the point was moot to me. Besides, we were only children."

"That's commonly how boys express their affection. The more they protest, the more they hide their true feelings," George said with a smirk, and to Louisa's horror, some of the uniformed men nodded in agreement.

"That is absurd."

"It is the truth. I was head over heels in love with you. But I never stood a chance, did I?" He pointed a finger at Will. "He stole not only my father's attention, but also you. I knew he was coming that evening because I overheard you talking in the forest that day. So, I hatched a plan. As soon as you appeared, my footmen would stop you and a third one would claim that you'd stolen the silver. I bribed them heavily, of course. I was the son of the house, and next to my father, my word had to be kept. Thought it was the only way to get rid of you. Figured they'd lock you away, and the engagement could go ahead undisturbed." He shrugged. "Worked like clockwork, too, up to a certain point."

Will exhaled. "Did you even consider, for more than half a second, the consequences I was facing?"

"I knew you'd be thrown into prison. I thought you'd be released eventually, with my father, Reverend Graham here, and Highworth sure to step up. Surely, his daughter would throw a tantrum, and her father would have him released in no time. Egad! That didn't happen."

"Because I didn't know he had been taken to prison." Louisa wailed. Will increased the pressure of her hand to comfort her.

"Neither did I, by Jove." Highworth shook his head.

"I confess I was somewhat taken aback when they said you had been shipped off for transportation," George continued. "Not sure how that came about. But the entire village knew by nightfall."

"What you're saying now is that it was a vicious boy's prank gone awry." Will's nostrils flared.

George hesitated. "I didn't like you, Will. But that didn't mean I wanted you dead."

"You could've fooled me."

Silence fell.

"But," George said, "It was all good for something, eh? He survived, he won the war, he got the girl, he got the house." He waved his hand about. "I didn't know that Ashford fellow who bought this crumbling pile of stones here was you. Not that it matters. It was a fair deal, and I got it off my hands. You got everything you ever wanted. Medals. Honours. A knighthood. You even got me to confess. Enemy vanquished and publicly humiliated. Revenge complete. What more do you want, pray?"

Will closed his eyes for a moment. When he opened them, he said, "All I ever wanted was to prove my innocence. That is what I lived for. To regain my honour. To clear my name." He looked at Wellington.

"I see now. The driving force behind all these theatricals." Wellington waved his quizzing glass about the room. "Honour. The desire to prove to me, in particular, that you're not scum of the earth. Am I correct?"

"Yes." Will swallowed. "Because you're my superior, someone I've admired since I can remember. Because it is of immense importance to me you all"—he emphasised the word and turned to make eye contact, one-by-one, with Wexford, Reverend Graham, Wilbur, Highworth and lastly, Louisa—"all know for certain that I am not a thief."

A heavy, suffocating weight pressed down on Louisa. She could have prevented so much suffering if she hadn't had that one moment of hesitation, of doubt.

Wilbur blinked his eyes and cleared his throat. "For what it's worth, Will, I never believed it. You were a whirlwind of a mischievous rascal, that you were. But crime? That just wasn't you. I always knew in my heart of hearts that you were innocent, and that you'd make it, somehow."

"Thank you, my friend," Will whispered. "You do not know how much those words mean to me."

"I am overwhelmed with gratitude to see how well you have done for yourself," Reverend Graham said. "Well done, William." He got up and squeezed his shoulder.

"Without your intercession, things would have gone badly indeed," Will said. "I felt like I never thanked you enough."

"Nonsense, boy," Reverend Graham said gruffly.

"It never mattered to me either way, because you never had to prove anything to me, son." Wexford stood beside him. "It's good to have the truth out, and I suspect this is all more for you than for us. We all believe you are innocent. Now we know it for a fact."

"At the root of all the trouble, a woman. The delectable Louisa. You play a similar role to the fair Helen, do you not? Men go to war over her," Wellington commented.

Miss Louisa's Final Waltz

Louisa looked ill. "Surely not!"

An amused smile played about his austere face. "Do not take it to heart, Lady Ashford. I was merely jesting."

But there was a kernel of truth in his words. Seeing George in the corner, scowling, she braced herself and said, "You have the honour of being my very first in a long line of rejected suitors, George. I suppose that counts for something. We were children then, and I think neither of us fully realised the consequences of our actions. Peace?"

He nodded after a moment's hesitation.

"She apologises to him, but not to me," Will grumbled.

"To you, I'll have to atone for the rest of my life," Louisa responded. "Knowing you, you'll never let me forget this."

At that, Will smiled. His hazel eyes lit up just like her childhood Will's eyes used to, full of happiness and sweet mischief, and she almost gasped.

George's voice intruded. "I must confess, I felt rather better after the long list of names of rejected suitors appeared in the Gazette. As for you," he turned to Will, "it pains me to say it, but dash it, very well, here it is. I suppose I owe you an apology."

"Hear, hear," said Wilbur, who clapped slowly.

Will looked at George with surprise.

George pulled up a corner of his mouth wryly. "You have to understand you embodied everything I ever wanted. You do so even now. Look at you." His hands motioned at his uniform. "I wanted to enlist; did you know? But Father wouldn't let me, flat out refused to buy me a commission."

"Well then, Milford." Will crossed his arms and assessed him. "I wonder whether you have it in you. I doubt you'd survive a fortnight marching with the occupation forces in France. What do you think, Your Grace?" Will turned to the duke, who steepled his long fingers together.

"A month at the most." The duke weighed his head back and forth.

"I wager less!" One of the duke's aides-de-camp spoke up.

"Agreed," replied another.

"Milford?" Will looked at him with a raised eyebrow. "If you pick up that gauntlet, know that I will watch you with a hawk's eyes. Everything you say and do will be under scrutiny and reported directly to me. By Jove, I'll make your life difficult, and I'm going to enjoy every single second of it."

George shrugged. "Do your worst, Major. You'll find I don't break that easily."

Will turned to Wellington. "Your Grace?"

He folded his arms. "Let him try. It's a suitable punishment for sure."

George stood up straight, as if a lightning bolt seemed to pass through him at those words. "It will be an honour to serve you, Your Grace," he said. "And you as well ... Major. I won't give you any reason to regret this."

He bowed curtly and left the room.

"Well," Louisa said slowly. "That was a rather unexpected turn of events. Ladies and gentlemen, after all this excitement, surely you must be craving some nourishment. I believe the supper table is ready."

Louisa only reluctantly let go of Will's hand, which she'd been holding the entire time. Wellington offered her his arm to lead her to the dining room, where he told everyone about his legendary exploits during the wars.

"Tell me, is Bonaparte truly the monster everyone says he is?" Louisa asked. "Because judging from your stories, you seem to have a considerable amount of respect for him, despite everything."

"Despite everything." Wellington leaned back in his seat thoughtfully. "Would you like the truth, Lady Ashford?"

"If you please, Your Grace."

"The truth is, I never met the man personally. We only fought against each other once in Waterloo. Even then I could not get a clear view of him because it rained that dark day. It is a fact that amongst all his field marshals, none could match his calibre. I believe his presence on the battlefield to be worth that of forty thousand men. Let us be clear. I respect his prowess as a commander, but do not believe he is a gentleman. But neither do I deem him to be the monster some claim. The true monsters on this earth are found buried deep within us, and we battle against them daily."

"Profound words," Wexford nodded. "I am entirely in agreement."

The last guests had retired, and the clock on the mantelpiece chimed the early morning hours.

"We are the only ones here now," Will commented, stating the obvious as he leaned back in his chair.

There was a moment's silence in the room, thick with unspoken emotion. Louisa traced the pattern of the crochet doily on the coffee table, unable to meet Will's gaze. When she finally dared to steal a glance at him, his eyes were already on her, a flicker of something warm igniting deep within them.

Will looked away, picked up his glass with cherry liquor and swirled the liquid round and round in the glass as if it were the most fascinating thing ever.

She could bear it no longer.

The chair scraped on the wooden floor as he got up. Then she was engulfed by his heat and masculine smell as he knelt next to her, wrapped his arms around her tightly, and rested his head on hers.

She was aware of him, how large he was, and the own thumping of her heart, which seemed tremendously loud and surely must be echoing through the room.

When she finally dared to lift her gaze, her eyes met his, and the melting intensity she found there stole her breath. Her stomach somersaulted.

"And now?" she whispered.

"Now, my lovely Lulu, madam wife …" He smiled slowly, and his low voice was filled with a promise that sparked a delicious shiver down her spine.

With one fluid motion, he swept her into his arms. She let out a small squeak of surprise as he carried her up the stairs, two steps at a time.

Chapter Twenty-Six

THE NEXT DAY, THE DUKE AND WEXFORD LEFT before dawn.

The carriage had pulled up. Wellington put on his bicorne and nodded at Will. "You know, I am loath to grant my staff officers any leave of absence. I shall make an exception in your case. I suppose a fortnight's honeymoon will do? I expect you to be back at headquarters in Cambrai in time for the manoeuvres."

"Yes, sir. I appreciate it. I wish you a speedy and safe journey, Your Grace." Will clasped his hand firmly.

"We will ride through without a stop, except at Dover." The duke bent over Louisa's hand. "Paris is beautiful at this time of the year. The social scene is vibrant, and you will make a charming addition to it. I look forward to welcoming you to my place in Mont St Martin."

With those words and another nod at Will, the duke and his three aides-de-camp left.

Will turned to embrace his father. Wexford then

drew Louisa in an embrace. "We will meet again soon in France." He swung himself onto his horse and left to join the duke's party.

"There he goes to join the Iron Duke. Next to Nelson, the greatest military hero our nation has ever seen," Will said.

"Says one hero about another." Louisa rubbed her arms in the chilly early morning air.

Will shook his head. "No. I may have brought home a medal or two, but I certainly don't feel like a hero, not even close. Wellington is a legend. He has changed the course of history."

The first grey rays of dawn crept over the horizon. The remaining guests were still sleeping, and would be until midday, if not later, after the late night.

Louisa and Will had not slept at all. A rosy blush covered her cheeks, and a warm glow of happiness engulfed her.

"Let us walk to the lake and watch the sunrise," she said impulsively.

Wrapped in warm woollen cloaks and shawls, they walked through the forest to the lake, holding hands.

"So, it appears we are going to France?" she asked.

"Yes." He gave her a quick look. "I have no intention of selling out. Not until I reach the rank of general, that is. I'm furiously ambitious, but you probably know that. Would it be a problem for you to come with me to France?" He held out his hand to help her over a fallen tree. "I won't force you if you'd rather not. You could stay at Wexford Hall if you prefer. Or anywhere else. I can buy you a house in London, even."

She shook her head. "No. I think I'd like that, to live on the Continent for a while. It would be an adventure."

"The troops are stationed in Cambrai, which is a charming town not lacking in social entertainment. His Grace entertains lavishly in Mont St Martin. Lieutenant Carey has found us a villa nearby, large enough to accommodate your parents should they decide to join us. You will be exceedingly busy and much in demand as a hostess, Louisa. You won't have a moment's peace. They'll adore you."

She supposed it would be a busy life, indeed. But she also wanted to do something other than being a society hostess. She just did not know what.

They reached the shore of the lake. Will dragged a tree stump from the undergrowth for them to sit on, for the ground was cold and damp.

"Are you happy with last night's events?" Louisa probed. "Did it all develop according to your expectations?"

Will picked up a twig and played with it. "It went well. Better than expected, actually. You can't imagine the weight that has been taken from my shoulders. I've been carrying it around with me all this time."

"I can only imagine how much it must have meant to you." A boy who'd never had the chance to prove his innocence could finally do so eleven years later.

"George is only partly right about this being part of an elaborate revenge plan," he said suddenly. "Certainly, it is gratifying to be the master of a place that belonged to my former enemy. But this is the only reason I bought this place." Will waved at the lake. "Glubbdubdrib. There is no other reason."

"Of course," Louisa said softly.

"And because of you." He looked ahead, the first rays of the sun now touching on his face. He closed his eyes as he spoke. "You are the reason I have made it all the way to where I am now. You're the motivation behind everything. That night, before they dragged me away, the former Milford told me I wasn't worthy of you; he told me to forget you, that our union was, and always would be impossible. That someone like me wasn't worthy of even kissing the tips of your toes. I'd expected your father to spew such nonsense, but surprisingly, he never did. It was Milford. And when I refused to let you go, he refused to help me in prison."

Louisa nodded. "Papa may come across as high in the instep, but he really isn't. When it comes to choosing family or fortune, he will always choose family. But Milford?" She shook her head. "How sad he turned out to be like this."

"Milford is cut of a different wood. It was he who wanted me destroyed. As for your father, I think he felt sorry for me, but he didn't spare me a thought when he packed you off to London. That night in gaol, when I was at my most desperate, I swore to myself that I would clear my name, get my revenge, and prove myself worthy of my girl. That gave me the will to survive, Lulu. I would prove them wrong. I would prove the entire world wrong. You were my light. In those dark, cold nights out on the battlefields, amidst all the horror and gore, you were the one who kept me going."

"And then I didn't even recognise you." Her voice wobbled. "As if that wasn't enough, I humiliated you and you became a laughingstock. That caricature!" She hid her face in her hands.

He laughed softly. "Yes, that brought me down a few notches. You wouldn't even give me the chance to explain who I was."

She frowned. "You hemmed and hawed. You should have just come right out with it and said who you were."

"But I did. And while you didn't exactly slap me like that other poor fellow, you slapped me verbally instead."

Louisa frowned. "You were just like the others. You uttered the same inane platitudes. Except then you went ahead and distinguished yourself by being even more asinine than the rest."

"I went up to you and said, 'Look at me, Louisa, don't you know who I am?'" As soon as the words were out of his mouth, awareness crossed his face, and he smacked his hand against his forehead. "Oh." He winced. "I see. That was indeed an asinine thing to say. You were surrounded by fools, each more pretentious than the other, and then I came along, vain and eager to impress, and promptly put my foot in my mouth. You must have thought me an arrogant ass, one who made an unforgivable social blunder by addressing you by your first name, to boot. No wonder you were angry with me before we even had a chance to talk properly."

She'd said some things that now made her wince. She'd been so unimpressed by him she'd merely given him a look that cut him to shreds and turned away.

"You gave me the cut direct." He uttered a short

laugh, as if he still couldn't believe it. "You were absolutely terrifying. I swear, Louisa, it would have saved us much trouble if you could've given the French forces the same look you gave me. You would've stopped the enemy in their tracks, and they would have retreated with their tails between their legs without a single shot being fired."

"You were ... annoyingly persistent. And annoyingly predictable. You'd had your introduction, your dance; of course, you'd take me out on the veranda where you'd spit out a proposal. They all did."

He threw up his hands in defeat.

"You started by boasting of your exploits on the battlefield."

"To impress you, of course. It had worked well with your father, but it was the wrong strategy with you. I only accomplished the opposite and gave you a disgust of me, and a complete refusal to listen to anything else I had to say."

"And I brushed it all off and called you a tin soldier."

"That still hurts." He placed a hand over his heart.

"I thought you were aggravating, impertinent, and too full of yourself." Louisa rubbed her eyebrow.

"You humiliated me in the worst way possible. My pride still smarts every time I think about it. You didn't think I'd just let that go, did you?"

"You've always been terribly efficient at devising intricate plans of revenge," she agreed. "I just never thought I'd ever be at the receiving end of it."

"I was flabbergasted and furious. I'd obviously put you on a pedestal and didn't know how to deal with the reality of you. I decided to teach you a lesson. But how?

One night at the club, I overheard your father ranting about you and your stubbornness. He was deep in the cups, otherwise he wouldn't have been so careless as to shout, '*Pon my word, and if it is the very next beggar she runs across, she will marry him!*'" He imitated her father's tone, which brought a slight smile to her lips.

"Indeed. I came up with a revised battle plan, and it was brilliant. I would be that beggar. I was convinced that you'd become cold and cruel, and that you'd deserved it. The plan was to give you a taste of your own medicine, to turn the tables on you and to soundly reject you at the moment of your vows, in front of witnesses, too. I'd humble you thoroughly, just as you did with me and all your other suitors. Well, my plan backfired spectacularly, didn't it?" he chuckled softly. "I expected you to recognise me eventually, if not as Will, then as that tin soldier you'd so thoroughly ridiculed. But to my utter astonishment, you didn't recognise me. To say I was stunned is an understatement. You were so beautiful, proud, and heartbreakingly lonely. And when I looked into your eyes, deep down, there was such sadness inside. It was then that I knew that I'd got you wrong. We all had. That icy shell was something you'd built around yourself to protect yourself. Deep down you were still the same Lulu. And it occurred to me that maybe that sadness had something to do with me. And I wanted, no, I needed to find out if that was true. It became an obsession. So, I threw out my beautiful, elaborately plotted revenge plan then and there. I couldn't keep it up for ten minutes in your company. Everything that happened afterwards—the marriage, the journey to Dorset, the hut

—none of it was planned. It was all because I followed you, because I wanted to know where it would lead us."

She looked at him in silence.

He crouched down on his haunches, looking searchingly into her face. "Louisa. And now? Are we good?"

She smiled sadly. "If you mean to ask whether I have forgiven you for trifling with me, pretending to be a costermonger, tricking me into marrying you, the answer is yes. If you mean to ask whether I can forgive myself for not having been there for you when you needed me the most, then I might still need some time."

He framed her face between his hands and leaned his forehead against hers. "I love you desperately, Louisa. You know that, don't you? I shall remind you of this daily from now on, for the rest of our lives. You have possessed my heart and soul from that moment I was alone on the lake in the boat and you by the shore. I thought you were a magical fairy princess, and I was so startled and entranced I fell out of the boat and nearly drowned. And then you saved me. Not only from drowning, but you saved me in many other ways. You were vulnerable then, and sad, and all I wanted was to make you laugh. It hurt me to see you sad, then, and it hurts me now. Do not carry regret with you, Lulu. Whatever happened to me was fate, and I made the best of it. I don't regret now that it happened. Not a single thing. So let us both stop looking backwards, for the past is of no significance. Let go of thoughts of 'if only I had done this', or what we could or should have said differently. Can we do that together?"

"I love you too, Will," she whispered. "I always have.

And I will try my best to let go and stop mulling over the past."

Then, being characteristically Will, he had to ruin the moment lest it was becoming too emotional. "And like you said earlier, you have the rest of your life to make amends. I like that notion immensely. I don't give my forgiveness easily, you see, and I will make you work very hard for it." There was a cheeky twinkle in his eyes that belied his words.

"Something tells me you'll remind me of this for the rest of my life," Louisa muttered.

For a while, they listened in silence to the water lapping against the shore. Will stole a glance at Louisa, her profile softened by the golden light. A wave of tenderness washed over him. He longed to erase the hurt he'd caused, to build a future worthy of her love.

"What a shame you really aren't a costermonger. I wouldn't have minded staying a costermonger's wife." She leaned her head against him. "Truly. I would have been rather good at selling those vegetables in the marketplace. We would have made excellent business partners."

"Alas, my Lulu. You will have to be content with being a mere tin soldier's wife." He chuckled as she hid her face in his arm with a groan.

"I was thinking, Will, about what to do now. I had such plans to open my own business in the market. You know. Soap, I thought. There is a shocking lack of proper soap here; it seems to be terribly expensive. Or I could paint porcelain vases and sell them. Or I could learn how to weave baskets. Maybe I could even teach the children in a village school. But now ..." She frowned. "I will be an excellent society lady and hostess, never fear. Our soirees and parties will be the best in all of Paris. But I would like to have some purpose other than that. I would like to set up an organisation, or a foundation. To help young ladies who, like Celeste, through the quirks of fate, have not been fortunate enough to find a suitable match. Perhaps a school for young ladies. And oh, speaking of Celeste, I would like it if we could invite her to join us. I would like to help her find a match. Especially now that her brother will be enlisting. Not that he ever did much for her." She made a face.

"Celeste is a sweet girl. I admit my enthusiasm for helping George marry off his sister is limited. But if that is what your heart is set on, then of course I will support you. I will support you in anything you want to do." He looked up and gazed across the lake.

"Look, the sun is rising over Glubbdubdrib," he said softly. "Isn't it magical? If the weather permitted, I'd have challenged you to a race across the lake. To see if I could finally beat you in swimming."

"Don't count on it. I practised swimming in the sea every summer when Papa would take us to the seaside at Bristol. I recall you used to thrash about in the water more than you swam. I wish I could've seen you swim across that river in Spain. I daresay I'd have made it through that river in half the time."

"Is that a challenge, madam wife?" There was a gleam in his eyes.

"Oh yes. One warm summer day, we shall have a race, you and I," she said. Her eyes fixed on his lips as they slowly approached hers for a heart-melting kiss.

Afterwards, they watched the island glow in the rosy rays of dawn.

"Watching the sunrise is wonderful and all, but I think we should head back to the house quickly." He reached out to pull her to her feet. "There's a lifetime of happiness waiting for us, and I wouldn't face it without you by my side."

Louisa smiled up at him. "Together," she whispered.

Epilogue

Cambrai, France, 1818

It was a sultry August afternoon. The women were having a picnic on the lawn by the picturesque lake. It wasn't as big as the one at Meryfell Hall, nor was it as cold.

It had been a long, dry, hot summer, and once the heat of the day was over, they ventured out to cool themselves in the lake and rest under the lengthening shadows of the trees.

"One can't properly call it a lake. It's somewhat bigger than a puddle and smaller than a pond. Is it a bigger fountain, I wonder? It defies any kind of definition," Will had mocked. It didn't have an island either. It was just big enough to splash about during the hottest part of the summer, or for a small rowboat to paddle around.

Their villa, with a surrounding park consisting of meadow and trees, was on the outskirts of the sleepy town of Cambrai where the occupying forces were stationed. Wellington's estate, Mont St Martin, was conveniently nearby. The duke was an excellent host. There were many grand dinners, balls, theatricals, and hunts for the men, which Highworth particularly enjoyed. Then there was the extravagant social life in Paris where they also had a townhouse.

The women sat in the shade of the large oak tree by the lake. On the lawn, in front of the blanket, toddled two chubby, dark-haired boys, identical to each other. Their faces were smeared with the juice of blackberries, and they took turns coming to the blanket to fortify themselves with more blackberry custard pie, then returning to chase each other and roll around in the grass.

Celeste shaded her eyes with her hand as she watched the boys with a smile. She was heavy with child, having married Will's aide-de-camp, the former Lieutenant Carey. He was a captain now, still faithfully at Will's side. Lieutenant Miller had changed regiments and taken up a post in South Asia.

"I vow, Louisa, it is a mystery to me how you can tell them apart. They are like two peas in a pod. And both are equally mischievous."

Louisa lay sleepily on the blanket beside her and smiled. "They'll make a pair of rascals when they grow up," she said fondly. "Nathaniel is the older one and already the bossy leader. He will grow into quite a personality one day. Jonathan is the one with the clever, mischievous ideas. Just like Will." She grinned.

"And this one will be a heartbreaker one day. Just like his mother." Louisa's stepmother Sarah placed a kiss on baby Jamey's honey-golden head. He had fallen asleep on her arm, sucking on his fist. Sarah gently placed him into a bassinet and sat down next to it. "What a blessing to have three boys so close together, Louisa." Never having had any children of her own, Sarah was thriving in her role as a grandmother. She and Louisa's father had followed them to Cambrai to be as close as possible to their grandchildren. Highworth was a doting grandfather and melted in the presence of his grandchildren. "I have never seen a prouder grandfather," Sarah said, before chasing after the boys to wipe their faces with a napkin.

"They'll make a holy trio of terror once Jamey learns to walk," Louisa prophesied. "Add yours to the bunch, and we'll have an entire regiment."

Celeste laughed and patted her stomach. "Unless it's a girl, of course."

Louisa stared dreamily at the foliage of the trees above her. "Yes. It would be lovely for our next one to be a girl," she added softly. "Though if it is a boy, that would be splendid, too."

Celeste lowered the pastry she was about to bite into. "No. You're expecting again?"

Louisa placed a hand on her stomach and chuckled. "Yes. I made up my mind. I think I'd like to have four boys and a girl last. That would be perfection." She sighed happily. "Imagine. The house won't stand long." She lay contentedly on the blanket, blinking against the sun's rays that poked through the foliage.

"Does Will know?"

"Not yet." Louisa chuckled. "He's in for a lovely surprise. He'll be terribly disappointed because he's been looking forward to our swimming race across Meryfell Lake all this time. It looks like he'll have to wait a while longer."

The hooves of their horses clattered on the cobblestone of the driveway. The men were arriving.

Celeste's husband was there, along with two other aides-de-camp—young lads still wet behind their ears, Will had said. Celeste waved, got up and walked towards her husband.

Will was now a colonel, his uniform adorned with the insignia that declared his rank. He dismounted and approached the group of women.

Having espied their father, the two boys emitted squeals of delight and raced towards him. Will picked up the shrieking bundle of boys, tossed them in the air, tucked one under each arm, and walked over to the blanket with long strides.

"I encountered these two rascals, madam wife. Perchance they may be ours?" He dropped a kiss on her lips, then bent over the basket to check on baby Jamey. The two boys clung to him like monkeys and refused to be put down, so Will held them in his arms as he lowered himself onto the blanket.

Louisa stroked a lock of hair from his forehead. "Has it been a difficult day? You look tired."

"Not difficult. Just busy. As you know, we're withdrawing the occupation forces in October. There is much to do. Logistics. Coordinating the withdrawal with the allied troops. Negotiating with the leaders here to maintain stability. And so forth. Ow, you little cannibals! They would eat me alive if they could." Nathaniel pulled at his ear while Jonathan bit into his nose. Then Nathaniel tried to pull off a button of his uniform while Jonathan sucked on the strings of one of his epaulettes.

She laughed and took Jonathan from him, who protested. She handed him a wooden figure, which Will had carved for them. Seeing Jonathan was playing a new game, Nathaniel struggled to be put down so he could join him.

"It will be lovely to return to England, of course," Louisa said as she watched her boys fondly. "We haven't been to Meryfell Hall at all this year, and I'm missing it."

They'd spent the summer with Will's father in Berkshire at Wexford Hall. Lord Wexford had retired and was eagerly awaiting their return from France. He couldn't wait to fill the hall with the sound of children's laughter, he said.

"Meryfell Hall. That damp pile of stone." Will shook his head. "I keep saying the best thing would be to tear it down and build it anew. Even so, I can't make myself sell the place."

"Because of Glubbdubdrib."

"Yes."

"I confess I'd be sad if you sold it. Has George shown any interest in repurchasing it?"

Will shook his head. "No. He insists on remaining in the army. He has astonished us all and is doing surprisingly well, even expressed an interest in being redeployed to South Asia. I may send him there on a mission or other.

Something complicated, something that will take him a long time to complete." A sardonic grin played on his lips.

"And what, pray, are your intentions upon returning to England?"

He pulled a leaf of grass. "The duke is attempting his best to pull me into politics. He has political ambitions and wants me to join him. I'm not convinced it's for me. I think I'd rather stay in the army. But I have received an offer from the War Office. They want me as an advisor, as does the Royal Military College at Sandhurst. I like the idea of training the next generation of military leaders. But we'll have to see what develops from all this." He placed his head in her lap and looked up. "If all things fail, I could help you set up your new business. French perfume and soaps. I can help you sell them at the market in Dorchester. I vaguely recall I used to be better at selling cabbages than you."

Louisa smiled, then looked dreamily out over the lake and the park. "I'll miss this place. We were happy here, weren't we? With our little family."

"Not so little now." Will watched the boys run towards their grandmother as she brought a tray with biscuits.

"Now that we're on this particular subject," Louisa said with a grin. "There is something I ought to tell you …"

When a scheming spinster is determined to help her sister find a match, she gets herself hopelessly entangled in a game of deception that will undoubtedly lead to disaster....or to love. Don't miss Emily's story in the next instalment of the Merry Spinster, Charming Rogues series:
Lady Emily's Matchmaking Mishap.

Also by Sofi Laporte

Merry Spinsters, Charming Rogues Series

Escape into the world of Sofi Laporte's cheeky Regency romcoms, where spinsters are merry, rakes are charming, and no one is who they seem:

Lady Emily's Matchmaking Mishap

A scheming spinster's matchmaking plans for her sister take an unexpected twist when she finds herself entangled in a charade of love.

Miss Louisa's Final Waltz

When a proud beauty weds a humble costermonger, their worlds collide with challenges and secrets that only love can conquer.

Lady Ludmilla's Accidental Letter

A resolute spinster. An irresistible rake. One accidental letter... Can love triumph over this hopeless muddle in the middle of the London Season?

Miss Ava's Scandalous Secret

She is a shy spinster by day and a celebrated opera singer by night. He is an earl in dire need of a wife - and desperately in love with this Season's opera star.

Lady Avery and the False Butler

When a hopeless spinster enlists her butler's help to turn her life around, it leads to great trouble and a chance at love in this rollicking Regency romance.

(*more to come*)

The Viennese Waltz Series

Set against the backdrop of Vienna's 1814 elegance, diplomacy, and intrigue, this series twirls through the entwined destinies of friends, enemies, and lost lovers in charming tales of love, desire and courtship.

My Lady, Will You Dance? (Prequel)

A Lost Love. A Cold Marquess. A Fateful Christmas Country House Party...

The Forgotten Duke

When a penniless Viennese musician is told she may be an English duke's wife, a quest for lost love begins.

The Wishing Well Series

If you enjoy sweet Regency novels with witty banter and a sprinkle of mischief wrapped up in a heart-tugging happily ever after, this series is for you!

Lucy and the Duke of Secrets

A spirited young lady with a dream. A duke in disguise. A compromising situation.

Arabella and the Reluctant Duke

A runaway Duke's daughter. A dashingly handsome blacksmith. A festering secret.

Birdie and the Beastly Duke

A battle-scarred duke. A substitute bride. A dangerous secret that brings them together.

Penelope and the Wicked Duke

A princess in disguise. A charming lord. A quest for true love.

A Mistletoe Promise

When an errant earl and a feisty schoolteacher are snowed in together over Christmas, mistletoe promises happen.

Wishing Well Seminary Series

Discover a world of charm and wit in the Wishing Well Seminary Series, as the schoolmistresses of Bath's most exclusive school navigate the complexities of Regency-era romance:

Miss Hilversham and the Pesky Duke

Will our cool, collected Headmistress find love with a most vexatious duke?

Miss Robinson and the Unsuitable Baron

When Miss Ellen Robinson seeks out Baron Edmund Tewkbury in London to deliver his ward, he wheedles her into staying—as his wife.

NEVER MISS A RELEASE:

To receive a FREE GIFT, exclusive giveaways, review copies, and updates on Sofi's books sign up for her newsletter:

https://www.sofilaporte.com/newsletter-1

About the Author

Sofi was born in Vienna, grew up in Seoul, studied Comparative Literature in Maryland, U.S.A., and lived in Quito with her Ecuadorian husband. When not writing, she likes to scramble about the countryside exploring medieval castle ruins. She currently lives with her husband, 3 trilingual children, a sassy cat and a cheeky dog in Europe.

Get in touch and visit Sofi at her Website, on Facebook or Instagram!

- amazon.com/Sofi-Laporte/e/B07N1K8H6C
- facebook.com/sofilaporteauthor
- instagram.com/sofilaporteauthor
- bookbub.com/profile/sofi-laporte

Printed in Dunstable, United Kingdom